# BURIED in TIME

*To Marsha
Happy trails
Susan Keene*

Buried in Time Book 1

# SUSAN KEENE

Copyright © 2025 Susan Keene
All cover art copyright © 2025 Susan Keene
All Rights Reserved

This is a work of fiction. Names, places, characters and incidents are either the product of the author's imagination or are used fictitiously, and any resemblance to any actual persons, living or dead, businesses, organizations, events or locales is entirely coincidental.

No part of this book may be reproduced or transmitted in any form or by any means, electronic or mechanical, including photocopying, recording, or by any information storage and retrieval system, without permission in writing from the author.

Publishing Coordinator – Sharon Kizziah-Holmes

Published by

Bent Willow BOOKS

Niangua, Missouri

ISBN -13: 978-1-964559-77-3

## Other books by Susan Keene

**Stand Alone**
Tattered Wings
The Twisted Mind of Cletus Compton

**The Arizona Summers Mystery Series**
The Wedding Cake Murder, Book one
The High Steaks Murder Book two
Bonfires, Barbeques and Bodies Book three
Mothers, Miracles and Mistletoe Book four

**The Kate Nash Mysteries**
Finding Lizzy Smith Book one
Who's Roxy Watkins? Book Two
The Untimely Death of Ivy Tucker Book three
Enough is Enough Book Four

**Children's Books**
We Are Not So Different After All

**Diggitty The Dog Series**
Diggitty the Dog at the Farm
Diggitty the Dog Finds a Friend
Diggitty the Dog Saves Christmas

# Dedication

To Nancy B. Dailey. Gone too soon.

# Acknowledgments

Thanks to Sharon Kizziah-Holmes and Paperback-Press, my publishing coordinator.

Jennifer Darnell, thanks for editing my work.

Many thanks to The Writers of the Purple Page and my critique group for your support.

Last but maybe the most important, a big shout out to Blenna DeHart who does double duty on the farm so I can write my books.

# PROLOGUE

On the clear, bright evening of June 7, 1929, six friends met at the Bailey House in Springfield, Missouri for a dinner and dance to celebrate their recent high school graduation. These six friends, two boys and four girls, were especially close.

The six were from a rural area where some folks still traveled by horse and buggy. One of the girls, Judith Izzard, came from a wealthy family. Not only did they own the local lumberyard sawmill, the girl's family was one of the richest in the area.

Judith's parents had just celebrated their twentieth wedding anniversary the month before. Judith's father presented her mother with a ruby and diamond ring that had once belonged to Queen Catherine of France.

According to Judith's parents, the nineteen-year-old had asked repeatedly if she could have permission to wear the ring to the graduation party. At the last minute, her parents said yes, on three conditions.

First, their hired driver would take her to the party.

Second, she was not to leave the hotel until Jackson, the family's long-time driver, came to pick her up.

Third, she was not to take the ring off her finger until she gave it back to her mother upon her return.

Of course, Judith agreed to the demands.

At exactly five-thirty on the evening of the party, Jackson had brought the car around, helped the girl with her long green velvet dress so it would not get caught in the door, and departed the residence for the graduation party.

Jackson, having been with the family for years, had been made aware of the rules surrounding the circumstances of Judith wearing the ring her parents had given them. He later told authorities how he had stopped the car in the circle drive in front of the hotel and helped Judith out of the car and up the stairs where her three giggling girlfriends waited and the two boys looked on.

The plan had been for Jackson to pick Judith up at the same place he had dropped her off, at ten P.M. later that same night.

The driver was exactly on time. The graduates came out of the Bailey House, in groups and some alone. Jackson waited a half an hour before he went in to see where Judith was.

None of the people left at the event center remembered seeing Judith for the last two hours of the dance.

Jackson was forced to go home without his charge. Nineteen-year-old Judith Izzard was never seen again.

Two weeks after her disappearance, one of the two boys was lynched for Judith Izzard's disappearance without one bit of evidence against him.

# CHAPTER 1

It was the end of May, but the humidity hung around one hundred percent and there was no breeze. I'd been working for nearly four hours but decided I might quit.

My dog, Indie, had given up hours ago and now was asleep under an oak tree in the middle of an entire grove of them. I picked up my water jug and walked over to join him.

I had a dilemma. It wasn't a moral dilemma. Mine was one of a more personal nature. My work ethic niggled at my brain trying to tell me I'd already been paid for this job. My independent self, the self-employed one, told me tomorrow was another day. I could start before the heat hit its peak or wait until evening when the heat of the day began to lessen.

The man who hired me didn't seem in any particular hurry for me to finish. I didn't know much about him. Information on him wasn't prevalent. Most people who wanted to explore a piece of land were right beside me. They didn't dig, but they were excited about what might be found under the ground they walked on and wanted to be on site when I uncovered it.

I knew his name was Barclay Simmons, he was from New Jersey, and had his hand in everything. He owned a couple of restaurants, an art gallery, dabbled in land speculation, and apparently had land all over the country. How he ended up with fifty acres on the infamous Izzard Farm outside a small town in Southwest, Missouri was beyond me.

He told me he enjoyed treasure hunting and, as he dug into the hobby, my name kept coming up. Since I belonged to the publish or perish group, I was glad to hear my name came up in lots of places.

What did a friend call someone named Barclay? Bar, Clay, or maybe Bark? Who knew? I guess it was a good thing we weren't friends so I didn't have to think to hard about it.

Mr. Simmons told me the Izzard farm was finally being split up and sold. Most of the acreage was bought by a big outfit called Whiting Land and Cattle Company. The company didn't want the house, so they surveyed it out along with fifty acres. Mr. Simmons had also told me he had done some research on the land and had discovered the Trail of Tears went through the farm and that the abandoned farmhouse sat on the Old Wire Road.

Since I lived in a town not quite twenty minutes away by car, I knew all about the Indian Removal. Part of the land behind my house was on the Old Wire Road, the first telegraph line from Jefferson Barracks near St. Louis, that ran all the way to Fort Smith, Arkansas.

I had accepted the job three weeks ago, but this was my first day to dig. First, I gridded the area. Some places were more likely to have buried treasure than others and I would start with the grid units with the most promising characteristics. After doing this type of work for more than ten years, I could usually get close to where items other than pop-tops lay.

Of course, it didn't mean I would find anything. Also, I had grown tired of traveling to different countries to work on archeological digs that took months and sometimes years. I thought I might be burned out.

After twenty minutes laying in the shade out of the extreme heat with my head resting on my eighty-pound German Shepard, I felt better. I looked at my phone to check the time, only one-fifteen. I'd go another hour and sooth my inner work ethic.

I went back to the place I'd been detecting earlier and began to swing my machine back and forth. It only took three swipes before I got what I called a "money ding". Metal detectors were just that.

They detected metal and the ding told me this grid unit had some in it.

I triangulated my spot and dropped to my knees to see what lay under the grass. I kept a bag near me. Out of it I took a trowel, a pin pointer, and a cloth. The best way to dig in the dirt is to make a semicircle shaped plug and lay it back on itself so I can check what's under it yet be able to flip the sod back over the hole. I'd done it for so long, I could sometimes be so neat no one would ever know I'd been there. On a farm, it wasn't as critical as if I were digging in someone's front yard. And I had experience with both.

The item was not in the hole. I put the pin pointer up to the plug of grass and dirt I had pulled from the hole, and it went wild. Most people would stop at this point and slip on a pair of gloves. I'd been cut and bruised so many times over the years I had taken to keeping gloves on ninety nine percent of the time and had automatically slipped them back on when I had finished my rest break.

Three inches down in my plug of dirt, I saw a flash of silver, then something hit the light and sparkled as only diamonds could. I took a brush out of my bag and began to gently remove the dirt.

I gasped for air in anticipation, then looked all around to make sure no one heard me.

What a nerd I could be. I knew no one was around but I guess old habits die hard. I could hear the traffic on Farm Road 87 beside me and except for the trees in the grove, the rest of the land was open, not a tree or animal in sight.

I'd found a ring. Once I cleaned the dirt off of it, I couldn't believe my eyes. I'd seen hundreds of pictures of this ring over the years. I hadn't found just any ring; I had found THE ring. I would bet my life on it being the exact ring Judith Izzard had had on when she disappeared ninety-four years ago. To be safe, I snapped several pictures of the grid, the plug, and the sparkling jewels revealed by my brush.

I couldn't begin to explain my feelings around this find. I'd grown up with the legend of the ring and the beautiful young woman who went to a graduation dinner and dance in 1929 and was never seen again. I believe every parent in the area, at one time or another, used the story of the missing girl to remind their daughters to be careful, not go into dark places alone, and to stay away from strangers.

Every year for at least ten years after her disappearance, my mom said the local papers wrote a story about the girl and the ring. As time passed and more relevant news came up, the story ended up on the archive pages where it was retold at five-year intervals. The value of the ring had been updated several times over the years. The last time I read anything about it, the appraisal was up to over a million dollars.

Indy must have noticed the change in my demeanor. He came over and laid his head in my lap.

"I'm okay, buddy. We can go in a bit." I reached over to my duffel bag and took a treat out and gave it to him. He seemed cool enough now to stay beside me.

I believe I could have been in a tornado or a blizzard and I wouldn't have noticed. My mind was totally captivated by the item in my hand.

I couldn't get over how warm the ring was. So warm I had to hold it in a rag to keep it from burning my hand. The ring was bigger than it looked in the photos. The rich red ruby was so clear it seemed bottomless as I examined it. Ten diamonds of perfect cut and clarity sparkled in the sunlight as I turned it to catch each one in the afternoon light. I wanted to study it some more but it was too hot to handle.

As I glanced back into the hole, I saw what I believed to be a small piece of wood. I wrapped the ring in a towel and laid it in my bag, hoping it would cool down. What I had initially thought was a chunk of wood turned out to be a small bone. I began to dig carefully, but in earnest. In all, I found nine small bones. When I arranged them in anatomical order, they made three small digits, the fingers of someone's hand. Had I just found the body of Judith Izzard? Or at least parts of it?

By the time the sun went down and the air became pleasant, I'd dug enough of the area around me where the ring and finger bones were, I was sure if the girl's body was around, it wasn't in the area where I was digging.

After the ring lay covered in the rag for several hours, I picked it up again to take a closer look.

It had cooled down but warmed instantly in my hand. I held the ring at arm's length. As I stared at the ruby itself, an apparition appeared. I closed my eyes tight and then opened them again. The phantom hadn't faded. It was Judith Izzard. She turned her head from left to right and then looked directly into my eyes.

Even I, who didn't believe in witchcraft or voodoo and had little faith in the supernatural, had no problem believing the girl in the ring was real.

The rational part of me shook my head and tried to tell myself it was excitement. After all, this was something that happened before I was born. The story of her disappearance was told to me when I was young. I listened until I could research it myself. To have what amounted to a local a fairy tale be true was a childlike way to think about the ring, but like other kids I had related to fairy tales as a child. My friends and I sometimes walked for miles to find the end of the rainbow so we could have the gold. How disappointed we were after years of searching when we realized there was no gold. My gut told me I was about to unravel the mystery of Judith Izzard.

Another part of me fell hook, line, and sinker for the image the ring sent as I held it. It remained warm in my hand. I tried to think of what to do. I decided to talk to the apparition before me. "Judith, where are you?" Although the image said nothing to me, the words, *stuck between two worlds* were vivid in my mind. The specter disappeared.

I picked up the nine little bones I had dug up and put them in a pouch I used to carry my finds. I sat down one more time and thought of the implications of my find. This was like a fairy tale come to life. I held the ring up again. The diamonds glittered in the sunlight. The ruby had a hue darker than any stone of its kind I'd ever seen.

I stood up, and pushed the ring as far down into my watch pocket of my Levis as it would go. As I prepared to leave the area, a serious thought came to mind. The fingers were human remains. According to the law, I couldn't take the specimens with me. The correct procedure was to mark the area of interest, call the police, and turn the investigation over to them.

I rationalized my decision to take the bones with me because I knew it wasn't a recent murder and had not in any way disturbed an active crime scene. No one would be able to take what I found and catch a killer who would be a minimum of one-hundred and twelve-years-old by now.

Besides, if the police took the ring it would sit in an evidence locker for years. I was sure if no one had solved the murder in ninety-four years, they were not going to solve it now just because I had found the ring.

To have the police come could be a calamity. They were like bulls in a China shop. They had a tendency to come in with road grading equipment and use it to dig up the area. I'd been hired in the past by police all over the place to try to find this item or that. If I had difficulty, they always wanted to bring in the big guns and make life easier for me. But it didn't, it broke pieces and in some cases buried what I was looking for under three feet of dirt.

I needed to see if anyone else had a reaction to the ring, or if maybe the ring had an effect on them. The first person who came to mind was Professor Jonah Thompson, a Professor Emeritus at Dorman College who lived on the campus In Benton, Missouri. Since I lived in the same town and we shared the same degrees, we often got together to discuss the latest finds from all over the world. I considered him a mentor.

We went home. I took a shower and fed Indy. It gave me some time to think. The walk from my house in Cali Acres to Professor Thompson's house took around thirty-five minutes. Indy and I chose to walk. It took care of two things at once, Indy's evening walk and more thinking time for me.

I also knew I could trust the professor not to go running down the street shouting about how I'd committed a crime by removing the items from the farm. He and I could look at them together. If the ring became warm in his hands or he saw anything in the ruby, he would either tell me or, most likely, I'd be able to tell by watching him.

The main differences between the professor and myself was experience, reputation, and expertise. He had all of it; I didn't feel I could hold a candle to him in experience. Experience was a given. He was in his seventies, I was thirty-two. As far as reputation went, I thought mine was solid.

Over the fifteen years I'd known the professor, we'd had most of our conversations outside on a bench under one of the giant hickory trees on the Dorman College campus, outside the Language Arts Building. He always acted like someone was after him. He'd look in all directions the entire time I tried to have a conversation with him. To get and keep his full attention, I began to show up at his house and suggest we have our meetings inside so I could garner his full attention. How he managed to do the kind of work he did, which required him to travel and be outside around strangers, amazed me. In spite of all of his weird quirks, he cut a handsome figure. In the years I'd known him, he'd remained timeless. He had the same amount of gray in his hair as when I took his Antiquities class fifteen years before. He stood about five feet nine. Society is funny: I'm five nine, which is considered tall for a woman but short for a man like the professor.

His clothes were pristine. His shirts professionally laundered, the crease in his pants sharp enough it could slice a tomato. He wore a bow tie he tied himself. I knew because on the occasions he loosened it, it hung like a silk ribbon around his neck. He wore Giorgio Armani Trousers, obviously custom tailored and Allen Edwards Oxfords. He rarely buttoned his sports coats. The labels were easy to read as he walked around a classroom or down the street. They all sported labels such as Nieman Marcus, Brooks Brothers, and Ralph Lauren to name just a few.

His head appeared to sit directly on his shoulders sans a neck. It didn't mar his elegant looks. He oozed confidence and his smile, when he chose to show it, lit up a room. Although a big man, he didn't have an ounce of fat on him.

I knocked on his door and as usual music floated toward me from an open window in the room, I knew was his office. Heavy drapes usually hung at every window. They were pulled so tightly, the house looked uninhabited except for the music and the one window.

The one story white stucco sat at the end of a cul-de-sac. Six houses were built on each side of the street with the professor's at the end totaling thirteen houses. The builder, I assumed, had no fear of bad luck.

What separated the homes in design was the color of the shutters and the flowers and shrubs in the yards. I knew the college owned the homes and kept the lawns mowed, leaves raked, and snow shoveled. Decorations were up to the tenant.

I knocked again; this time a bit louder to drown out Mozart's Piano Concerto No. 21. It had been a favorite of my father's, and I recognized it immediately.

The music stopped. I heard the professor say, "Hold your horses, I'm on my way."

Once he opened the door, he stepped out and looked around in all directions. It made the hair stand up on the back of my neck. The way he studied his surroundings every time he stood in the open doorway made me think of a criminal who knew if the right person identified him, he would be a dead man. Maybe he'd been bothered by an intruder or once been mugged. I'd never had the tenacity to ask him. Today he acted more strange than usual. He moved me gently out of his way, looked in each direction a second time and stepped back inside.

I took a step back and looked him in the eye.

"Alexa, what are you doing here at this late hour?" he said when he acknowledged me.

"It's only seven-forty-five. I need a moment of your time. I hate to let this wait."

He opened the door a bit more this time but didn't look out. "Come in," he said. When I didn't move, he waved me in with his hand. "Well, come on."

My dog, Indy, fell in step beside me.

"You know that dog can't come into my house. Give him one of those commands he knows so well and tell him to wait here." He pointed to the steps.

I nodded to Indy and pointed to the porch. He laid down and rested his head on his paws. As we entered the house, I heard him let out a big sigh.

The first time I had visited the professor at his home, I had been awestruck. Photos covered every inch of the walls in the room to the right of the door. It was the only room he'd ever invited me into. The pictures depicted him in different locations around the world where he had been invited to identify artifacts. They showed a good-looking young man with a full head of dark blond hair, medium tall, with a trim build and a knowing look on his handsome face.

The pictures were hung in chronological order. The more mature he got the bigger his arms and legs became. He had to have spent a lot of his youth in a gym. You don't get that sort of muscle just working at a dig. I walked and dug holes nearly every day and my muscles developed over the years but it made me look athletic, not like a body builder. That type of muscle building took specific training and probably a ton of weightlifting.

Except for some fine lines and graying temples, the man in the pictures looked like the man I knew now.

Then there were his eyes. The summer before I entered the fourth grade, Mom took me to see an old movie about Jesus, called King of Kings. The star was a man named Jeffrey Hunter. I'd never seen eyes so blue, until the professor.

I snapped to attention when he asked, "Well, Dr. Ford, what is so important you felt the need to interrupt my work?"

He pointed to the one chair in the room not stacked high with books. I sat and crossed my legs near my ankles. "I found something today I feel is important. I want your opinion on it before I notify the police," I said.

He looked at me over the top of his readers. He always had them with him. The glasses were either on the top of his head or on his face. "Intriguing, why would you have to call the authorities? Were you somewhere you should not have been?" He leaned back in his chair and pushed until it hit the bookcase behind him. He stretched his arms out in front of him, rested them on the desktop, and waited for me to speak.

I didn't get up. I already knew every horizontal surface in the room had from one to a hundred items on it. To me, it seemed like nothing more than unidentifiable clutter, but I knew better than to remove anything and expect the professor not to notice immediately.

I lowered my head and looked up with my eyes. My mother had called it my "flat-eyed stare". While I waited for him to tell me where I should set my treasure, he said nothing. So, I reached in my pocket and took out the ring. Carefully, I set it on his desk with the ruby facing him.

I looked up and realized he had moved closer to the desk and leaned forward to get a better look at the ring.

"May I pick it up?" he asked.

"Of course, and I have these." I laid the three parts of the fingers on his desk in anatomical order.

I loved his mind. He had the distinction of being one of the top five antiquities authorities in the world. To be fair to myself, I was no slouch. After all, I had earned a BS in Archaeology and a Masters in Anthropology. Last year I finished my Doctorate.

When a rare piece of jewelry, metal or perhaps a bone, never seen before needed to be identified, those in charge put up the money to fly the professor to the location and see to it he had everything he needed to keep him comfortable until the job was done. Last time I had heard him speak in a formal setting he had recently returned from Egypt from that type of trip. He had mentioned he'd identified objects and their origins in all fifty states as well as fifty-six foreign countries.

My finds were boring compared to all the exotic destinations he'd traveled and all the accolades he'd earned for his work. He still had the good manners to take every item I brought him seriously.

Professor Thompson had helped me identify my findings before, but never anything as special as what I had with me on this particular visit.

Had I not been a treasure hunting nerd, I would never have been close to the professor. I originally met him when I attended Stanford, where I earned my undergraduate degree. There he had taught a class called "The Social Life of Bones." He also invited me and twenty other students to accompany him on a dig in Peru.

"Follow me," he said. We walked down a long narrow hallway. No light penetrated the thick dark drapes on the one lone window at the far end of the hall.

He reached up and pulled a chain and one light bulb, no brighter than forty watts, came on. It swung by the cord and cast shadows on the walls on both sides as it made a fast arc from one side to the other. The more times the light made a pass, the smaller the arc, the less light it put out.

We passed two closed doors on each side of the hall. Though I'd come to see the professor before, at least a half dozen times, he'd never ask me to accompany him to another part of the house.

The treasure hunter in me would have loved to have thrown open each door we passed to peer inside. It seemed as though he only used the one room, or at least the only one he invited guests into.

Maybe, I didn't know him as well as I thought.

The door stood open to the room he entered. The professor walked across the room to a large oak table. The polish was so deep I could see his face reflected back at him. He pressed a button near the middle of the table and lights came on. The difference was like we went from twilight into the noon day sun.

I looked around. Another smaller table held a microscope. Another held at least a dozen magnifying glasses and jeweler's loops. I hoped my mouth hadn't gaped open as I looked around the magnificent room.

I watched as he put the cloth on the table and looked down at it. This time he took the time to study what I brought with me.

"This room is amazing. Is this where you do your work?" I asked.

"One of them," he said. "It depends on what I am trying to identify, and it keeps me from wasting time going around to look for what instrument I need for a specific item. I assume this is a treasure. I can say you never come here unless you have something extraordinary to show me. I appreciate it."

"You saw it. The look on your face and our walk down to this room let me know you know exactly what it is," I said. "I dug it up this morning."

Thompson looked me straight in the eye. "Where was your dig?"

When he finished his examination of the item. he took in a short quick breath. "I don't have to look this one up. You didn't either or you wouldn't be here. This ring belonged to Judith Izzard. I'm sure you know the story. Supposedly she left for a graduation party in June of 1929 and was never seen again. Where did you say you found it?"

"I didn't say, but I don't mind telling you. It lay about six inches down in a field at a farm in Seymore, ironically, the old Izzard farm."

He'd left the bones on the pile where I'd put the three parts of each finger the way they would appear on a hand. "You forgot these." I had the little bones in my hand and laid them down on the corner of the table.

He stopped, put down the magnifying glass he'd been holding and looked at me.

I became extremely nervous under his stare. The look on his face was of a person who was lost in thought. I finally began, "The land has been sitting for years, but someone pays the taxes on it so it stays in the Izzard name. I haven't taken the time to search the tax rolls yet. The man who hired me and claims to have recently inherited it did some research and found out the Trail of Tears went directly through the property."

"He said he doesn't want to sell it with a bunch of wealth under the ground," I continued. "The strange thing is, he isn't listed as one of the owners or heirs. So far, my research on him pegs him as a land speculator. It's possible that his claim is so new it isn't searchable yet."

"How do you know he even owns the land? With a piece like this ring," he picked up the ruby and diamond ring again, "there could be a fight over who owns the land and if you even have permission to explore it. Where were these bones found?" He had tweezers in his hand now and delicately arranged the bones back into fingers as I had earlier when I found them. When he finished, he asked, "Is this how you found them?"

"Yes, I took plenty of pictures before I picked anything up. I know I'll have to notify the police. I hate to turn it over, but I bet the rest of her body is around there someplace. It might even be where I had my detector. Had it not been for the ring, the bones might have been in the ground for years longer."

"Are you going to turn it over when you leave here?"

"I'll wait until morning and put everything back the way I found it. Then I'll call the police and the University of Missouri."

"Do you have the photographs on your phone? I'd like to see them. This case is extremely important to me. I have spent years trying to track young Miss Izzard's journey the night she disappeared. About twenty years ago, I made it a class assignment and now I give it as one of the topics for a term paper. The ideas the students come up with as to what happened to her is fascinating." He chuckled, clearly thinking of some of the stranger theories.

"I put all the information collected over the years in a folder. If anyone could solve the mystery of her disappearance, I would take him or her on my next out of the country dig. It wasn't for lack of trying, but at the end of the semester, we never made any progress, so I tucked it away and take it out only if someone chooses it for a term paper or when the press highlights it on the anniversaries of her disappearance. Dateline has all the information I have. I believe they will, one day, make an episode out of the story."

While he'd been talking, I had taken out my phone and pulled up the two dozen or so photos and handed it to him. He said nothing until he had studied each angle, I had captured several times. As he handed it back, he said, "You might want to reverse your order on that. I'd call the school first. After they arrive and grid off the area, then notify the law. The authorities will be out there with a bulldozer if they get the call first. It is in their DNA. They care nothing about history. Meanwhile, do you have a safe?"

"No, I don't."

"Leave it here then. until morning. What time do you plan to go back to your site?"

"We shoot for eight. We actually leave at around six-thirty, but we stop at McDonald's and Starbucks."

"I'd like to go with you," he said.

It was obvious he didn't have a reaction or interaction with the ring. Also, it didn't need to be in a safe. Not another person in the world beside him and me knew it had been found.

"I'd be more than happy to take you with us. Thing is, no one knows the ring has been found so there really is no need for it to be in a safe."

"Indulge me," he said. "The paper I was working on when you arrived is nearly finished. I'd like to have more time to study the ring before you put into someone else's care. And those bones don't belong to Judith Izzard. Did you really take a good look at them?"

I walked around the table so I could look straight at him. "No. I would have later. I also knew who's ring it was. I assumed the bones with it would belong to Miss Izzard."

It was a rookie mistake not to look more closely at the bones. He still studied the material in front of him so I doubt he saw the beautiful flush I felt on my cheeks. In my defense, I had been a bit distracted by seeing the ghost of Judith Izzard in the ring.

"I let the excitement of the moment keep me from doing the job I was hired to do".

"Now that you've seen them laid out anatomically, what do you see?" He handed me a magnifying glass he'd picked up from the table. "I'd say these bones have been in the ground less than five years."

He didn't give me a chance to look. The way he was acting was not what I expected. Had I known he'd want to keep the ring and finger bones, I wouldn't have brought my finds to him. I was a grown woman, but I was sure anyone who just saw a girl in a ring try to communicate with her might be as shook up as I was. Seeing a ghost had caused me to make a novice mistake. I knew better than to let the excitement of a find cloud my mind. But this wasn't any find. It was the find of my lifetime.

He smiled at me, a rare occurrence for sure. "It could mean several things. First, it means the owner of these bones was murdered. It could lead to the conclusion this is not the original Izzard ring. But I'd stake my reputation on the fact that it is. I don't have to test the ring; it is a Forstner, as was the original."

I interrupted him. "They were best known for bracelets, pendants, and broaches. I read the story. Mr. Jacob Izzard had it made for his wife on their twentieth-fifth wedding anniversary. It has a little F/Nj on the inside. He told the police at the time that his wife let Judith wear the ring because it was such a special occasion." What I didn't add was, only Judith's ring would react the way the one I'd found had if it belonged to the missing girl.

The professor clasped his hands under his chin as though he intended to hold it up.

"Lexi." It was the only time in fifteen years he'd used my nickname. "You not only found a 94 year old ring, but you uncovered a five year old murder. My philosophy on everything is unless you are locked in a bathroom, all by yourself, when you do something, someone somewhere knows what you have done, found, sold, or who you slept with. I believe we will both sleep better if the ring and fingers are in a safe tonight.

The Professor stood. He walked over to the other side of the room and from a drawer in a long chest he took out two red velvet pouches. "Gather your things. Put the bones in the larger one and the ring in the other."

I took my time and put all the bones but one in the bigger bag. In the other bag I slipped the smallest bone. I made sure I didn't hold it too tight because I wanted the professor to believe it held the ring. When I finished, I pulled the drawstrings, tied them together, and set them back on the table and hoped since they were tied separately and together, it would be too much trouble for him to undo them to take one more look.

In my right pocket I carried a pocket pistol, a Ruger LPC .22 with a six-shot clip. I had a spare clip in my back pocket and two in the car. I'd only had to use it once in the nine years I'd owned it. Once, while on a dig, a pack of dogs, led by the biggest Husky I'd ever seen, had approached and despite my warnings had kept coming closer and closer to me and Indy. Indy had tried to defend me, but there were five of them and only one of him. He had growled and snarled but they had kept coming. I had taken my gun out and shot three times right in front of their feet, getting so close to one, he had jerked his foot away. They had hightailed it out of there after that.

Why the gun came to mind again made me uneasy. I learned a long time ago to trust my instincts. While I wasn't sure about that, there were two things I was sure of. I couldn't tell the professor I had no intention of letting him keep the ring. I would deal with his ire in the morning when the time came. And the second was that for the first time ever, the professor made me uncomfortable and being in his house gave me the willies.

I took another, closer look at him. The professor had the same demeaner as the man I'd known for years. He had always kept a proper decorum with me and all of his students. I knew this because any time he posted a notice that he needed student workers for one of his digs, sometimes as many as thirty people signed up to join him. Several had gone with him on digs numerous times. It told me he maintained the student teacher relationship.

Unfortunately, my schedule and his had never come together again so that I could join him on a dig.

Professor Jonah stood in the doorway waiting for me. "Are you doubting my plan?"

I didn't move. "What if you aren't here and I need these things?" I asked as I pointed to the two velvet bags.

"It won't happen." He said matter-of-factly. "I will have the two bags and meet you at the front door when you are ready to go back to the dig in the morning. To satisfy your uneasiness even more, I will give you the combination to the safe. Does that help? I hope so." He said not giving me time to answer. "After all these years, it would be a shame for something to happen to the artifacts."

A chill ran down my spine for the second time. I trusted the professor, so why did my gut feel as if electric eels swam circles inside by belly? I'd never heard an unkind or inappropriate word come out of his mouth. In the professional circles I ran, he was the equivalent of a benevolent king. At any conference where he made the keynote address, it was always standing room only.

Another chill hit me. I believed it to be in anticipation of him confronting me about the ring in the morning. The foreboding feeling I had unsettled my entire being. I couldn't pin down its source of my anxiety. It wasn't as if this was the most exotic or expensive item I'd ever found. And surely it wasn't because it had been heating up since I put it in my pocket. How did it know me from others? It was just a ring after all.

There was the time I had found a jar of gold coins at the bottom of an oak tree and the time I had dug up an old safe nearly two feet down in a marsh. It had been filled with artifacts from World War II and had caused quite a stir among the war collecting community. I sold the items for a six figure sum seven years ago on my twenty-sixth birthday.

As a result of that find, I became the keynote speaker at several conferences. Because I used a metal detector and didn't work on an actual dig, some of the professor's colleagues didn't consider me in the same class as them. I held my tongue. Mostly they dug at sites where they were sure there were artifacts. I started with nothing and no real expectations. Maybe I was a snob in reverse.

# CHAPTER 2

I remembered a lot of the lessons my parents instilled in me, but the one I used most was to follow my instincts. It had kept me safe many times when I set out to explore in the middle of nowhere, alone. I had bought Indiana Jones as a puppy and trained him to alert me to danger. Unfortunately, he currently lay sleeping on the professor's front porch, and I couldn't draw from his reaction to my emotions and mood.

Once we were settled back in Jonah's low light, messy office, he took out a pad of paper and began asking me questions. "Tell me how you ended up with the job to search these fifty acres?"

"Word of mouth, I guess," I answered.

"I'd believe that. I can't pick up a book about antiques or metal detecting where your face isn't smiling back at me. I heard through the grapevine you have a YouTube channel on coins and another on TikTok. You're getting quite a reputation.

"Tell me again the name of the man who hired you and how he contacted you? I'd like to look into him. I know you have already done so, but I'm sure different facts interest me than interest you."

The tingle I had in the hall doubled when he told me different facts would interest him. "Such as?" I asked.

"Alexa, I've been all over the world. I have identified items for over six thousand people in my career. Some people paid me, some cheated me. I have been involved in a shady deal I didn't know was illegal until it was over. I've learned what is true and what is made up in a person's background. Red flags stand out like beacons in the night if you know what to look for.

"Trust me to look into this man. How many times since you began finding things for a living has anyone bought fifty acres in a little town of fifteen hundred people and paid a small fortune to have someone with your reputation clear the entire place to see what you find? Did he ask you to also use an earth magnet?"

He didn't pause to let me answer. I was beginning to think it was a bad habit he had. I hadn't noticed it before because he'd never questioned me like he was now.

"I say the man knows there was something there. He might not have known of Judith Izzard, but he knows something of value is buried there," was my answer to him.

I stood and began to walk around the room. I purposely looked at every picture, news article and diploma I saw. I didn't know what exactly I was looking for; I only knew after I saw his entire life in front of me, out in the open. My bad feelings settled down a little. But they didn't go away.

"His name is Barclay…"

Before I could finish his name, Professor Thompson said, "Barclay Simmons?"

"Yes. He lives in New Jersey, said he was retired, but when I Googled him, the only Barclay Simmons I could find in New Jersey was a day trader. Simmons is a common name, but Barclay isn't. I didn't look at it the way you are. As I said, the other article I dug up referred to him as a 'land speculator'?

"I figured it would be a boring few months scouting fifty acres looking for who knows what on an abandoned farm. I shot him a price twice what I usually charge and he took it. He's already sent half the money, so I don't lose anything if I don't get another penny."

"At the fear of being rude, may I ask what he is paying you?"

"One hundred thousand whether I find anything or not. He said my reputation preceded me and he knew I could and would do the job. The check he sent me cleared my bank, so I decided he was on the up and up."

The professor pushed his chair away from his desk and put his feet up on a foot stool to his left but turned to face me. His hair fell to his forehead as it always did. Casually, he pushed it back with his fingers, using them as a rake.

For an instant I saw the young man he used to be. The one in the pictures on the walls, but it was gone as quickly as it came and the old man once again showed through.

"He could be a day trader. It would be a good way to hide money and have lots of cash. If you're good at it. Did he say what he thought you might find?"

"Answer a question for me first," I asked. "Why it is you knew his last name when I said Barclay? Have you had dealings with him before?"

"I don't know him, but one of my friends from Cambridge certified a painting for him when we were there for a symposium. I remembered his name because in that case he also paid much more than the job warranted. Maybe he does it because at those rates he knows he won't be turned away. However, my friend didn't have his doctorate yet. I wondered if anyone would consider him a professional at that time. Simmons didn't seem to mind. I remember the picture was a Monet. Even I knew it to be valid."

"If I've answered your question, tell me what he said to you when he phoned."

"He told me the Trail of Tears went through the property. He said he was almost sure there was a bank and a grocery store owned and run by Native Americans, most likely and an Indian burial ground on the property. The Cherokees were swept up in the Trail of Tears and there might well be relics both Calvery and Native American on the parcel. I let him know the law prohibited me from digging in an Native American burial ground. I explained to him it was sacred ground, and if I found one, I would have to report it to the Bureau of Indian Affairs.

"I went to the county courthouse and found out the Old Wire Road was also on the property. I knew I'd find something. Just didn't expect to find a murder and a famous ring. I spent my first two days walking and gridding. I walked every inch of the acreage. Using instinct and experience, I flagged and marked all the spots I thought I might have the best chance of finding an artifact."

He motioned for me to sit. Maybe he got tired of turning his head to follow me as I paced around the room. "Didn't you think the money was a little much and the request out of the ordinary?"

"Yes and no. People ask me for what he wants me to do every day. They just don't hire me because of the price I command. But rich people do silly things. Maybe he does this to all the properties he buys and he picked me because I lived near the farm. Seymore is only twelve miles from the farm."

He stood, "It is already after nine. I need my beauty sleep. Come with me, we'll put this in my safe until tomorrow. For one thing, I'd like to have another look at the ring."

Reluctantly, I pulled myself up and followed him. He opened the first door we came too. He used a key so old it looked like a skeleton key. I noticed he didn't use a key to get into his work room. I wondered what was so valuable in the floral-patterned room he needed to keep it locked. A strange habit if one lived alone.

The room was pristine. The carpet, a rich chocolate color, looked as if it had never been walked on. A couch sat against one wall opposite a fireplace. I could hardly take my eyes off the mantle, a four-inch-thick piece of a tree, not planed, yet sanded to a glossy shine. It had two huge moose horns holding it up. A Greek Urn sat on top.

A loveseat rested perpendicular to the sofa. A table separated the two pieces of furniture. They were both muted rose floral patterns. Normally I'd say the carpet should have been gray not chocolate, yet somehow it worked. The table legs were zebra wood and the mantel I guessed to be cherry, worm holes and all. The room we left and the next room we entered were day and night apart.

Nothing in it was even close to my taste. It was full of mismatched chairs, lots of throws, soft crochet pillows and a roaring fire, but they looked good in the room we were in. The walls were painted a medium brown and as usual, the heavy drapes didn't let in any light. In the corner, away from the rest of the furniture sat a mahogany shift robe with handles of zebra wood.

He opened it and to my surprise, the massive outside doors opened to another equally massive set of doors. The second set needed a combination to open. Inside the second set of doors a safe took up nearly every inch although I couldn't see it until he removed a false front.

He leaned down and fiddled with the combination lock. He turned his head toward me. My butterflies were back with a vengeance. I handed the two pouches to him and he laid them inside the crowded safe on top of several more artifacts. I prayed when he said he wanted another look at the ring he didn't mean now. I was hoping to be home if he discovered I'd swapped the bone for the ring. I can't express how relieved I was when he closed the door, twirled the lock, and stood without so much as a glance at the two pouches.

The professor walked over to the desk, took out a small envelope and a piece of paper. "I don't expect anything to happen to me, but inside are the combinations. The top one opens the combination doors and the bottom one is for the safe itself." He sealed it and handed it to me. "I'd like to have your word you won't open this," he flicked the plain white envelope he held in his left hand with his right index finger, "unless I'm not around to do it myself. And I don't mean *not around* like at the college. I mean not around, as in if I died. Of course, I don't expect that to happen. I'm only seventy-one."

"I understand," I said.

# Chapter 3

We walked together silently with him two steps in front of me until we were back at the front door
"We'll see you in the morning, "I smiled at him and snapped my fingers to Indy who got up to come walk beside me.

The professor's mood had changed again. He smiled at me more than once during our conversation.

"See you in the morning," He parroted back at me.

I stepped out onto the porch. I didn't look back but I heard him close the door and lock it behind me. As I reached the first step, I heard him slide on the security chain.

I knelt next to Indy, who I could tell had been snoozing the entire time I was inside with the professor. I gave him a treat, I always carried some in my pocket and told him what a good boy he was.

"Let's go home."

## Chapter 4

Every street in Benton had a sidewalk. Indy and I walked most everywhere, unless I had a dig. Carrying all my tools would have been a struggle. The town of twenty-one thousand people had everything you'd want. The movie theater had a new release twice a month. Small markets dominated a street, appropriately named Market Street. Downtown had a section of restaurants and cafes. I had never been able to name a cuisine not readily available. There were five churches last time I checked and one Synagogue. Kroger sat at the edge of town. So far, the people in high places had kept Walmart out, but the time was near when they wouldn't be able to hold the front line. Their company sent out flyers, whether they were true or not, and made it seem as though they sold their grocery items for the lowest prices within three states.

More and more people moved to our little city. No crime, good schools, summer sports and a municipal swimming pool were a great draw. They were even working on a program where longtime residents whose kids graduated from Benton High School, Home of the Hornets, could attend Dorman for the first two years free.

The entire town reminded me of a big, round wave pool with Dorman College as the center. The wave began and went out in all directions. I lived in Cali Heights, nearly two miles from the college. My mom had died several years ago in an auto accident and Dad had died two years later. They said cause of death was a heart attack, but I know he died from a broken heart. My mom was his life. Except the times I went away to school, Stanford, Carnell and UCLA, to get my education, I had lived in Benton.

Seems to me at least a dozen of my friends either stayed and took over family businesses or moved back after school. There was something about the town. As I pondered over what it might be, Indy and I walked the two miles along the tree-lined streets and dark pieces of property and not once did I get spooked.

By the time we arrived home, it was after ten. I went ahead and packed the Jeep before I went to bed. I'd never settled down from my visit with the professor. I could count on one hand the number of times I'd gone against my gut. The feeling that something was off didn't leave me.

I spent an hour looking for the right place to put the ring. Finally, after I stared at it and looked at it from every direction, I decided I would put it under my pillow.

There were no apparitions like last time. I held it up eye level and instead, an entire phantom vision began to play out in front of me in full color. Of course, I only recognized one person, Judith.

A thought flickered in my mind and I wondered if I should take notes, but after the first three seconds, I knew I would never forget what happened…

Judith was at a dance, standing on the sideline talking to a girl. She smiled and waved to someone across the room. Young men and women were dancing. I couldn't hear the music, but their movements made it evident what they were doing.

Judith had on the green velvet dress mentioned in every telling of the story of her disappearance, with its gold brocade trim. I could see the famous ring on her right hand.

A thought flashed through me, *this could not be real.*

She turned, left the girl she had been talking to and walked down three stairs to what turned out to be a huge open room with upholstered armchairs, coffee tables, and settees .

I could see Judith as she picked her heavy skirt up a little to keep from stepping on it as she descended the stairs. She pushed open a door with the word *WOMEN*, painted on it in glossy black. Under the sign was the silhouette of a woman in a long formal dress.

Judith went into the bathroom and several minutes later, having finished, she started to open the door to exit. She heard a noise and quickly closed the door, leaving it open only a slit so she could watch and hear what went on outside. My view allowed me to peer over her shoulder as if I was standing behind her so I could see from her perspective.

Two men were shouting at one another. Judith acted as it she didn't know why they were fighting. I had to use body language to fill in some of what was happening as there was no sound to go with the vision. She opened the door a bit wider, and I understood then I was seeing what Judith had seen that fateful June night in 1929.

They were young men. One faced Judith's direction while the other had his back to her. I could see the one facing Judith, and me, so clearly. His eyes were green, his hair long, in the style of the times. He had a handsome face and stood a good two inches taller than the man whose face I could not see.

However, I could see the other man's coat was a dark tan and his pants matched.

Within a few minutes, the men began to throw punches. The one with his back to me took out a knife. The way he faced, I could only see the long blade and an intricate carved handle.

He stabbed the other man in the belly, pulled the blade out and sank it again , higher this time. The knife went into his opponent's chest.

I saw Judith abruptly bring her hands to her mouth. She must have made an audible sound because the man with his back to me turned around to face where we stood in the bathroom door.

She closed the door and leaned her back against it. She looked straight at me, fear clear on her face, and mouthed *Help*.

The ring changed back to a solid ruby and the scene faded away. I could see nothing else.

Surely, I had dreamed what happened. How could a simple diamond and ruby ring have such a secret in it?

I didn't get much sleep. I put the ring to my eye more than once. Nothing happened. Was that all I was going to get or would I get another picture of her night when I had deciphered the first one?

I sat up in bed. So, Judith Izzard saw a murder take place and the murderer saw her. Could it be the answer to her disappearance?

Were there two homicides the night of the dance? And if that were the case, why was the hotel so quiet? Wouldn't there be law officers there because of the dead man?

Now the entire story didn't make any sense. Why, in all the years the Judith Izzard story dominated the news, hadn't anyone mentioned the murdered man?

The bones came to mind. I went over what the professor said about the bones not being in the ground very long. I pulled all of the photos I'd taken on my phone. I looked at them over and over, I knew he was wrong. And I'd stake my reputation on my conclusion.

They had all the ear markings suggesting they were there the entire time. The bones looked old to me. They were beginning to crack longwise from loss of calcium and the color suggested age. Why, with his vast experience, would the professor have tried to convince me that the bones were too new to have been Judith Izzard's?

My heart pounded with excitement and trepidation. In the morning I would have to face the professor. It would be easiest to say I didn't have the ring, but I knew I couldn't pull off lying to him. And, I didn't want to go to the dig, I wanted to go to the library and search for a young man, murdered the same night Judith went missing.

At three-fifteen, I climbed into bed and patted the space next to me. Indy jump up got comfortable and soon began to snore softly. I, on the other hand, laid awake looking at the ceiling and then gave up the struggle and got up an hour before the alarm went off.

## Chapter 5

The Jeep Rubicon I drove stayed in the garage in case of rain. Indy and I both preferred the top off. We were stubborn about it. The weather had to prove it would be a gully washer before we put the top on or up depending on the time of year.

I had on cargo pants so I could zip the ring into one of the pockets on the front or side. The closer it got to the time to pick up the professor, the shakier and more nervous I became. It wasn't in my nature to go against the people I looked up to in my life. It also wasn't fair for him to ask me to leave the ring when he knew he'd see it today and could have it all day if need be.

My normal dress, when I worked, included long pants, a long sleeve Mountain Hardware shirt and Ecco boots. I wore a leather pouch around my waist to carry my small equipment. I kept my Ruger LCP22 in my pocket. I had a knife. Sometimes I liked to use a knife to dig with rather than my digging tools. A Mine Lab Equinox 900 was my detector of choice. It and an Ace 400 were always in my car. There might be better detectors on the market. I knew you could spend thousands on one if you were so inclined. I had bought mine while I was a poor college student. By the time I finished they were a part of me and I loved them.

At one time I worried someone would take my equipment. I only had to leave it once to realize Indy would never let anyone take my goodies. He could go from a gentle sleeping dog to a snarling toothed mad mamma-jamma in less than ten seconds. I doubted he would bite anyone, but so far, no one had been willing to get close enough to find out.

Okay, I admit I haven't had to buy my own detector for over ten years when my trusty original detector had finally worn out. Seems I had become well known enough that the companies believed if I tried out their brand, sales would go up. The same went with my preferred work clothes. Those companies were also willing to pay money for me to wear certain name brands of clothes, even if I was not on a job. Who was I to say no? Most likely it would be what I wore anyway.

Over the years it had become less and less of a problem. I signed with a clothing company out of New Hampshire to have my own line of clothes. They added a new item or two every year. Right now, there were T-shirts, wrist and headbands, tennis shoes, jackets and hoodies.

My only staunch rule went like this: *If I don't like your equipment, or your shoes pinch my toes, you can never use the photos of me using or wearing your products.* So far, so good.

Indy got excited daily at the thought of a ride in the car which he knew was getting ready to happen as he watched me gather what I needed for the day. He was four now and had been going with me on every local trip I took and some across country. If I needed to fly, he stayed with my dear friend Emily Smart. We'd known one another since kindergarten. Emily even made him a bed near the inside of the backdoor of the kitchen in the restaurant she owned so he didn't have to stay home alone. She went to Europe for a few years to study the culinary arts and now ran the most popular high dining establishment in Benton.

Okay, the only really truly high end dining place in Benton.

On our way to the professor's house, I drove through Starbucks for coffee and a Danish. Indy preferred a blueberry bagel with strawberry cream cheese.

When we pulled up to the house, Indy didn't dance and whine to get out as he usually did. I had to walk around and invite him to go up the stairs with me. I really couldn't blame him. The professor had never spoken to him, except to ban him from the house. He acted as if the dog wasn't even with me.

I knocked. I didn't hear any music, and no one came to the door. After a good ten minutes of knocking and waiting, I tried the door.

It creaked open. Indy stayed behind me as I stood in the open doorway and called, "Professor, are you there?"

My voice echoed back. I didn't think it would happen if the other doors were closed. I stepped inside. Indy hugged my left leg and went in also. He stayed lockstep with me. We checked Jonah's office first.

It had been ransacked. The books were out of the bookcases and thrown all over the floor. Papers were tossed around and all of the pictures he had collected over the years were taken off the walls. They also had been taken out of their frames. Someone had thrown them to save themselves time. Glass crunched under my feet. It had been a violent break in.

I ordered Indy out of the room and into the hall. I went to find the professor. I stuck my head into each room and looked around. I found him in the room with the safe. It didn't look as though anyone had gone through it and the doors to the cabinet where the safe was, were closed.

The professor lay on his back with two obvious bullet holes in his forehead. I ran back to the front of the house and sat on the floor behind the desk where no one would see me. I needed to think. For a reason I couldn't begin to explain because I didn't know why myself, I didn't call 9 1 1.

I don't know how long I sat there, hidden, not being able to regulate my breathing. Any normal person, when they found their friend murdered in their own house, would have called the police. I chose to ignore protocol. Instead, I reached in my pocket and took out the ring.

I didn't yet know why it warmed up when I had it near my body. I didn't know if it was Judith I saw in the ring or if I was projecting because of the excitement from the find. And now, since I didn't leave it in the professor's hands and because I didn't want to give it up until I knew more about it, I didn't want to be questioned about why I was at the professor's house at seven-thirty in the morning.

Fear coursed through my body. Why would someone kill the professor? Was he right that you couldn't do anything without someone knowing your secret? Did someone know about the ring and the bones?

I held the ring up, there wasn't enough light in the room for me to get a proper look. My brain began to function a little more. Two things occurred to me. I needed to get out of the house and I'd let Indy walk to me over all the glass on the floor. Some dog mom I was.

We heard a noise from the back of the house. Indy barked once. I took the pistol out of my pocket and went down the long hall with the window at the end. As we passed a room, I stepped in and cleared it like I'd seen on *Blue Bloods* so many times.

The difference between them and me was, their hands didn't shake like mine and they didn't have to stop, lean against the wall and try to get a breath so they wouldn't throw up or pass out.

We went toward the noise. It got louder as we went. About three feet from the back door a room went off to the right, the kitchen. The back door was open and it banged against the cabinet behind it in a four-four beat. We went out and I closed the door behind us.

My actions could have been explained away, I realized later. Professor Thomson's murder could not.

I'd created a mess and it wasn't even noon.

# Chapter 6

There was no need to worry about any fingerprints I may have left; I could prove I'd been in the house the evening before. About halfway home I stopped and took stock of what I'd done. I knew there would be a penalty for not reporting a homicide and, worse yet, I left the scene of a crime.

My biggest mistake, the one I made that started the chain of events of yesterday and the morning, came when I found the ring and bones and like a little kid, went to show them to someone.

I don't think the professor was murdered because of my visit.

Maybe no one knew I was in the house last night or this morning. My fingerprints were not on file. Wait, yes, they were. I had to have an FBI background check to get my Conceal and Carry permit.

The ring, legally, belonged to Barclay Simmons. My only claim to it was the money I got paid to see what might be found in or on the property.

What a mess, all created by my lack of professionalism. I began to go over what steps I should have taken. But what good would it do now? I would have to wait and see.

Indy wanted to run ahead and then back. He needed to burn off some energy.

I stopped dead in my tracks. My Jeep was parked on Janice Street, right in front of the professor's house. In my shock I had forgotten I'd driven there.

I ran as fast as I could back to Jonah Thompson's Street. I stood beneath the trees to see if there was any movement. There was none and why would there be? Every house on the street was either occupied by a professor, teacher, or retiree from Dorman. They were an older crowd.

Casually, I got in the car. Indy, who had caught up with me a mile back, jumped into the back. He thought it a great adventure. I didn't speed down the street. Also, instead of going straight home, I went through McDonald's drive through and got Indy a hamburger.

As soon as I got in the house, I put my phone on private and called 9 1 1.

"9 1 1 what's your emergency?"

"There was a murder at 2335 Janice Lane."

"What's your name? Are you at the address you gave me, right now?"

I hung up.

# Chapter 7

I heard the grandfather clock in the downstairs hall strike two. Still afternoon. Lots could go wrong before the day was over. My clothes were filthy and somehow, I had blood on my pant leg and on my wrist.

I took a shower and put on an old pair of Nike sweatpants and a faded Dorman sweatshirt, brushed my wet hair, and put it up in a ponytail. I went downstairs and stuck the bloody clothes in the washer with a half cup of bleach. I knew I didn't need as much as I used, but I wanted to remove all the stains.

I opened the refrigerator door when I passed it on my way to the den. The thought of eating made me nauseous. I poured a glass of wine. It broke another one of my rules: never drink when you are upset. I poured the wine back into the bottle and closed the door.

I rarely watched TV so it took a while for me to find the remote. I looked at my Fitbit, which I used as a timepiece, among other things.

I figured out apprehension and nerves were what was keeping me in front of the TV. When the news picked up the professor's murder, I wanted to hear what they had to say.

My only hope was the mistakes I made had nothing to do with why the professor lost his life.

The doorbell rang. I glanced at my wrist again. Three-thirty, it didn't take long for them to find me. Why pick my house out of all the rest. I ran upstairs to put the ring in my pocket; I felt it belonged there

Most importantly, I didn't get to look in the newspaper archives to see if the young man who was stabbed had actually died the night Judith disappeared. If what I saw was the way it had happened, I'm sure he died.

I ran up the stairs two at a time, grabbed the ring, shoved it in my pocket and ran back down. They must have been talking outside because they only rang once.

I looked out the window and saw two cars, a police car and a black SUV. The cruiser sat in the driveway, the SUV behind it but parked in the way so no one could drive in or out.

My heart skipped a beat. All I could think of was how fast they found me.

A tall, uniformed man with dark close-cropped hair stood on the porch with his back to the door.

I opened the front door and the man in uniform stepped back. Behind him, stood a tall, blond man dressed in a navy pin striped, three-piece-suit. His light blue shirt looked as if it had been freshly laundered. His stylish navy tie matched the stripe in his suit.

He was a handsome man. I pegged him at about six-foot-two. He definitely lifted weights.

In his hand he held a leather ID wallet. Blake Wade, Special Agent, FBI, the shield and his picture were prominently displayed.

After he showed me his badge, he stepped forward. "May we come in?"

I stepped back and let Indy come closer to the door where he could be seen. "What is this about, Agent?"

He took another half-step forward and the Benton City Officer stepped closer to him. "I'm sure you know, Dr. Ford."

My stomach rose to my throat. I put my hand down and touched Indy's scruff. "Bed, Indy," I said, before I moved out of their way and gave them access to the foyer.

Both men walked into the hallway with purpose. "Is there somewhere we can sit and talk about your whereabouts yesterday evening and this morning or would you rather talk at the station?" He nodded to Officer Orval Johnston, according to the policeman's name tag.

I turned around and began to walk toward my living room. "We can talk here," I said, "I don't want to leave my dog here alone."

The officer, who I didn't recognize, glanced around the room and took a seat in my recliner next to the front window.

The FBI agent looked around the room too, but his assessment wasn't the same. When he finally sat down, I knew he could close his eyes and recite where every item in the room sat and what they were. He sat on the sofa and patted the other end for me to sit.

The room remained quiet for a long minute. The only sound I heard came from my parents' grandfather clock in the hallway. I broke the ice. "Since I don't know either of you gentlemen, I realize this is not a social call. Would you like to get started?"

"Get started on what?" Agent Wade asked.

"You tell me," I said.

"Okay, Dr. Ford. I'm getting weary of your attitude. You know as well as I do your friend Professor Jonah Thompson was murdered last night. We know for a fact you found his body. At this point we don't believe you killed him, but we need you to begin cooperating right now."

Special Agent Wade paused and leaned toward me. "You're trying my patience. The longer you stall, the more I think you have something to do with all of this.

"I'll make this easy. We have you on film arriving at Professor Jonah Thompson's home at around seven P.M. yesterday evening and leaving at around nine. Several cameras followed your progress back here to your home. We know once you arrived home, you didn't leave again."

I took a deep breath and then said, "I admit I went to see the professor. We are friends. I have visited his home dozens of times over the years. I don't see a problem with that."

"Neither do we, Dr. Ford. But you went back this morning and stayed about an hour. On your way home, you realized your car still sat in front of the professor's house and you ran back to get it."

I looked at the Benton officer. He sat leaning with his forearms on his knees and his hat in one hand. He must have been new to the force because, I swear, he looked twelve. I caught myself leaning forward to see if he had any kind of facial hair. His eyes were so dark brown I could see the reflection of my face in them when he leaned toward me. He smiled at me and nodded his head up and down. I guessed it to be a signal for me to talk.

I sat up a little straighter and turned to face Wade head-on. "I don't know much. Last evening, I took some artifacts I found on a dig earlier in the day to the professor's house. He helped me identify the items. I left and walked home.

"The professor wanted to go with me this morning to my dig and search the site further. I went there this morning to pick him up. He didn't answer the door, which was ajar.

"I walked through the house while I called his name. I found him dead in his den. I wasn't sure what to do. Indy, my dog, and I came home. I wanted to get out of there. On the way, I remembered I'd driven over there and I ran back to get my car. That's the end of it."

"I doubt that is all there is to it. You have the same degrees as Thompson. Why would you need him to help you with an artifact? You don't recognize me, do you Dr. Ford?" the agent asked.

"No, I don't. You'll have to refresh my memory."

"It was UCLA. You had your master's and I went there to study criminology. Some of the required classes I needed to take, you taught. I couldn't tell you the exact names of the classes anymore. It seems like a lifetime ago.

"You were less than thrilled when someone stopped to question one of your statements." He gave me a grin showing his perfect white teeth. It made his eyes sparkle and reminded me of Dudley DoRight.

I relaxed a little. "Now I don't feel as bad. There were between one hundred and two hundred students in the lecture hall at any one time. I didn't even try to take roll, it was useless. I doubt I noticed you unless you were a burr in my saddle. "

"I find that a very reasonable answer." The grin again, then he added, "I wanted you to know I have seen your temper flare. It's a common trait in a murderer.

"Again, my question is why would you, a famous antiquities expert, need to ask Professor Thompson's opinion on anything?"

"It had to do with a missing piece from years ago. It has always been sort of an unwritten bet among treasure hunters around here as to who would find it."

"And you believe you found it?"

"Yes, but it has nothing to do with why someone killed him. I found it while I worked on an old farm around here. No one knows I had it. I went straight to Jonah's house with it."

"Again, why would you need to ask him to identify a piece for you?"

"I didn't need him to identify it. Haven't you ever had a case, and you knew you were going in the right direction with it, but you talk to a colleague just to see what they think?"

He didn't answer so I went on.

"We might have the same letters behind our names, but he is nearly fifty years older than I am. And has lectured, taught, and dug in all fifty states and fifty-nine countries. It would be like a novice soprano wanting to take over for Barbara Streisand because she was out with a sore throat." I smiled at him, "And we were friends."

The entire time I spoke, he had been taking notes on a pad and pen he took out of his breast pocket. "What are the items you took to show the professor?"

I leaned back and took a deep breath. "I'd rather not say."

He looked at me, he smiled a cold fake smile. "Dr. Ford."

"Could you please call me Alexa? Few people call me doctor."

"Okay, Alexa, will the name change help you loosen up a bit?"

I stood. "I need a cup of coffee. Would you two like to join me?"

Neither of them answered me, but they both followed me into the kitchen.

# Chapter 8

I wanted a cup of coffee like I wanted a hole in my head. My mind hadn't had time to absorb what I'd seen at Jonah's house, much less what my dig might have to do with it. I took my time to make the coffee and set cream and sugar on the table along with three mugs I bought from an antique shop near Fisherman's Warf in San Francisco. They were made by a young blind man.

The cups were amazingly the same size and color. I didn't know how he did it.

My mind whirled. I had no intention of giving up the ring, or telling him about it for that matter. So, knowing there were no identification marks or tags on the bag of bones, I decided to only talk about those.

"Agent Wade," I said after I served the coffee, "I'm afraid I made a mistake yesterday. But I don't believe it had anything to do with the Professor's death."

The two men looked at one another before Blake Wade answered me. "We are ninety percent sure his murder is connected to artifacts from World War II, and art from some of the great masters that have gone missing. We can track most of them to Dorman College and then we lose track of them."

"So, you think my friend, the professor was an artifact thief?"

"I didn't say that and I shouldn't have told you that."

"Well, you're barking up the wrong tree here. I found some bones that at one time were fingers. I wanted to know how old they were. I guessed over fifty-years. To run tests, I would have to go to the lab at the college. Professor Thompson had everything I needed right in his house so I went there. We didn't agree on how old the bones were. He said they had only been in the ground for five or six years.

"We decided I would pick him up this morning and he'd go to the site with me. Maybe we could find some artifacts to help age the bones. A couple of major events happened on and near the property I'm searching."

I took a sip of my coffee and sat the cup on the table. I was prepared to stop talking.

Agent Wade looked at me over the rim of his cup as he took a drink. "Let's stop right there. I have a couple of questions. Can you go anywhere you want and begin to dig for treasure?"

"No, it takes permission to go on personal property. Anything we pay taxes on we have a right to use. I always ask permission except for schoolyards and parks."

"So, you ask or someone gave you permission to dig where you are searching now?" Wade asked.

"No, I was hired by a man who bought the land. He researched and realized the Trail of Tears and the first telegraph line went through a part of the property. He wanted to have someone go through the fifty acres he bought and see if there is anything of value there."

"Do you have any idea why he hired you to do the work?"

Officer Johnston said, "I can answer your question, Agent. Dr. Ford is world famous for her work, plus she is a guest speaker at conferences all over the world. She's been on the cover of *People*, *National Geographic*, and *Sports Illustrated*, unfortunately not the swimsuit issue." His face turned the color of a maraschino cherry before he got all the words out of his mouth.

My demeanor must have changed noticeably because Indy came into the room and sat beside me. "It's okay, boy. I'm fine. Do you want to go outside?"

He got up and exited the kitchen through his doggy door.

Both men looked at me. "He's my best friend. He knows when my mood changes. If he thinks I might be in danger, he comes to me."

"Did you train him?" Officer Johnston asked.

"No. A wounded veteran who once trained dogs for the military trained him. I took some time off so I could be with the two of them while he was being trained. Indy is who led me to Jonah's body this morning."

"What is the name of the man who hired you?" Wade asked.

"Barclay Simmons."

He looked at me. "Barclay Simmons who is listed as a land speculator from somewhere in New Jersey?"

"One in the same," I said. "I did a background check on him before I agreed to search the land. There isn't much about him until he was thirty. It is like he showed up one day. When I could only find vague references on him, I shot him a price twice my normal fee and asked for half down.

"I figured if he didn't pay anymore after the retaining fee, I at least wouldn't get hurt financially."

"So how did you know how to grid off the land?"

I smiled. "I've done this since I was a kid. My dad and I went out with a metal detector every chance we could. After a while, you know where things are buried. Remember, I studied antiquities for many years."

Agent Blake Wade nodded to me. "Finish your story."

"I picked my starting place and within five minutes I'd dug up the bones of a hand. Actually, nine small bones equaling three digits.

"I intended to show them to the professor, put them back and call the authorities. He insisted he keep them."

The agent stood, walked to the coffee urn and poured himself another cup. "Anyone else," he asked as he presented the glass carafe to us. The police officer said no and I shook my head to indicate the same. "Are you always as reckless with items you find or is this an isolated incident?"

I could feel my face and neck begin to burn. This guy was some piece of work. I wanted both of them out of my house. As soon as I relaxed and told him my story, he attacked me. I turned to face him head on. "You have no idea who I am or what I do. The only mistake I made was to take the items to the professor instead of having him come to me.

"Now, either charge me with something or go. I'm growing weary of your attitude."

"Slow down. I didn't mean what I said quite the way it came out. I have nothing to charge you with, Alexa. Do you know the combination to the safe?"

"No. Now if you will excuse me, I have work to do."

I began to walk toward the front door. He had no other choice but to follow me or sit and drink his coffee. With in a few seconds I heard both men behind me. "I need the address of your dig. And don't leave the area. I might need to talk to you again."

The officer cut in and said, "I know where it is. I hunt deer out there every year. The deed is still in Ben Izzard's name, or it was. He is a couple of generations back. I'd check so I'd know whose permission I would have to have to hunt there. Seemed no one was around to care."

Once we were outside, Agent Blake Wade put his hand out to me. I looked at it. When I didn't move to shake it, his face turned pink and he withdrew the offer.

"It was nice to meet you, Alexa."

"I'm sorry I can't say the same. And you can call me Dr. Ford."

Halfway to his car, he turned toward me. "Where are the bones now?"

"I left them with the Professor."

# CHAPTER 9

I went back inside the house, locked the door behind me and fell onto the couch. Indy jumped up beside me. "I should have told you to bite him."

Indy yipped once and rested his head on my lap before I got up.

As I cleaned up the mugs and emptied the coffee pot, I went over the entire event in my mind. What happened when I arrived at Jonah's house. How he acted about the ring. How he knew who Barclay Simmons was.

There must be a good reason why the rules are the rules. Call the authorities, call an institution of higher learning and go from there.

It could not have been the ring and fingers that caused someone to want to rob and kill the professor. Agent Wade said war artifacts sometimes disappeared once they reached the Professor's house. What the FBI agent had told me seemed a more plausible reason for the professor's murder. The only question I had was did the professor know they were stolen artifacts or was he caught up in something he didn't know to be illegal?

Or was my old friend a Trojan Horse?

Personally, I couldn't picture it. Jonah Thompson had been an upstanding man since day one. On the other hand, everyone in law enforcement seemed to know the name of Barclay Simmons. I couldn't help but believe they had something to do with one another. It was curious that the professor, the agent, and I were all involved with a man named Barclay Simmons.

I believe the old adage, you never really know someone is true.

No one could have known about my finding the ring. Not until I told the professor. I left early yesterday morning. The sun had barely risen when I went through the Starbucks drive through. I saw no one. As a matter of fact, the barista commented I had the first cup of the day.

On the way to do the job I contracted with Barcley Simmons I didn't pass a single soul.

On my way to the site, I had considered the likeliest places to begin looking. There were always hints, trees, planted an equal distant apart, in a straight line was a favorite. The problem there, the trees grew over the years and many times the roots were grown over the area the ancestors hid the bounty.

In the past, I'd had to break glass jars and dig currency and coins out of the ground. This was a direct result that for years, farm folks hadn't trusted banks. After The Depression, no one trusted banks. They hid money, jewelry, and heirlooms out on the property.

After putting my flags thirty feet out from each tree, I had looked for the first of the hints: stands of trees. Farms called them glades or natural pastures. Most folks with theft on their minds didn't want to walk or dig in cow manure to try to find something of value. That wasn't a problem with the Izzard farm now. No one had grazed an animal on it for at least seventy-five years.

Then came the springs, if there were any, or natural waterways. They were usually a treasure trove, especially if the water ran down hill to them the way they did at the Izzard farm. Rains over the years would change the lay of the land and previously buried items would wash up and be carried in creeks and streams during flash floods or years of rain.

---

The Trail of Tears, a forced relocation of Native Americans, namely the Cherokee and Osage went through Missouri. It had taken the Northern route from 1837 to 1839. This path also had promised the possibility of artifacts.

Once I had marked out the most likely spots for success, there never ended up being much left. I guessed that to clear the fifty acres and do it properly would take me about ninety days. And then just one day in, everything had changed.

The equipment I used was kept in the car unless it needed to be charged. All the small items took batteries. I made a snack and a big jug of water for me and one for Indy. I put my gun in my pocket. We were ready to pick up where we had left off yesterday.

It was a lot of preparation to go downtown to the library, but if I was being followed, I didn't need to raise any more red flags.

Indy and I spent the next few hours at the library. Of course, Indy stayed in the car. No way would he let anyone take anything or, for that matter, get near the car. He would not take a treat, drink, or toy from anyone but me. Even a sirloin steak wouldn't get his attention. He'd never bit anyone, but once the hair on the back of his neck bristled and he snarled, folks cut him a wide berth.

---

It didn't take me long to find the stories from June of 1929. The avenues the news, the papers, and magazines followed were the death of eighteen-year-old Nathan McGuire of Seymour. Who, according to those sources, had been stabbed by an unknown assailant at the Bailey House the same night Judith went missing.

There was one story about the hotel closing early, but it was attributed to a plumbing problem. The one and only article about it stated that all of the teens from the graduation dance had been picked up before the hotel closed its doors.

Once it was determined Judith Izzard didn't make it home, the murder, the odd closing of the hotel, and the investigation of the murdered boy were never mentioned again. It was like it never happened. To me, it meant it did happen, and that made it all the more important than ever.

The Benton Library didn't carry old stories from the national papers except for major events. Those stories included Marilyn Monroe's death, the Kennedy assassination, Nixon's debacle, the moon landing, the plane crash with the Big Bopper and Rickie Valens and more of the biggest events in history.

On page four of the Kansas City Star, four days after the dance, there was an article about the death of Nathan McGuire. It said: *Nathan McGuire of Seymour, Missouri was found dead in the woods near his home, he had been beaten and robbed. Nineteen-year-old McGuire was the son of Roger McGuire, the President of the Bank of Seymour. The cause of death was a fatal stab wound to the chest. The police are searching for the killer but have no leads at this time.*

I looked up Roger McGuire. In 1929 he was not a popular guy because of The Depression and bank failures. The only other article about him and his family said, "he and his family moved away from Seymour after the death of their son, Nathan."

The ring moved in my pocket. Surely it didn't know what I was doing at the computer in the library or even what a computer was? I reached into my pocket and took it out.

Instantly I was back in the bathroom at the hotel with Judith. The young man I couldn't see had turned around and faced Judith. His face was purple with bruises and rage.

He strode toward Judith, closing the distance between them in long strides. He pushed the door she was leaning against so hard she flew against the vanity. He picked her up and slapped her across the face, twice. The man was short, his clothes expensive. He wore an initial ring on the ring finger of his right hand. The first time he hit her the ring cut into her face and caused it to bleed. The second time he backhanded her, he hit her nose and broke it.

Gaging him in size with the man he had stabbed, he was significantly shorter. Judith must have been tiny because she was much smaller than him despite his lack of height. His hair was shorter than the other man's and a dirty blond. He had a sturdy build, not quite fat, but not thin either.

He pulled her close to him with one hand and said something in her ear. I could see the initial on his ring was a T. She began to cry. The man grabbed her arm, pulled and manhandled her through the common room and out a back door.

The stone cooled down, and she was gone.

I hated to jump to conclusions, but this had to be Judith's murderer. I heard Indy bark more than once. I closed the machine down, thanked the librarian and headed toward the car.

When I rounded the corner, Indy had half of his body extended as far out of the car as he could. He was barking at our friendly FBI Agent, Blake Wade. Geez, didn't the man have any sense?

"Don't harass my dog," I said.

He gave me a look I couldn't read. "I wasn't bothering him. I went to your dig and you weren't there. On my way back to the hotel, I saw your car parked here." He looked at his watch and then back at me. "Since it is already three--thirty, I decided you were not going there today. Just being nosey, wondering what you're up to."

I tried not to change my expression. I knew he wanted to get me to react, but I wouldn't. "I went to the library to do some research."

"On what?"

"Since it has nothing to do with the dig in Seymour or the death of the professor, I don't have to tell you." He looked at me and said nothing, but his eyes flashed and I knew he was angry.

"I really need to get home. I need to feed Indy and take him for a walk." I moved past him and got into the car.

"Later, then," is all he said.

Indy and I went home. The events of the day had killed my appetite. I fixed him a bowl of food and sat on the floor next to him as he ate.

We went for our evening walk and called it a night. I hoped I could get Judith, the dead boy, the killer, the FBI agent and Professor Thompson out of my mind so I could rest.

## Chapter 10

I woke up with a start. Darkness still owned the sky and a quick glance at the clock told me it was only four-thirty in the morning. A flash of lightning lit up the room followed by a giant boom and rolling thunder. I hated storms before daylight.

I knew I wouldn't go back to sleep; I grabbed my robe and went downstairs to make coffee.

Something had been bugging me. Until I found Judith's ring, I had always kept a journal of my jobs and so far, I haven't written a word. Now was as good a time as ever.

I took my coffee and went to my office behind the garage. Indy dragged along behind me. It was apparent he, at least, could have slept longer. I reached down and patted his head. "You can sleep in your bed in the office," I told him.

It didn't take long to make a permanent record of the job, beginning with Barclay Simmons and then continuing to the ring, the death of Professor Thompson and Agent Wade. My only stumbling block was explaining the ring and I had what I decided to call my *human interaction* with it.

Once I had what I believed to be an accurate and honest record, I went back to the kitchen to grab another cup of coffee before I went back to searching for more information on Nathan McGuire and to track down the young man with an initial ring with a "T" on it.

I began with the graduating class of Benton High School in 1929. There were only twelve students, seven girls and five boys. Using Google images, I was able to procure a photo of the class. The girls in the front row were on a bench. They all wore their hair down. As far as I could tell, there was one blond, one redhead and three brunettes. Even though the photo was black and white, Judith Izzard's hair was red when she appeared in the movie clips I saw in the ring.

Nathan McGuire stood in the back row. It was all the information I gleaned from the picture.

I looked up an image from 1928 and no student's last name began with "T". In the years 1927, and 1926, there were students named Thomas, Thurman, and Terry; all were girls.

The photo from 1925 had a boy named Thompson, Morgan Thompson. It was the boy I saw in the vision with the help of Judith. If my memory served me correctly, Professor Thompson had three brothers and his father also had several siblings. I needed to go to Ancestry.com and look up the professor's family. It meant most likely Morgan Thompson was his uncle or cousin.

I began to look at the Thompson Family one at a time. Of the professor's three brothers, the youngest had two daughters, his middle brother had two boys and a girl, the oldest brother had four boys, Michael, Mason, Matthew and Mark. No Morgans there. I would have to keep looking. I moved further up the family tree. The professor's father was a senator, like their father before him, and had one brother. Bingo – Morgan Thompson.

No wonder the professor gave out the mystery of Judith as a term paper choice. The boy who fatally stabbed Nathan McGuire to death was his relative as I thought. It didn't necessarily mean he did something to Judith, but in the vision, I saw him pull her along with him after the murder and she was never seen again.

I shook my head. There were some people in the world who would believe in the power of the ruby and diamond ring, but they were few and far between. I needed to solve the mystery myself with actual evidence. I doubted there were any folks a minimum of one hundred and twelve years old for me to interview.

Indy came up to me and began to whine. I looked at the clock, it was nearly eleven. As smart as he was, he couldn't get his own breakfast.

The sun had come out and the ground had dried. I thought we needed to go to the Izzard farm. I took one more look at the ring, in case Judith had more to say, but the ruby was dark and the ring relatively cool.

My next obstacle would be another interview with the local police and Agent Wade if they'd found any part of my story they disputed. Since the only fact I'd changed from the truth was to not admit to finding the ring, I wasn't worried.

My experience told me the uncovering of the ring and the fact the ring ended up on a finger not belonging to Judith Izzard, so the professor had believed, would be a major, nationwide news story. However, knowing someone was murdered the night Judith went missing, that the professor knew the illusive Barclay Simmons, and the FBI had been watching the professor for a long time and were familiar with the name Barclay Simmons made me think there was more to the story than I was being told. I didn't know what to think. I didn't always consider myself a wise person, but one lesson I learned over and over again was nothing is as it seems. And the less you say, the better off you are.

The story had been legend in the area for nearly a hundred years. I would bet new details would come out none of us knew. I was both excited and perplexed.

The entire afternoon at the farm, I had a nervous feeling. I stopped more than usual to look around. Indy would not let anyone, or anything, come near me. I believe it was just the excitement of the find. Thank goodness, dogs, especially mine, guarded their owners diligently. Back at the hole where I found the ring and bones, I began to dig for more parts of the girl. I certainly didn't think someone buried her hand and a million-dollar ring and then dumped the rest of the corpse elsewhere. The body lay on the farm; I knew it.

I took out a Garrett pin pointer and stuck it in the hole I'd left after I found the ring. It beeped nearly continuously. People had partied in this area over the years. I fully expected to find an abundance of bottle caps and pull tabs. The cedar glade covered what I gauged to be about five acres.

The trees were no more than ten feet apart in any direction. It would have made an ideal location to hide a body.

What puzzled me was, the hand lay at the far northeast side of the stand of trees. Had it been me, I would have buried it in the middle, where no one could see me get rid of her.

The horrible thought that someone might have chopped up the girl's body made me shudder.

I knelt on my toes and rested my lower legs on my boots. I looked from tree to tree. Nearly one hundred years ago something happened to a nineteen-year-old girl. I had been looking at it from a modern viewpoint. When I got home, I would look at the original maps and abstracts. There might not have been a road through the area fifty years ago. Everywhere they went, especially a young girl, would have gone in a carriage with a driver.

# Chapter 11

One-half of all the money ever minted in the entire world remains lost. Folks were no more inclined to pick up a penny a hundred years ago than they are today. The difference is, some of those pennies can now be worth hundreds and even thousands of dollars. I fully expected to find some of that here on the Izzard farm long before I found anything more helpful or related to Judith's ring.

Instead, I found a pendant less than two feet from where I found the ring and finger bones. Someone had probably given it as a gift. On the front a dragonfly had been etched and on the back: *We are so proud of you, MJ, June 13, 2019.*

The professor hadn't been far off with his estimate of the age of the finger bones. If the pendant belonged to the same person the fingers had come from, she'd have only been in the ground for six years instead of five. He knew his stuff. Or it could have been lost a week ago. A closer look showed it to be fourteen caret gold. A small number 78 was printed near the clasp, a jeweler's mark. I happened to recognize this particular mark as belonging to Marcus Jewelry. Dragonflies were popular gifts for girls graduating from high school and college since many people believed they represented transformation and personal growth.

I'd found pieces with the Marcus brand before. I'd most likely be able to find out when it had been sold and perhaps who bought it. It looked expensive and usually numbered pieces from Marcus were on the company database.

Before Indy and I sat under a pine tree to take a break, I put the pendant in one of the zipper pockets in my cargo pants where it would be safe. Offhandedly, I wondered why it didn't have a chain with it. Maybe I'd come across that later.

I took the ring out of my pocket and held it up to the light. My world became distorted. The tall straight pines began to wiggle and move into odd shapes. The sky turned black and the surface of the ring seemed to grow to the size of an outdoor movie theater. Judith was underground. I could see jars of canned food, beans, and something made from tomatoes. There were other objects on shelves plates, urns, and even old paintings in ornate frames.

Standing at the bottom of what looked like a ramp, were Judith and the man who killed Nathan McGuire, Morgan Thompson.

And here I was at this point in my investigation with nothing but questions for which I had no answers.

# CHAPTER 12

My latest spectral vision, seemingly brought to me by Judith Izzard from beyond the grave, marked the end of my day and time for me to head home to try and process everything going through my head. After I fed the dog, showered, put on sweatpants and a tee shirt. I went downstairs, it was like a light had gone on in my brain and I was now super aware of thoughts I hadn't had until now. First, the bones. I looked at the thirty or so pictures I'd taken at the dig on my phone. This time I saw the obvious; the growth plates were attached proving the person they belonged to had finished growing. I also remembered the ring would have fit me and I wore a size six. I slid it on my finger. It slid on as if it were made for me.

When I had uncovered the ring, it showed no dirt, mud or grime matted to the stones, the settings or the prongs. Almost as if it hadn't lay buried in the dirt for the past 96 years.

I sat the phone on the desktop, crossed my arms and laid my forehead on them. What was wrong with me. My mistake had been so amateurish. I wanted to follow my thought pattern from yesterday, but I couldn't.

Ten years of digs had flown out the window. I could only think it came from the shock of finding the famous Izzard ring. And maybe a little bit from the strange things that kept happening around that ring. I raised my head and pulled up the photos of the fingers. They were the same, no crust, caked on dirt and no scuffing. They were perfect.

What did it mean, I asked myself? It meant the artifacts had only been in the ground since before the last rain. My calendar hung on the wall behind my desk. The last rain had been eleven days earlier.

All the weather facts were on my schedule. I recorded the rain, sunrise, sunset, moon phase and how many hours of daylight we had. I guessed it to be the nerd in me.

Where was I on the eleventh of May? According to my notes, I went shopping with Emily who always insisted it was best to shop on rainy days.

I took a few deep breaths and realized I could never get on with my discovery if I didn't forgive myself for the awe I had when I saw the ring. It caused everything I'd studied so hard to learn, fly away.

Indy had turned restless. Who could blame him? No one was in the house, nothing seemed out of order yet I'm sure he sensed my unease.

"Indy, let's take out the trash and walk around the block."

I didn't have to ask twice. He ran around me in circles.

The sky sparkled with stars, the moon stood high in the sky, nearly full, which illuminated the homes we passed. To not ruin a lovely night, I forced my mind away from the obvious conclusion I had reached. Professor Jonah Thompson had set me up. No wonder he knew the name Barclay Simmons. Most likely they'd both been involved in my once-in-a-century find.

Why else wouldn't he see the fingers as he laid them out were out of order. He had third, first and little, the first two should have been switched. It brought up three questions. First, why did he do it; and second, why didn't I notice it? And third, what did it mean?

I had to admit to myself, I had put the bones from the fingers in the same order the professor did when I photographed them. We might be adults, but the excitement on my side was palpable. I would put the bones out of my mind and go on with what Judith showed me today.

After our walk, I stayed in the backyard with Indy and ran him through his paces. He could shake, give me five, roll over, play dead, heel, get up on an object, and stay for indefinite lengths of time and much more. He wanted to do more but I was calm enough to go in.

But, before I put the subject of the bones away, there was one more thing I needed to admit to myself. I could guarantee the professor, in his fifty years on the job, would never have missed such a blatant mistake. It could have only meant one thing.

# Chapter 13

A habit I tried to keep included at least one healthy meal a day. I had a glass of wine. The ring was lukewarm in my pocket, but my nerves were on edge anyway. I'd always been a pragmatist. The ring showing me visions of happenings so far in the past, unnerved me. I'd heard many stories about gems and precious stones and how they influence behavior. I put it out of my mind as folklore.

After today and all the heavy thinking, I couldn't muster enough energy to cook. I called Guido's Pizza and ordered a large veggie pizza and a garden salad.

While I waited, I drank a glass of Pinot Noir. I knew in my present mood and physical condition, and on an empty stomach, I should have passed on the third glass of wine and switched to water. Problem was, I didn't always do what was in my best interest.

By the time the doorbell rang alerting me my food had arrived, I'd dozed on the couch. It took me a long minute to shake off the fog and remember about the pizza.

When I opened the door, there stood FBI Agent Blake Wade, with my pizza balanced on one hand and my salad in the other.

I stepped around him and looked out the door and down the road in both directions. "Where is James, my delivery boy?"

"I told him he could go on."

I turned and walked into the house. "Tell me you tipped him."

He smiled a killer smile I might have liked if I hadn't already considered him a jerk.

Oops. I promised I would not prejudge situations anymore. I took my food out of his hands and turned to walk toward the kitchen. "Why are you here?"

My robe began to slide open and I remembered I hadn't dressed again after my bath. My evening plans had included a pizza, another stint on the back porch while Indy took his last time out for the day, and then bed.

Before I turned to face the man, I pulled my robe tight and tied the inside belts, which I never did. I tied the outside belt and turned toward him.

"I told you earlier, I wanted to ask you more questions after the CSI teams left the crime scene at the professor's."

Once I sat the pizza box on the table, I got out a plate and looked up at him. "Are you hungry?" I asked.

"Sure, if you have enough. I didn't have time to eat dinner. I came straight from the murder house."

I shook my head at him. "Do you have to call it that? Jonah Thompson was my friend."

Instead of sitting, he hovered. When I turned to put our dishes on the table, I bumped into him.

"I realized you were friends when we found the extensive file he kept on you."

"That surprises me. What kind of file? Most of the time except when we met one on one, I thought he just tolerated his students, me included.

"I brought it with me. It's in the car. Let's eat first. The man clearly admired you. He kept track of all your digs and assignments, copies of all your papers, and several photos.

"I'd actually call it more of a dossier with the depth and quality of information he kept. He had several more of them on different people. The agency is tracking down who and where the others are. I'm hoping you might be able to help me out with the list.

"The most interesting item comes at the end of the biographies he had compiled. He adds a list of strengths, as though he were a recruiter."

We ate in silence for a minute or two while I pondered this new information about my now dead friend. Indy must not have liked the quiet. He came into the room, sniffed Wade up and down and sat next to my chair, between the agent and me.

The old saying, *you catch more flies with honey than vinegar* came to mind. So I asked, "Would you like a beer or a glass of wine?"

"Beer," he said nodding and I made an effort to change my attitude.

Clearly, Thompson's murder involved more than a simple home invasion or robbery. If I played ball with the agent, I could get information of my own. I wanted to know who killed my friend and why a man from New Jersey happened to call me to search a piece of land with a body on it. And why the professor had let me make a fool of myself by not having me look once again at the bones before he whisked them away and locked them up. I believe he did it on purpose. I know now he knew more about the murder and his family history than he let on. Maybe he was the one who displayed them wrong because of nerves.

I set a plate in front of Agent Wade for his pizza, handed him a beer from the fridge and gave him a bowl and a fork so he could share my salad.

I needed to know the entire story about the professor. For that, I could play nice with the Special Agent.

# Chapter 14

When Agent Wade began to talk, he opened right up. He still wore the same suit he had on earlier in the day. He reached into the inside pocket in his coat and pulled out a small notebook. "Do you recognize any of these names? This is everyone Professor Thompson had a dossier on." He took a piece of paper out of the notebook, unfolded it, laid it on the table and slid it over to me.

I read the names out loud and added what I knew about each as I went down the list, "Markus Darnell and I were lab partners while I earned my doctorate at UCLA."

"What do archaeology lab partners do?" he asked curiously.

"We paired up to learn how to identify artifacts, rocks and gems. Nothing nefarious. We didn't keep in touch. According to the college's newsletter, he is a professor at Dartmouth, married and has three kids."

"Alice Dean," I continued, "and I were roommates at Stanford. Another person I didn't keep in contact with. I don't know anything about her life now. She could be anything from a nun to a hooker." I smiled so he knew I didn't mean anything bad.

"Isla Moore is an Assistant Professor at Dorman College. She teaches Archaeology Field Methods, and several more classes. I only know her by sight. I'd say she is near retirement age.

"I don't know John Sears or Samuel Smith."

He stared at me for a long minute. "That helps," he said. We finished eating in thoughtful silence.

Wade helped me put the dishes in the dishwasher after we finished eating. I gave him a second beer and took my wine into the den. Indy walked close to my leg. He stayed between the agent and me.

Agent Wade took a coaster out of a holder on the end table and sat his bottle on it. "I'll get the files from the car. Maybe going over the information will jog your memory of the two on the list you don't know."

"They all went to at least one of the schools you did and all of them at the same time as you. You all didn't have the same major. John Sears studied International Banking, Samuel Smith, tackled Forensic Science and is a coroner in Washington, DC. Somehow you all had to have crossed paths with the professor.

"Dr. Alexa Ford, are you with one of the government's underground initial groups, CIA to name one?" He asked suddenly.

I started to laugh but when I looked into his blue eyes, I saw how serious he had become.

"Why would you ask that? My life is an open book. If you follow my trips and the papers I've written along the way, you'll see I don't do anything in secret."

He leaned forward, "Is that a no?"

I still believed he couldn't be serious. "Of course not. Why would you ask such a question?"

"Because Professor Thompson worked for the government, as did three of the people on the list I showed you. If you were not recruited, you were being groomed. How old are you?"

I stood and took a step back. "Agent. This conversation is going downhill. I am not an agent for this government or any other. What is this all about?"

"An official from Homeland Security called me today. He informed me some of the people on this list are CIA, or Homeland Security. Maybe even a different agency altogether. They told me on the phone today that the professor had the highest security clearance on our whole list.

"Things are topsy-turvy. No one wants to share information. I'm going to ask you one more time, are you a government agent?"

"Absolutely not. I'm an archeologist. I have a minor in accounting because I knew I didn't want to work for anyone and I didn't want to go to jail for not being able to keep my own books.

"This is ridiculous. I found artifacts at the dig today. They might shed some light on who our fingers belong too. It is my only interest. I wanted to share it with you so if the girl is missing, we can find her and ease her family's pain."

Agent Wade stood up and went to the front window. He opened the drapes and stared out to the dark, empty street. He didn't turn toward me when he said, "I'm sorry. It's frustrating. We all work for the same country, for the same outcome even. When we come up against another agency, it's the worst thing imaginable. Today, I felt more like the enemy than an agent."

What do I say? Nothing, I decided. "Is the dead girl, the one who's finger bones were found at the dig, important, or are you now going in another direction?" I asked.

"She's important, I'm just frustrated with the powers that be."

"Which do you want to do first? Look at the dossiers on the names I gave you or address the items you found today?"

"The items," I said.

# Chapter 15

I got up and headed for the garage where I had lockers for the artifacts I found, along with shelves, bins and tons of equipment. He put his hands in his pockets and walked around looking at all the equipment and artifacts I stored there. I was thrilled he didn't try to touch or pick up any of my precious treasures. And I'm including my equipment in that description.

The pendant I'd found earlier that day lay in a drawer of a locked chest I bought at Sears. It had drawers and each one locked independently. It was supposed to hold tools, but it worked marvelously for my work. Before I put the necklace away, I'd wrapped it in a piece of black fabric. I picked it up and shoved it in my pocket.

When we got to the kitchen, I laid it gently on the table and unwrapped it. "While you are looking the piece over, I am going to take the opportunity to put on some clothes. I'm embarrassed I waited this long."

He looked up at me and smiled, "Don't get dressed on my account."

I shook my head at him and headed for the stairs.

While I got dressed in some real clothes, I heard Agent Wade go outside through the front door.

He didn't knock before he came back in. Indy barked at him.

"It's okay, big guy." I heard him say.

It didn't deter Indy. He stayed with our guest every step of the way and when Wade sat on the couch, Indy jumped up and sat close to him.

Wade looked at the dog. "Protective, aren't you?"

He looked up at me as I walked down the stairs, now dressed in Dorman College sweats.

"Can you call him off? I really want to go over these files. You are the only one I know who can spot something unusual."

I sat on the other side of the agent and patted the open space beside me, but not between us. I clicked my tongue. Indy jumped down, but not before he gave the man another look and growled. He laid down next to me, put his head on my lap and stared at our guest.

"I would rather not tell you. Not knowing will keep you on your best behavior."

He leaned over to touch Indy's head, but the dog moved. He looked straight into the dog's eyes while he replied, "Indy, I am always on my best behavior."

I looked him right in the eye and asked, "If you have me on camera several times, why don't you have the professor's murderer in custody?"

He smiled. "Good question. We know who did it and where he is. What we don't know is, why? He is under surveillance. We can take him any time we want.

"That's why the FBI is involved. They have a huge operation. It's in nine states and four countries that we know of. The man who shot the professor is an enforcer. We think they killed him because he wouldn't work for them. We think when they tried to recruit him, they told him so much he could have hurt the operation, so they felt they had to silence him.

"If we arrest the killer, it won't help us. We want the leaders of the group. They have bought artifacts that shouldn't be owned privately and sold them to people who have so much money they believe they are beyond the law."

I let out a big sigh. "So, Professor Thompson was not a criminal. He was killed because he wouldn't be dishonest. Is that right?"

"It would be the obvious answer, but some of the art and artifacts sent to the professor to be appraised, already dated and with their origin established, were never seen again. We haven't determined if the professor had anything to do with the disappearances, or if it happens after they left him. "

The pains of indecision twiddled their thumbs in my belly. The one and only time I'd gone against the rules, I'd done it big. All my work and my reputation could be ruined if someone found out I took human remains from a dig without calling the authorities. The more I spoke with Wade, the more I realized he had no idea how I worked or the rules I needed to go by.

He stood, walked over to the chair where his coat lay and picked it up. He reached into one pocket and brought out the velvet pouch I'd left with the professor with the bones in it. "These were clearly marked they came from you and where on the Izzard farm they were found. He gave a detailed report, which is enclosed in this folder." He held it up for me to see. "In this report, he ages the bones as most likely the fingers of Judith Izzard. They have nothing to do with our case, although, I don't understand why he told you he thought it was a missing girl and the report says something different.

"It further makes me think Jonah Thompson is not and has never been the man he pretended to be." He handed me the pouch. "What will you do next?"

"In the morning, I'll call the University of Missouri and ask them to send a crew to help me search the rest of the dig site."

"I faxed a photo of the nine little bones and the record Thompson wrote. I sent it to headquarters and once they established there was nothing else like them in his finds, they believed the story you told me about having him look at them. The bones have nothing to do with his death. You can go on with your dig. We are not going to muddy the waters by adding any notes about the bones."

"Thank you." I was thrilled. No one knew about the ring but me and now the bones would get handled correctly with the help of the University.

The clock in the hall, which had the Westminster chimes, sounded twelve before we finished with the files Agent Wade had brought in. At first, he made it seem as if the packets about each of us were kept for dark reasons. However, as we looked through them it seemed as though, the professor had a reason for meeting with each of us on the list. His notes gave the impression he thought of us as the "cream of the crop".

"I need to take the dog out and get some sleep. The murder and all that accompanied it wore me out." I picked up the pouch and looked at it. I laid it on the kitchen table. I had lost fifty pounds of worry when the agent had said the bones had been determined to not be part of the murder investigation.

He stood, "Same here. I'll be going. I know how much you thought of the professor. I will keep you posted. Thanks for dinner."

I walked him to the door. "I am thrilled to get the bones back. Thanks again for going the extra mile."

He leaned down to pet Indy, but the dog took a step back. Wade looked up, smiled, shrugged his shoulders and left.

# CHAPTER 16

I spent the next hour trying to find a place to hide the phalanges and ring. In my heart, I knew it wasn't necessary but after everything including Agent Wade's assurances that they didn't think the bones had anything to do with Professor Thompson's death, my nerves were shot.

I put them in a drawer in my chest. If someone came in, I'd have plenty of time to prepare. Indy knew when the slightest out of place movement or sound happened.

I noticed one change in the ring as I looked at it again; it pulsed. This time Judith appeared in front of me and looked at me with her big, green eyes. She didn't blink or say anything. In about twenty seconds she disappeared in a mist.

In an effort to shake off what I had just seen, I brushed my teeth and laid down. My body had been through enough for one day but still I tossed and turned. The professor's dead face flashed in front of my eyes. To get killed because you would not go outside of the law seemed doubly sad. Would it be different if I found out at the end of all of this that he was a dishonest man? How would it affect me and his life's work?

By three-thirty, I couldn't keep my eyes open. As a result, I didn't get up as early as usual. Indy must have gone through the doggy door because he didn't wake me to take him outside. At a little after eight, Indy jumped on me, stood on my stomach and licked my face.

I pushed him away twice, but he continued. I opened my eyes and looked at the clock on my bedside table. "Wow, no wonder you think I should get up. We are usually at the job by now."

He jumped off the bed, ran in circles and barked.

"Okay, I get your message. Are you hungry?"

He barked twice. His way of saying *yes*.

We didn't arrive at the farm until nearly ten. I parked near the hole where I found the ring and bones. I couldn't believe it had only been two days since the find and the professor's murder.

I had covered the area with a tarp held down with tent stakes. Moisture had collected under the cover. The temperature had already reached eighty-one degrees. It would be eighty-eight before long and the dig, although in the trees, would be in the sun for another hour or two.

It took one of those hours for me to replace the bones where I found them. I didn't know why I thought that necessary. No one would question the location. When I finished, I walked back toward where I had left my Jeep and called the Seymour police department.

"May I speak to Chief Davis?"

"Who's calling?" A voice on the other end asked.

"Alexa Ford. I found human remains at a dig site I'm exploring."

"A body?"

"I haven't found the entire body. Just the fingers from one hand. And I found some coins and a locket. I don't know if everything is from the same person."

"Just a minute, I'll get the Chief for you."

I didn't have to wait long. "Hey Lexi, what's up?"

"I'm doing a search of some farmland in Seymour. I dug up some coins, a locket and the bones of three fingers."

"Do you think it's a relic?"

"I don't know yet. I'm on the old Izzard farm, maybe I'll find Judith."

"Okay, I'll be right there. Do you want us to excavate the area?"

"I'd rather you didn't. I am about to call the University and have them do it. I don't mean to insult you, but you guys sometimes do more damage than good when delicate artifacts are involved."

The chief laughed. "I'd like to dispute you, but I can't. I will keep a guard out there until they get here. No telling what's there. Tell me where you are."

"I'm at the inside edge of the stand of pines near the north end of the farm. You can even park on the road and walk in. It is much shorter. You can see my Jeep from Farm Road 74."

"Okay, on my way."

"Thanks, Chief."

We hung up and I had nearly the same conversation with Professor Adaline McGuire at MU. The quickest way to reach McGuire was to connect with Swallow Hall where all the classes pertaining to my field of science were held.

She didn't have a class and answered the phone herself. After I explained what happened she said, "Let me check my schedule."

The other end of the line remained quiet for a long minute. "I can't come tomorrow but I can come Wednesday. I'll bring a couple of grad students with me. They have been chomping at the bit to do something outside the regular humdrum. I've been having a hard time getting the funds to send them very far. They'll be thrilled."

I told her I would text the directions and since the grad students were men, I would arrange two rooms somewhere close. One for her and one for her students.

When I hung up, and pondered the dig site my stomach still told me something didn't feel right. I couldn't put my finger on it, but my gut assured me I didn't have the entire story about the murder, the ring, the fingers, or the professor's part in the entire mess.

Indy moved closer to me. I reached down and scratched his back. "Let's go back to the car and get a drink."

Before I could take a step, Indy stood up on her back legs and lunged toward me. He used his entire body weight to push me. I fell hard. As I hit the ground, I heard the shot. Maybe my imagination had the best of me, but I'd swear I heard the bullet whiz by my ear.

I moved close to the tire to have something between me and the shooter hoping Indy sat behind another tire when he moved away from me. He twitched. I knew he wanted to run toward the shooter.

I turned my body around. Indy was crouched down, ready to run. I shook my head "no." He whined and began to crawl my way. "No, Indy. Stay where you are."

Two more shots rang out. One hit my passenger side rear tire, and one hit my front tire on the same side. Whoever held the gun had decided they didn't want me getting away and had now stranded me out here in the middle of the farm.

I couldn't wrap my head around why anyone would try to kill me or scare me.

Thank goodness, the police were already on their way.

Speak of the devil, an SUV with "Seymour City Police" stenciled on the side, pulled in and parked about ten feet from me. Sounds from the trees across the way let me know my attacker fled the arriving cavalry.

The chief smiled at me as he got out of his cruiser. Chief Bill Davis and I went to high school together. He was a senior when I was a sophomore. Everyone knew him, the football star and Prom King. Mostly, a nice guy. Law enforcement had been his dream since he was old enough to shoot a gun.

Another officer got out on the passenger side. I didn't know him.

His smile faded as fast as it came as he watched me pick myself up off the ground where I had been huddled. "What's wrong? Are you hiding?"

"Someone has been shooting at us."

The officer came and stood by the chief. "Maybe we have a poacher."

I looked at his name tag. "I don't think so, Officer Matthews."

"Oh, I'm sorry," Bill said, "this is Sam Mathews. He's been with us about a year now."

"It's not a hunter. Whoever shot, blew out both tires on the other side of the Jeep. And before that, two shots went over my head."

They both crouched down.

"No need for that," I said. "They are long gone. They left weaving in and out of the trees as fast as the four-wheeler they left on would go."

He looked toward the stand of trees beside us. "You would either have to be a great driver or know these woods to get out of here quickly on a four-wheeler. Did you see which way they went? Did you see what color or brand it was? You keep saying they, how many were there?"

"No to the color, west for the direction and I believe there were two, a man and a woman. They shouted at one another. A male voice and a female voice.

"Actually, I was scared. I'm going by sound as to what kind of vehicle it was, and I could tell the direction as the sound faded that way." I pointed to the west. It also made sense. The east went toward town, the north and south were woods and overgrown fields. To the west a paved farm road would have taken them to the most rural part of the area.

"I see," he said. "I think we need to talk. Exactly what have you found?"

"Can we talk while someone comes to tow my car and fix the tires? Someone wanted me stranded here. What do you know about Professor Thompson's murder?"

He took his hat off and wiped the sweat from his forehead with a handkerchief from his pocket. "I read the report. It was pretty vague. They called it a home invasion. It said you had an appointment with the professor the next morning and found the body. Mostly it referred all questions to a Special Agent Blake Wade. He is the lead on the investigation. I guess the professor was part of a case or maybe one of their experts."

I pointed toward my tires.

"Sure," he said. "I'll get a tow truck out here. We also need more guards. I'm not leaving one officer tonight against an unknown shooter."

"Can I put my equipment into your patrol car and you can take it home for me? It is too expensive to leave in the car. After they fix the tires, they'll just park it out of the way until I get there to retrieve it."

He looked at Mathews. "Carefully take what is in her car." He nodded in my direction. "And put it in the cruiser."

# Chapter 17

"I don't know how much I can tell you. There's much more going on here than I originally thought.

"I found a pendent while going over this land for the owner. It belonged to someone with the initials MJ and was engraved with the date 2019. I also dug up the phalanges of a small woman.

"I took lots of pictures of the pendant and the fingers when I dug them up and took the photos to the professor. He said he was almost certain the fingers hadn't been in the ground very long. He said he could tell from the pictures that the bones were not very old.

"Yesterday morning, the professor was going to come out here with me and have a look for himself before anything got disturbed and before I called the University. No one knew about the dig or that I was even out here, so I thought it would be okay. But when I went to pick up the professor, he'd been murdered. It was a horrible scene. I believe he fought with the killer before the person shot him."

Officer Mathews looked me straight in the eye, "I'd say someone knows you were here."

I stopped, took some deep breaths and prayed I didn't say anything to get me on the wrong side of Agent Wade.

I stepped away and took Agent Blake Wade's card from my pocket and called him. He answered on the first ring. "You're the last person I ever expected to call me," he said. "What can I do for you, Alexa?"

"I'm out at the farm in Seymour. Can you come here? There has been a development in our case."

"I didn't know it was *our* case."

I ignored him, "Can you come or not?"

"Alexa, what's wrong?"

"I'll tell you when you get here."

"I'm on my way."

# Chapter 18

It seemed like forever before the FBI Agent arrived. He wore faded jeans, a *Life is good* tee shirt, with a man holding a drink sitting on an Adirondack Chair, printed on the front. He had on a navy-blue ball cap with three large gold letters, FBI. In a leather holster on his left side, he wore a nine-millimeter Glock 19.

I prided myself on how observant I'd become over the years. Imagine my disappointment when for the first time I noticed how good-looking he was. His dark blond, close-cropped hair barely showed under the hat. He stood ramrod straight. His arms swung casually at his side as he walked on the balls of his feet, lithe, like a cat ready to pounce. He sure was easy to look at.

He walked up to me, ignoring Chief Davis and Patrolman Sam Mathews. "What happened here?"

"I was continuing my dig to see if I could find anything of value where I dug up the bones. Someone shot at me. Luckily, they missed. Indy and I hid behind the Jeep's tires. Whoever it was wanted to strand me here. They shot out both tires on the other side of the Jeep."

"I'd already called Chief Davis and as he drove up, the shooters left."

"Have you found anything else?"

"No, I didn't have time to look. The shooting started before I got my equipment out of the car."

He turned toward Davis. "I'm Special Agent Blake Wade, FBI. I was sent here to see if some expensive stolen art made its way to this area. Professor Thompson worked for us as an expert. The bones are a coincidence, I hope."

Davis introduced himself and his deputy. "Since there were bones I kind of figure the murderer is upset Lexi dug them up."

Wade looked at me and then back to Bill. "Lexi?" he asked.

Davis smiled. "We went to high school together. It would be odd to call her doctor or Alexa at this point."

Blake nodded his head, then asked for more details about the shooting, standard questions much like Davis had wanted to know.

He walked off in the direction of the trees. He looked back and hollered. "Bring one of those metal detectors. Let's see if we can find some shell casings."

I walked over to my Jeep which still held all my equipment since Officer Matthews was interrupted before he could start moving it to the cruiser and picked up a Minecraft Equinox 900 and began to follow the agent.

Davis caught up with me. "Here, let me carry that," he said.

For the next hour we followed four-wheeler tracks and found four shell casings. They all agreed the bullets came from a 30-ought 6, a common deer hunting rifle for the area.

The three of them said little while they scoured the area. Indy barked twice. Once he found a casing and another time he showed them a scar on a pine tree with a trace of red paint.

Once they were satisfied they had searched the entire area, they walked back toward the cars. A dark blue truck with the words, AFFORDABLE TOWING on it in bright orange letters pulled up, the driver got out and began to hook up the Jeep.

"What happened here?" The driver directed his question to me. "How'd both tires go flat at the same time?"

"Someone shot them out."

Agent Wade interrupted, "If you find any lead in either tire, call me, will you?" He took a card out of his pocket and handed it to the tow truck driver.

"A Fed. I don't think I've ever seen a real Federal Agent before." He reached for Agent Blake Wade's hand and when he found it, he latched on and began to pump it up and down in some kind of strange enthusiastic handshake.

Blake stood still and the man let go after a long minute. They smiled at one another.

"It would be best," Davis said, "if you didn't tell anyone about this. We don't want too many people out here sightseeing."

Wade glanced at the area above the pocket on the tow truck driver's uniform shirt where the name, "Homer Jones," was embroidered. Wade said in nearly a whisper, "Homer, I know we can count on you. I believe you can see how important it is that we keep this quiet."

"Yes, Agent, I surely do." Homer looked down at the card in his hand before he slipped it in this shirt pocket. "You can count on me."

# Chapter 19

The two cops, the agent and me along with my trusty dog were still at the dig site well after dark. One of the problems had to do with the size of the Seymour police department. The whole department consisted of only two school resource officers, three patrolmen and the chief.

No way could the four of them maintain a two-person team around the clock to keep people away from the dig site. If word got out a crime had taken place at the farm it would prove even more difficult to keep the site secure when the university team arrived.

Once the UM team's backhoe and other equipment arrived and the students began to show up at local cafes and restaurants, the rumors would start. Add the professor's murder and the scuttlebutt the FBI had a hand in things and the small town of Seymour would become as popular as the Kansas City Chiefs. Everyone loves a scandal after all.

Two more police cars pulled in. We did the only thing we could do, we decided to take it one day at a time. The biggest worry for the night was the man with the rifle. Anyone who ever pulled an all-nighter knew ninety-nine out of one hundred people could not stay awake from two-thirty a.m. to five a.m.

We discussed the men taking the night in shifts, yet one man could not look in all directions to try to see someone wanting to kill. With the kind of gun he had, he didn't have to be close to hurt someone.

Davis leaned on one of the cruisers. "He'd have to be a trained sniper to make a long distance shot in this area at night. It gets so dark you can't see your hand in front of your face."

Everyone agreed.

Most of the evening, Indy lay in the back of a police cruiser. He would not let me close the door. But I wanted to get him off the ground. I guess one could say I spoiled the dog.

I knew from listening to the conversations all evening, the main concern was the safety of the men who would be out all night to guard the area. The men decided we needed more bodies to cover shifts. Chief Davis called the Highway Patrol and the Justin County Sheriff's office. Agent Wade said he would call the nearest FBI post in Joplin, Missouri.

---

By the time the three agencies talked, we had the promise of twelve men in three shifts. Two cars would remain parked with lights flashing and one would circle the field around the stand of trees. No one wanted to wait until the university team arrived with their crew in two days.

Agent Wade and Chief Davis put two strands of crime scene tape around the outer row of trees. They put one up as far as they could reach and the other at knee level. In all my life, on TV, or in real life, I had never seen two levels of crime scene tape.

My old high school friend, Sheriff Bill Davis, took me, Indy and my equipment home. On the way we talked about what we knew about the disappearance of Judith Izzard all those years ago.

We both admitted we had lost interest in the saga and hype of Judith Izzard and her ring a long time ago, but we were both familiar with the ring. We'd seen it year after year since we were kids.

Agent Blake Wade's black Yukon, sat in my driveway when we arrived at my house. "Fancy meeting you here," Davis said.

Blake had taken a seat on the front porch before we pulled up. "I got to thinking about it. If the shooter was after Lexi, he might come here to try again. I'd feel better if I stayed here tonight."

I put my hands on my hips. What was it with men? I wasn't helpless. I took a deep breath. "I know you mean well, but Indy would never let anyone come in the house. And I can shoot the wings off a grasshopper at a hundred yards. I have a license to conceal and carry." I raised my shirt to show him my pistol in a holster at my side.

"That is all very impressive, but it is my job to see no one gets hurt. Maybe you would rather your buddy Chief Davis stayed with you?"

I saw Bill make a slight nod of disapproval at the comment. "Sorry, Agent. I agree someone should be here, but it can't be me. I have eight-week-old twins at home. I need to go there and help my wife. I'm sure she is exhausted by now."

"You go on home, Bill. The agent and I can work this out. Tell Elly I said hi and kiss the boys for me," I said.

He glanced away from me and up at Wade who had about five inches on him. "Are you sure?"

"Absolutely."

"Let me unload Lexi's equipment from the cruiser before I head out then," the chief said.

Agent Blake Wade walked with the chief to the cruiser. "I can get that. I don't want to hold you up any longer, Chief."

Bill Davis didn't say a thing. His face said it all. He thought the agent might not be the great guy he pretended to be. Thank goodness for restraint.

# Chapter 20

Despite the fact I could hardly stand up due to exhaustion, none of us got to bed for another two hours. Indy ate and went outside. As I watched him eat, I realized I hadn't eaten since breakfast.

I looked in the refrigerator to see what might be hiding there. Nothing I could fix quickly. Blake came up behind me and looked over my shoulder. I could feel his warm breath on my neck.

The sensation confused me. I took a step back so he would have to move and turned around. "About all I can offer for dinner is a bowl of soup."

"I passed an all-night sub shop a few blocks away. I'll order ahead and pick it up."

"Are you sure you can leave little old me alone here by myself?" Sarcasm practically dripped out of my mouth with every word.

"I take it you're super independent." Before I could answer he asked. "What kind of sandwich would you like?"

"Veggie with everything and add jalapeño peppers and a small amount of ranch dressing."

After he ordered the sandwiches he asked, "Are you a vegetarian?"

"No, but it sounded good. Shouldn't you be going after our food?"

"They said they deliver for free, so I told him the address, and they are on their way."

We sat at the kitchen table and I wondered if he thought I had done something illegal and needed to be watched.

"Tell me more about the ring and Judith Izzard," he said settling in as if he were getting ready to hear a bedtime story.

"First, I need to tell you something else about Professor Thompson. When I showed the photos of the hand bones to him, he said nothing about the fingers not being in the correct order. The ring finger and middle finger had been reversed when I took the bones from the hole. I have no other excuse than I was excited about the find to explain why I didn't see it. There was NO reason for the professor to miss it. I believe he was nervous, nervous the bones were found. I just don't know why.

"He had microscopes and jewelers' loops when he looked at the bones. He even took the time to arrange them the way they were in the photos before he put them in the safe. I believe you might have a case you are following him on, but I believe this is something different. I believe the professor was involved in the murder of the girl who is missing if indeed those bones don't belong to Judith Izzard, which in my mind, they do. Of course, not involved in the girl's original killing, but there is a connection somewhere.

"But you asked about the story of the ring and Judith Izzard. For a long time I thought the story of the ring to be a myth. Supposedly, a beautiful young girl, Judith Izzard, begged to wear her mother's ring to her high school graduation. Eleven children Judith's age attended a one room schoolhouse about four miles from the Izzard farm. Altogether, stories have it 12 kids in all were enrolled. The twelve children included first grade to twelfth. The numbers are hard to pin down. There were supposedly more kids at the graduation party than reportedly went to school with Judith.

"The Izzard's owned the local lumber yard, sawmill and several hundred acres of woods. Everyone said Judith was a beautiful girl with impeccable manners and a quiet demeanor.

"She had a Tennessee Walker named Whittaker. She rode him everywhere. He'd been trained to come home if anything happened while they were out riding."

The doorbell rang, interrupting my story. Blake stood and walked to the door. He took a second to move to the left of the door to the huge bay window taking up most of that side of the house. He looked out, confirmed the restaurant delivery and smiled back at me before he opened the door.

He reached into his pocket and brought out enough money for the bill and the tip. Out of nowhere, Indy jumped up and knocked him into the delivery boy. They both fell. The boy hit the ground first and Blake fell on top of him, both landing outside on the porch. A shot rang out.

Blake scrambled to his feet, grabbed the boy by the collar of his shirt and dragged him into the house slamming the door behind them. The kid couldn't have been over sixteen. Crocodile tears ran down his face.

"You okay, kid?" Blake asked as he drew his gun and headed for the back door.

Indy began to follow, but I called him back.

Blake was no longer there for the kid to answer so he looked at me and said, "Yeah, I think so. Why did someone shoot at me?"

"It isn't you," I said. "I believe it's me. I promise we'll get you home safely. Right now, sit right there on the floor and stay down until the agent comes back."

"That man's an agent? Like FBI?"

"Yes. Let's just wait here and be quiet until he comes back."

Blake came back in through the front door about five minutes later. "What time do you stop deliveries?"

"At midnight."

Blake looked at his watch. "It's ten till so there won't be any more tonight. Just sit tight while I call the police."

I picked up my cell phone. "I'll call."

Within a few minutes, Chief Bill Davis knocked on the front door. "What happened?"

We explained the events while Bill shook his head. "I wonder what we have gotten ourselves into. I can't believe it could be the Izzard girl. That happened nearly a hundred years ago. I think it has more to do with Lexi and what someone is afraid she'll find out there."

Wade and I both agreed.

"I told the boy to have a seat. He's still pretty shaken up."

"Can I get you a drink?" I asked the boy. "What's your name?"

"Dakota Mussman. Can I just use your bathroom?"

"Sure," I pointed to my left. "At the end of the hall."

"I'm with you," Blake said. "We happened to be in the wrong place. I'm going to stick around though, just in case this has something to do with the professor's death."

"I'm not sure they want to harm Lexi. It might be a scare tactic to convince her to give up the dig. The only reason for them to do that is there must be something on the farm these folks don't want found." Dave said.

"I went after the shooter, but by the time I got around the house, he was already down the street. It was a truck. I couldn't see the color. Just that it was dark."

Chief Davis looked from Wade to the boy who'd returned from the bathroom. "Do you deliver in your car or does it belong to the sub shop?"

"It's mine. I have one more delivery to make."

"Where?"

"Two blocks down the street."

"At the Anderson's?"

"Yes."

"Listen Dakota, I'm going to follow you down to the Anderson's and then follow you home."

"Do you think the guy will come to my house and try to shoot me?" Dakota still looked spooked. Understandably.

"Absolutely not. He only shot while you were here because the door opened at that time. I want to make sure you get home okay because I can tell how upset you are. But honestly, I'm sure you are not going to be bothered again." He put his hand on the kid's shoulder. "Okay you two, stay safe. I need to get back to my wife and kids. We don't get any sleep as it is and we," he pointed to Wade and me, "can talk in the morning."

He didn't leave room for discussion. He told the kid to follow him. A couple of seconds later he opened the door and handed Blake the sandwiches. "Here, you might want these?"

Unfortunately, they had landed first, under both Blake and Dakota and were now a little worse for wear.

# Chapter 21

You'd have thought all the commotion from the gun shot and the police would have taken away my appetite, it didn't. I put two paper plates on the table, took out two bottles of water from the refrigerator, opened the bag and took out my somewhat flattened sandwich.

Blake had not said a word since the chief left. I could almost hear his mind whirl as he thought. Finally, he spoke up, "Did you train the dog yourself? He's the smartest canine I have ever been around."

"His name is Indiana Jones; he doesn't like to be called *the dog*. He stayed all day for six weeks at Paw Paw's. The owner trains all of the police dogs for the Highway Patrol and all of the local law enforcement agencies. Before then, he trained dogs for military combat. I was between assignments and stayed with him as he trained."

"He saved our lives tonight." He looked at Indy. "I didn't think he liked me."

"It's why I knew I would be safe here alone. Indy would never let anyone hurt me."

"What about if you open the door or stand in front of a window?"

"I would not have opened the door," I replied pointedly.

We ate the rest of our sandwiches in silence. Later he said, "I can sleep on the couch. Do you have an extra blanket?"

"There's a guest room at the end of the hall. It has a Jack and Jill bathroom, so you won't have to come out in the hall to use it. The bed is made up. If you need an extra blanket, there's one in the closet. As hot as it is, I doubt you will need one.

"My room is upstairs. I'll see you in the morning."

I felt a little guilty about not going down the hall with him and showing him where everything was, but not guilty enough to go back.

Indy followed me up the stairs. I heard our self-appointed bodyguard check the front and back doors to make sure they were locked before he went into the bedroom. He didn't close the door. I smiled to myself. I guess his hearing wasn't as good as Indy's.

The problem with a sandwich after midnight was it kept me up. My mind went straight to the events of the past few days. Even though I thought over the years I'd learned all about Judith Izzard, I hadn't paid attention to any news about it for at least ten years. It would not be on my mind at all had it not been for the ring and Professor Thompson's death.

His death had been the number one news story on local and national news since the morning we found him. No one could tie it to the Izzard death because only I knew about the ring being in my possession.

I gave up on trying to sleep. I set my computer up at my dressing table in front of the window before I thought better of it and moved it to a chair, siting on my bed to type.

I Googled Barclay Simmons. His background didn't tell me a lot. The lack of information made him sound like a shady character. What he did for a living wasn't clear. One article I read said, *Barclay Simmons does it again.* A land purchase of some kind helped someone. I read it three times and still I couldn't get a clear picture of what went on.

Another time he donated a painting to a museum in New Jersey and yet another instance said he donated fifty-thousand dollars to the *No Child Goes Hungry* group in his area.

I remembered his name didn't show up on the deed to the property I had contracted to search. I'd go to the courthouse and look for myself.

So far as to the professor's evil deeds, I didn't believe there were any. I'd bet my last dollar he had a job with the FBI trying to track artifacts down. It could have been anything, but if our friendly FBI agent knew anything more, he did not share.

I intended to forget the artifact case and his job with the FBI and focus on the ring, the bones and the farmland. The other had nothing to do with me. I hoped.

I believed the shootings and my findings had everything to do with stopping me from finishing my search of the Izzard farm. Whatever was buried on the land meant a whole lot to someone. I also didn't think they were out to kill me. They shot at the car tires when I was out in the open. They shot through an open door. I couldn't help but think someone wanted me to give up and go away.

I finally laid down around three a.m. and woke up to the smell of coffee wafting up the stairs and someone knocking on the front door at eight.

Soft voices floated upstairs. I brushed my hair and teeth, slipped on a bra, a Golden State tee shirt with a hole in one sleeve and a pair of jeans with the knees torn out. Within five minutes, I was downstairs. Blake poured me a cup of coffee.

"What did I miss?" I asked.

Bill held up a box from where he sat at my kitchen table. "So far, only first choice of donuts. Have a seat."

Blake took a notebook out of his shirt pocket and said, "I'll go first. Barclay Simmons was not born Barclay Simmons. Barclay didn't show up anywhere before 1995. There are no records on or about him before that time."

Bill and I sat silent and looked at him. When he realized we were not going to say anything, he went on. "Since 2011 he, at times, is a hedge fund manager out of New York City, other times he is a professional poker player. He owns a Nissan dealership in Seattle, he's an art dealer and, last but not least, a philanthropist."

Bill reached for another pastry. "Why would he have changed his name?"

"Good question," the agent said "We can't seem to find him doing anything illegal. It isn't illegal to change your name. Believe it or not, he even pays his taxes, for each of his enterprises including declaring his poker winnings and losses."

"Come on," Davis said disbelievingly. "Surely he's done something wrong."

"A Barclay Anderson Simmons died in Juno, Alaska in 1973 before his first birthday. This man we now know by that name, took the name, got a Social Security Card, forged the papers he needed and popped into the world in 2011 at age twenty-two. He is now thirty-five.

"When he showed up on the radar, he already had lots of money. He could have been a bank robber in another life or maybe he inherited his money but didn't like the circumstances of his life.

"Whoever he was before, we don't know. There are so many people and thousands go missing every day. According to our records 2,300 every day and 563,000 give or take a few each year. There is no way anyone can keep track of the whereabouts of so many people.

"We've never been able to get fingerprints on him. Our informants tell us he puts clear Hard as Nails polish on the pads of his fingers.

"We would like to find out what he's up to. This time, I think if he is involved in this, and there is evidence he might be, he's finally gone too far. The men who killed Professor Thompson showed up on several cameras and we have the license plate number on the vehicle they drove away in.

"They didn't leave town without dropping by McDonald's first." He took a photo out of his pocket. "Have you ever seen either of these men before?"

"No, do you have them under arrest, yet?" I asked looking at the photo and then passing it back to Agent Wade.

"Not yet. When they left the professor's home, they had a box. Thing is, three men went in and only two left. We think the third man shot the professor, but we aren't sure where he went after that. I also don't know what was in the box the other two men took when they left, but it was so heavy the bigger of the two had to carry it with both hands. By the time we found the camera footage, they were gone from the area and had had time to stash the box somewhere. If we arrest them now, chances are we will never find out what they took, or who the third man was.

"We know for a fact those two men pick up and deliver art and artifacts for Simmons when he is managing his art gallery.

Problem is they also deal in art in nine other states. We believe they are fences. We have not let them out of our sight since we identified them.

"Sooner or later, they will try to get rid of the items they took, and we will be there to arrest them."

Bill asked, "What do you intend to do?"

"I believe Simmons is behind all of this. I'll be very surprised if whatever those men took from Thompson's house isn't connected to Simmons. And the third man who disappeared had to have had some stealth training, because the only way he could have left without being detected was if he was dressed in black and crawling on his belly in the dark of night."

"Simmons has bought and sold land and then given the money away on more than one occasion. This is the first time however, we have known him to hire someone to search for artifacts on land he has purchased. Maybe the Native American history or the Civil War interests him."

Bill Davis said, "I don't think it does. I believe someone knows a secret we don't. When will we know how old the bones you found are?"

"Depends," Blake said. "Will the University of Missouri team be here tomorrow?"

"Yes, they will meet me at the site on Izzard farm."

Bill and Blake both voiced separately they didn't want me to be out without a security person.

"Okay with me," I said. "I don't really like being shot at."

"At this point we have to believe someone does not want you to dig up anything else at the Izzard farm. Thing is, they have made such a ruckus about it now, they are on everyone's mind. And the more we want to dig the place up. I'd say they aren't the sharpest knives in the drawer," Blake said.

Bill took a notebook from his back pocket. "Before we break up this little get-together, I took the liberty to look up every case of a missing girl over the past ten years, both here and in the neighboring counties. There are five. I'm going to spend my day looking into the cases."

"I don't mean to one up you Chief, but the FBI has a larger data base. Do you mind giving me the list too. We can compare notes when we're done."

Bill smiled, "I have an extra list. I anticipated this." We broke up the meeting at nine-fifteen. The chief went to his office, I changed clothes and wanted to go to the dig site. The agent said he would escort me.

# Chapter 22

The officers left to guard the area of the dig looked relaxed when we arrived. They each had a cup of coffee and biscuits and gravy from McDonald's and were eating and drinking together, using one of the car hoods as a table.

"Morning, Agent," one of the men said to Wade

"Morning, Officers. I take it you fellas had a quiet night."

"Sure did," the men looked at me and managed a nod of the head in hello. One man who seemed to be finished with his breakfast asked, "Are you here to work, Alexa?"

"Yes, I am. But not here. I want to go down to a gully I saw the other day. There isn't much topsoil here. The water runs past this area and down the hill to the creek at the bottom. I usually have good luck in places like that."

A young cop walked over and stuck out his hand for me to shake. "I'm Tony Asbury, I've only been on duty since nine this morning. I can go with you to make sure you stay safe."

Since the agent, Indy and I got out of the car, Indy had been mesmerized by something outside the perimeter the men were in. He looked up and whined. "Go see," I said.

Indy took off at a fast run. When he got about ten yards past the police cars, he stopped and began to root around.

He barked, turned in a circle and barked again. Blake, the young officer, Tony, and I went to see what he found.

The tall grass had been smashed down. It was obvious someone had been laying there. And for a long time. An army blanket lay a little shy of the indentation. "I'd say someone slept here last night," Blake said. "I believe you officers were lucky you didn't get hurt. Whoever is keeping an eye on this place doesn't seem to fear much.

"I don't know if it is our shooter but whoever he is, he is serious about knowing what's going on."

Indy came to sit by me. I rubbed his head, then I turned to Wade. "All of my equipment is in your car. Mind driving it down to where I'm going to explore. I'll call at lunch time and try to find out about my Jeep."

"Sure," is all he said. The four of us began to walk back to the other men and the police cars.

Tony looked at his fellow officers and said, "Someone watched you all last night. He might have gotten closer than that. I believe we need to quit thinking about this as an old case." He looked from man to man, "You could have been shot during the night."

The tension became palpable. One man said, "I'm off duty, I'll see you guys tonight." He walked away as if the warning we gave him didn't mean a thing.

The second officer said pretty much the same thing. They left together in the same car. The man left at the site said, "I'll stay here and keep lookout. I doubt much will happen in the daylight." He shook his head at the officers who left.

How wrong he turned out to be.

## Chapter 23

Tony and Blake drove me down to the spot I wanted to have a look at. Blake went back up the hill and parked halfway between us and the cop we left behind at the entrance. "I'll be busy on the phone running down the names of the missing girls, but I'll park here where I can keep an eye on all of you." Without waiting for either of us to reply, Blake put his car in reverse, turned around and headed up the grade. I wasn't afraid and I could tell by Indy's demeanor, he didn't sense danger.

I kept my eyes on Tony until he settled above me. He leaned against a Short-leaf Pine, and seemed pleased after he looked in both directions, and gave me a thumbs up. What he couldn't see, I felt sure Blake could see from his location.

Satisfied I had professional men with eyes on me, I began to work.

Once I gridded off a smaller section with small orange safety flags I could easily stick into the ground, I took out a metal detector and began my search. I took my phone out of my back pocket and looked at the time. I'd been working for two hours and my shirt didn't have a dry spot on it. I'd put my hair in a ponytail after the first half an hour. Indy was on his second full bowl of water. I heard Blake start his car once in a while, I guessed to turn on the air conditioning. Must be nice, I thought.

Tony sat about thirty yards above me. When I looked at him, he had taken his hat off and unbuttoned his shirt. He waved at me so I knew he still had his eye on me.

My metal detector began to beep. It gave a completely different sound when it was picking up money in the ground. I went back and forth until I'd triangulated the sound. My digging shovel had a saw edge on both sides. The heat hadn't as yet dried out the soil and it went into the grass and then the dirt with hardly any effort. About six inches down, my shovel hit an object.

I took a pin-pointer, a small detector about a foot long I could move around in my exact area of interest. In this case, a hole about nine inches deep and five inches in diameter. No matter where I moved it, the annoying high-pitched squeal let me know a metal object lay beneath it. With my trowel I took my time to dig the dirt loose around the object. A little at a time I scooped out the packed soil around whatever lay beneath the ground to see what I'd found. I dug out a penny, a dime and a quarter. All of them were within ten years of being new. Sometimes a lot of work gave little reward, the opposite of the other day when hardly any work had given a huge reward.

As I moved the tool around the dugout spot, the pointer went wild. I dug deeper and deeper. When I finally hit something, I could not believe it, more bones. The long bone could not have given out a signal. Metal detectors were just that, machines made to find metal. There had to be something more in the immediate area.

I turned back to motion to Tony, but he wasn't there. "Tony," I called. There was no answer and I assumed he had gone to relieve himself or check on something he could see from his point on the farm. I shrugged to myself.

I heard Blake shut off his car as I went back to my task. It took so long to remove the bones which turned out to be humerus bones and a skull, I was exhausted by the time I was finished. I laid the bones out anatomically along with the rest of what I had found.

The items the machine had detected were three more coins, a silver pendant and earrings. I sat back on my heels and looked over the array of body parts for what was there and what wasn't. It could have been the same girl the finger bones had come from;

there were no bones from the lower part of either of the legs or feet.

The strangest thing was, I had dug in exactly the correct place yesterday to find something the first time I dug and then the exact place today. How could it be? I was not psychic. It had to be luck merged with experience. The terrain where I dug yesterday didn't have the same grade as the area where I dug up a new set of bones. If they were all from the same girl, I couldn't imagine how they had all ended up where they did.

How I decided where to dig rivaled the way a golf pro reads a green. I took into account which way the water flowed through the area and if the grade changed abruptly as it did where I stood.

The entire area sloped downhill, yet this particular spot went uphill instead. The rise only went twenty yards or so before the natural slope continued down to a creek a hundred yards below it.

I leaned back, moved my feet and let my butt hit the ground. It was not possible for digging and finding artifacts to be so easy.

There had to be a clue somewhere. Whatever and wherever it was, I needed to find it, or them. I'd done this kind of work for years. I knew how difficult it could be to find one item, much less to find two hot sites so quickly.

I said a silent prayer, "Please don't let me be in a killing field." Immediately I wished I'd never even thought it in my mind.

I glanced up. Tony again sat under his tree, chewing on what I guessed was a pine needle. I beckoned him to me. He ran down the hill. "Are you okay?"

"Yes, but you won't believe what I found."

"Don't keep me waiting."

"More bones," I replied, pointing at where I had pieced them back together.

He took his hat off with two fingers and wiped his forehead with the rest of his hand. "What do you make of it?"

"It's strange. It's one of two things. First, it's a bone yard or second, there were subtle clues left here to persuade me to dig in these two places. By the way, where were you earlier? I looked up and couldn't see you."

"Oh, I heard a rustling sound in the grass. It was a covey of quail. I'm surprised you didn't see or hear them flutter off."

"Do you mind watching this place while I go get Mr. FBI?"

"Yeah, sure, no problem,"
Indy and I headed up the grade to Blake's car.

# Chapter 24

Before I had a chance to talk to Blake, my cellphone beeped, signaling a text message.
*Lexi, we are at the Holiday Inn Express on Highway 160, five miles west of Seymour, Missouri. Please advise. Adaline McGuire.*

Blake jumped when I knocked on the driver's side window. "What kind of FBI Agent are you? You let me sneak up on you."

His face reddened. "Give me a break. I saw you coming and went back to work. You walked faster than I expected you to."

I smiled at him and got to the problem at hand. "I must have divine intervention, because I found more bones, some change and a silver pendant with an early Christian fish symbol and earrings to match. Maybe it will help us to identify the victim, or victims."

His eyebrows rose into a near perfect half circle. He looked down at the papers in front of him and only lifted his eyes to look at me with a flat-eyed stare.

My father used to give me the same look when I brought home something less than a perfect paper from school.

"I'm as surprised as you are," I said. "After years of doing this kind of work, I am pretty good at spotting subtle differences in the surrounding landscape. I'm usually right. But what are the odds of digging up two bone sites on a fifty-acre piece of land. I'm not that good, I don't know anyone who is.

"I need to take some time and scout this place. As I told Tony, there has to be some subtle clues to guide me. If there are, whoever buried this has a vast knowledge of treasure hunting or is one lucky son-of-a-gun."

I stepped back so he could get out of the SUV. "Give me a 'for instance' example."

I turned my head and looked around the immediate area where we stood. "Look to your left. See how the land slopes gently downhill for almost a hundred yards? There is a large divot and then the land continues to follow the same trajectory.

"Most likely, someone buried something in that spot, or dug up a tree. To make a long story short, the dirt settled in that particular spot at a lower level than the surrounding dirt. Makes me think there is something there."

"Let's go see," he said. "You have your detector in your hand."

I reached down and petted Indy's head before I turned on my heel and began to walk Wade to the area I'd pointed out.

Why I became suddenly angry perplexed me. What he asked was a perfectly reasonable question and was a perfectly good idea. All I could discern was that his tone of voice came out similar to an adult telling a child what to do or as if he was testing me. Geez. Or lack of sleep, or maybe I'd worked alone too long.

The detector picked up a signal almost immediately. I knelt down, took my trowel out of the pouch around my waist and began to cut a circular plug of grass. Once I had ninety percent of the earth loose, I folded the grass out of my way and reached for a pinpointer.

When I stuck it into the hole nothing happened, but when I ran it over the plug, it went crazy with its high pitch sound. I reached down and picked up an aluminum tab off some kind of soda can. "I didn't say everything I find is valuable, just that I can usually pick out where an object is buried."

I grinned up at him. He didn't smile.

It was at that moment I realized good looks do not trump a friendly smile. Indy, who had more compassion in one paw than most people did in their entire body, moved as close to me as he could, leaned against me and put a paw on my lap.

The FBI agent stared down at us for a long moment, then reached down, extended his hand and helped me up.

At that moment, most of the tension between us, melted away

# Chapter 25

Indy and I walked back to the dig site while Agent Wade drove slowly behind us. Patrolman Tony Asbury knelt peering into one of the trenches. "Don't touch anything," I yelled down to him when I saw him pick up a bone.

He placed the bone back, stood and began to walk toward us. "Sorry, wanted to see for myself what you found."

I must have given him a less than friendly look because he immediately said, "Look, I'm sorry. I find all of this exciting. Been with the department a year now and this is the first really cool thing I've gotten to do."

I hadn't realized before how young he appeared to be. As I gave him a closer look, I noticed it was already three in the afternoon and he had no sign of a stubble on his face. Had he been light skinned I would have dismissed it, but he had a deep tan and black hair. My analysis told me he didn't have to shave every day.

Despite his height, which I guessed at over six feet three, and his body builder look and stance, he couldn't have been over twenty, twenty-two at the most. "Excited or not," I said, softening my look, "this is a crime scene and needs to be treated as such."

He looked down. "Sorry, Dr. Ford."

Blake didn't overhear our exchange. He had parked the car and began stowing my gear in the back. Tony rushed off to help him, possibly to avoid any further embarrassment.

Before we left, Blake ask Tony to stay at the site and guard it until we came back. Even though I didn't think he overheard the earlier exchange between Tony and me, I was soon proven wrong. "Don't touch anything," I heard the agent say.

Blake turned around and looked in an entire circle, surveying our surroundings.

"See that tree," he put his hand on Tony's shoulder and pointed further down the hill. A huge hickory tree stood at the bottom and behind it a rise. "You'd be safe to sit under the hickory down there. It gives you a panoramic view of the entire area. I doubt anyone would try to come up the hill behind you since a creek runs on the other side of it. With the recent rain, it would be prohibitive."

Tony gave a mock two finger salute and jogged toward the tree. Blake made no effort to move toward the car until the young cop seated himself, leaned up against the tree trunk and waved at us.

Indy ran to the SUV. I walked beside the agent. "Odd kid," he muttered.

We had nearly a mile ride back to the main road where the police guards were parked immediately outside the yellow crime scene tape. All was quiet. The only sounds were Indy's panting and the occasional rattling of my equipment.

A trained FBI agent and an adult German Shepard must have a better sense of danger than I did. We were a football field away from the two police cruisers when Blake stopped the car and the hair stood up on the back of Indy's neck and he began to growl.

"What is it?" I asked.

Blake had turned off the ignition and lowered all four windows. Outside, no breeze stirred. The eerie silence was palpable. The agent turned to me, "Stay here. Something's wrong."

He opened the door and Indy jumped down as if he would follow the agent. "You should stay here and protect your owner," he said. Indy fell in beside him anyway and walked with him, paying no attention to his suggestion.

About ten feet from the first car, Blake drew his gun. He crouched next to the car and made his way to the window.

Indy beat him to the other car. They repeated the same maneuvers. Blake turned around, leaned against the fender of the cruiser and slid down until he sat on the ground.

He took his phone out of his pocket and made a call. He also motioned for me to join him. When I got closer, he said, "Neither man is responsive. I tried to shake them. They each have a pulse but it's weak. I called Chief Davis and 9 1 1. An ambulance should be here soon."

In less than a minute, I heard sirens. Then I remembered, First Responders were housed at a local fire department, less than a mile from where we stood.

The first to arrive on scene was Chief Bill Davis. He jumped out of his car before it fully stopped. He jogged over to the first car and then to the second, unknowingly repeating what Agent Wade had previously done. When he turned to us, I now stood next to the agent, "I don't understand. What do you think happened here?"

"I wish we knew." Wade said to the chief. "It isn't the only strange thing happening here today. Alexa found another bone site. It contained bones, coins and jewelry."

The chief clearly didn't have control of his emotions. He was understandably upset. "Where's that ambulance? These men could die. We don't know how long they have been like this or what they have in their systems."

Davis walked back to the first car and took the man's pulse as Blake did earlier. It was steady. He walked to the second car and did the same thing.

Davis hurried back to where we stood, as the First Responders pulled in. They immediately set to working on stabilizing and reviving the two downed officers.

"Where's Tony?" Davis asked us. Looking back the way we had come.

"We left him to guard the second site," Blake said.

"Are you sure that was a good idea, considering what has happened here?" He nodded from one car to the other.

"When we left him behind," I said, "we didn't know about this."

The chief sprinted to his car with the agent hot on his tail. "Stop!" Blake shouted. "You stay here and take care of your men, I'll go."

Indy looked at me once, barked and headed out like a dart to get into the SUV with Wade before he left.

Amazing. I wondered what he saw, smelled or heard that we didn't have the senses to know about.

Without waiting for an answer from Chief Davis, Wade opened the door for Indy and headed back the way we'd come to where we'd left Tony. Davis sat on a log outside the tape.

"I notified the Highway Patrol and the Sheriff's office. Where are they?" He looked at his watch.

"I don't think you called anyone, Bill. Maybe you'd better check."

He took out his phone, looked at the screen and said something I couldn't understand.

Only a few minutes passed before sirens approached from all directions. I turned and walked in the direction Blake had driven with Indy. By the time I arrived, Wade sat next to Tony with a cloth held to the man's head.

"What happened," I hollered as I jogged in their direction.

Blake answered, "I'm not sure yet. When I got here, he was unconscious. I dripped some water on his face, other than this huge goose egg on his forehead, he seems alright."

"Tell me what happened?" I asked coming up to sit with the two men on the ground.

"I'm embarrassed to say I fell asleep. Before you judge me, let me explain. The sun was shining down on me, it was quiet and I got sleepy. I heard a noise and when I opened my eyes, a guy hit me."

"What guy?" Blake asked.

"A dark-skinned man with red hair and a C-shaped scar on his cheek. He put his hand over my mouth and hit me with a rock he had in his other hand."

"Are you saying he was black?" I asked.

"No, just dark complected. I know it sounds strange, but his red hair looked natural. Never seen him around here before. Meanwhile, a small woman stood up there," he pointed to the dig site above us.

"She had a bag and began to put all the bones and things you dug up today in the bag. I didn't get a good look at her. She was too far away. And the guy hit me before I could say or do anything."

I walked to the first dig site of the day. Every bone, the fingers, and the pendant with the fish on it lay broken in the dirt as if someone had stomped on it and then ground them into the dirt with their shoe.

At the second site, not only had someone taken every item I'd found, but someone took their foot and pushed as much dirt as they could over the holes. I looked around. It was as though someone had taken a leafy branch and smoothed the entire area. I wasn't wrong because about half-way between there and the trees lay a broken branch from a maple tree.

Blake came up to me as I finished.

I sat next to the ruined area and put my head in my hands. What was happening? First the professor. Then I get shot at. Someone takes a chance on killing a delivery boy in hopes of getting off a shot in my direction.

Two policemen are in horrible condition in their cruisers. Now my guard had been knocked out and my treasures were gone.

My goal was to stop digging and start tracking. I needed to find out if all the events we'd encountered thus far led us back to the long, lost Judith Izzard disappearance. Or were we in the middle of other unconnected crimes we knew nothing about?

Was it all about the ring or did no one know it had been found? All of the jewelry could not possibly be from the Izzards. One pendent was dated 2019. What did Professor Thompson have to do with any of it? Bill and Blake were sure he was not involved. I wasn't so sure anymore. Was it a coincidence the professor got killed the same night I showed him the ring? While the two men thought it unlikely, I thought it was getting more and more likely.

The murder of Professor Thompson, the ring buried with a different, younger body and the assault of the officers. It would be much harder to determine the answer without the artifacts I'd dug up. I leaned against the agent's SUV and tried to make my brain stop spinning.

# Chapter 26

The agent looked behind him at the hill. He jogged up and stood on what looked like a ledge and looked in both directions. Then he disappeared. It was a good ten minutes before he came back down to where I was, now half holding Tony up.

"There is no sign, track or broken twig to show they went up the hill. It's a wet weather creek. The other side goes straight down to what looks like a spring. It's nowhere anyone would want to go. It's marshy. With the rain, it looks like you might sink up to your knees. I would have had to slide down it on my butt if I truly wanted to go to the bottom. Then I believe it would take a tractor to pull me back up the hill.

"My other question, Tony" Blake continued. "Is how do you know it was a man and woman if he came up behind you and hit you on the head, and she was too far away for you to see any of her features?"

I had the same thoughts but had chosen not to voice them. Blake

Tony tried to stand and did so with a great amount of effort. A blank look came over him. "Just guessing, she just looked like a female. They stand different, look different and move differently. You know what I mean." He looked at Blake while he talked. When he looked at me, he blushed.

"But you are sure it was a man and a woman?"

"Yes, after he hit me, I was more in a fog than out cold. I watched them take everything. It was like watching shadows, I couldn't see details and everything was foggy. One moved like a man and one moved like a woman. One was big and one appeared small.

"When I could no longer stand the pain in my head, I closed my eyes."

"Where is your gun?" Blake asked.

The officer reached down to his utility belt. "It's not here. They must have taken it."

I walked to the dig. "Guess I need to see what they destroyed and what can be salvaged." I knew I didn't say it loud enough for anyone to hear but Indy. But I didn't care.

My phone rang. Dr. Adaline McGuire said, "Did you forget about us. We have been waiting here at the hotel for hours." She was definitely annoyed.

"I am so sorry. Many things have gone on this morning. I promise to tell you all about it. I'll be there in thirty minutes."

Davis walked up behind me as I said, "I need to go to the Holiday Inn on the highway and pick up the crew from the university."

He stepped closer to me. I thought he would poke me in the chest but he only raised his arm to push his hair back from his eyes. "Have Agent Wade take you and get back here as soon as you can."

"Where *is* Wade?"

"He stayed behind to get Asbury into his car and drive him down here. I don't know what's taking them so long."

"Maybe I should go have a look," he said.

Before he had time to get to his car, I saw Tony and Blake coming down the hill.

Tony's head rested on the passenger side window. He looked out of it. Blake looked to see what was ahead of him and back to Tony. He did it several times before they reached me and the chief.

Bill ran to the passengers' side of the car and opened the door. He had to catch his officer before Tony fell out onto the ground.

"I have you," he said. Bill raised his head and nodded to Blake. He pointed to the two police cars. "I want Tony to go to the hospital first. There is nothing we can do for or about the other two. EMTs said they were poisoned and are already transporting them to the hospital. Not much they can do about it until they find out what it was."

Once Wade turned Officer Tony over to Davis, we left to get the archeologist and her group from the hotel. Chief Davis told me it would be best if they didn't come until the next day. I nodded and said I would talk to them.

The first part of our drive to the hotel was quiet. I finally asked, "How can I get my car back? They don't want to deliver it unless we take their driver back to the shop."

"Tell them to set the car out, put the keys under the floor mat and we'll pick it up this evening. Will that work?"

"Sure," I said. "If you don't mind."

I called Sam at the shop and he agreed to set the car out.

At the hotel, the students sat on duffel bags to the side of the circle drive. Adaline sat inside and came out when she saw me. "Sorry," I said. "This has turned out to be much more than a normal dig. This morning someone stole every item I dug up. I'll show you and we'll talk when we get there."

I didn't care what the chief said, I intended to take them back to Seymour even if they did nothing more than sit in the car.

McGuire didn't introduce her crew. They just piled into the SUV and off we went. In the rear-view mirror, I saw each of the students shrug their shoulders to one another. I couldn't blame them.

# Chapter 27

No way could the authorities hide the fact something had happened on the old Izzard farm. By the time Blake and I arrived with the college crew the area had turned into a circus of people, as if a fireworks show was about to begin on the Fourth of July.

Three ambulances, from four or five neighboring towns, as many police cruisers from the same towns, as well as the highway patrol and the sheriff all sat together near the entrance to the farm. Every one of them had their bubblegum lights spinning. Blue and red shadows flickered in the sunlight.

As we tried to drive through, a man in a blue suit and an obvious shoulder holster put his hand firmly on the hood of the car and stopped us.

Our agent lowered his window, looked out and said, "Hi Roy. I heard you were in Missouri. Didn't expect to see you out here."

"It's a long story, buddy. We'll talk later. I need to get your car out of the way."

The lawman stuck his head in the window opening as far as he could and eyed each of us. "Since we're restricting who can be let in, want to introduce me?"

"Sure." Agent Blake Wade pointed toward me. "This is Alexa Ford; this is her dig site. The rest of my group includes Dr. Adaline McGuire, University of Missouri, and her post grad crew."

I read their names off of the text she'd sent earlier in the week. "We have John Wilson, Terrill Jones, and George Drake."

Each of the students nodded when I said his name. "Due to the age and history of some of the items that have been found, it was decided this crew and their expertise was needed."

"Okay, Blake, pull your vehicle to the left as far as you can get it. Don't plan on moving it for a few hours. Dylan Austin, the head of the SW Missouri FBI office is here, and he wants to personally interview everyone involved before he will let anyone leave."

Blake said nothing. He moved the SUV to an empty spot as he was told, and we all got out. No one knew exactly what we were supposed to do so we all leaned against the SUV or stood around. "I'll go see where they want us to go and what they want us to do," Blake said to me. "I'll be right back."

"Wait," I said as I caught up to his long stride. "I'm going with you. Who is Dylan Austin?"

"He is the Agent in Charge of the Regional Office located in St. Louis. I don't know how he got here so soon."

"Geez, I didn't realize taking a simple excavation job would start all of this." We found Bill sitting on the tailgate of an ambulance. He looked as though he might pass out any minute. I went up to him. "I'm so sorry, Chief. Have you heard anything more about what happened."

He shook his head. "A call just came in from the hospital. My men are awake, and in stable condition. They should be released to go home in the next couple of hours.

"Some guy they didn't know drove in about six and said I sent him with dinner for them. He brought fried chicken, mashed potatoes, gravy and green beans from Lilly's in town. I have someone on the way over there to see if anyone at the restaurant knows the person who ordered and picked up the food.

"They also delivered two large coffees from McDonalds to my officers. He'll go there too. The guys believed him. He left and they sat on the fender of one of the cruisers and ate.

"Neither one of them remember anything else about him. One said he looked about six feet, the other said he was shorter. It went like that the entire time I tried to talk to them.

"Doc said after they sleep some more their brain fog might clear enough to be of some help. There was Benadryl in the food. Not enough to kill them but enough to put them out."

"I've never heard of such a thing," Blake said. "I believe you can make a drug out of anything. I got a report the other day, some kids were sick and one even ruined his lungs getting high on the accelerant used to make whipped cream come out of the can. I can't remember what it's called."

Chief Davis patted my shoulder. "Where did you leave the crew from the school?"

I pointed toward the parking lot. "I know you told me not to bring them here, but honestly, I had no idea what else to do with them. They're over there." I pointed to the general direction of the car. "I haven't told them what's going on yet. I'm sure they're sorry they're here."

"Can you get them started on a new dig? Maybe somewhere their luck won't be as good as yours? Make it as far away from this area as you can. We have enough volunteers to post men around where they are. Didn't you say you're supposed to look over the entire fifty acres?"

"Yes, the entire fifty acres. Should I call Barclay Simmons and tell him what's going on here?"

Blake answered for Bill. "No, let's wait a few days. Our guys who are watching him said he's acting normal. He hasn't made or received any phone calls or texts to make them think he's involved in any of this, including the professor's death."

I shook my head. "I feel somewhat responsible. I didn't think to check him out. Who buys a farm in a town of 200 people and then starts attacking people? I know we don't know much about him, but all I know for sure is his check didn't bounce."

"I'll move them closer to Farm Road 181," I shrugged. It was the farthest point from where all of the excitement had taken place yet kept them on the farm.

I gathered the group and their goody bags and had them follow me. I decided not to go all the way to the Farm Road in case someone tried to shoot at them. I led them to one of the spots I determined might have an artifact or two.

"I need to get back. I think this is as good a place as any to get started. When will the equipment arrive?"

"I'd say by ten in the morning. I asked for a skid steer and a tiller. What about the explanation you promised us about what all of this is?" Dr McGuire moved her arm in a sweeping arc to take in all the activity happening around where we stood.

"I promise I will. Unfortunately, I'm a key player in what happened and I need to go give my statement. Until then, don't wander about looking for a better spot. Don't go off on your own. I'm sure the people who were here got what they wanted, but I can't swear to it. I'll take you all to dinner and tell you about it."

Not waiting for an answer, I turned on my heel and left.

"Stop," Dr. Maguire yelled in an authorial voice. "I need to go to the site I came here to work on. And, I don't intend to go another minute until I find out what is going on. We'll not be pushed aside to do busy work while whatever this circus you have here goes on without us."

She had a point. I walked back to her group and sat on the ground in front of her. The good doctor and the rest of her group sat in a semi-circle around me.

I took a deep breath. "Okay, I'll do the best I can, but I'm not sure what is connected and what isn't. Also, let me start with the fact that I made a mistake. You'll know what it was when I get to it."

"Will that be anytime soon?" Dr. Maguire asked, testily.

Again, I really couldn't blame her. I called her, made her rework her entire schedule, find a few post grads who could accompany her and then I left her at a hotel for hours waiting for me only to be pushed to a piece of land on a farm, not knowing if it had any connection to what I had called her for originally. The least I could do was give her a run down on what was happening.

"I was hired by a man from New Jersey to scan this fifty-acre farm we are on, to see if there are any artifacts. The first day, I walked the entire acreage and decided on a place to start.

"I only worked a few hours when I dug up some bones of a hand.

"I'm Agent Blake Wade, FBI," said Blake interjecting as he settled in the grass with the rest of us, "I'm here to try to solve the case of some stolen art. Or at least, I thought I was. I'll let Lexi go ahead with her story in a minute. However, I do want to interject this is about murder and theft. Nothing you hear while you're here is to be repeated. Does anyone have a problem with that?"

The four of them signaled they could keep the facts to themselves.

"My mistake," Lexi said, "was I took the bones I found to a professor at Dorman College. The next day he was found dead in his home. The killer didn't get the bones. They were locked in the professors safe. I wasn't here long before I began to find more bones." I felt a little guilty but it was close enough to the truth for what they needed to know.

"The local authorities posted guards around the farm to protect the site from anyone snooping. Later that day, someone also shot the tires on my Jeep and shot at my door when the agent opened it to get a delivery.

"When we arrived this morning, the two officers posted overnight were unconscious. We thought they'd been murdered, but fortunately it turns out they'd only been poisoned. Not fatally.

"The cop assigned to stay with me was attacked and knocked out while Agent Wade and I were helping the two unconscious officers and is now on his way to the hospital for a checkup."

"So now we have three assaults. Whoever poisoned the two policemen took all of the artifacts I'd gathered.

"I shouldn't say the same people did everything that's happened. None of us knows how big the group doing all of this is. Once your equipment gets here, I'm hoping we can dig deeper in the places we find anything."

I scanned the faces looking at me intently. They were awestruck. No one moved. Blake took over. "I think it best if the four of you go to the original site. I have a gut feeling there's more to find." He looked at his watch. "It's nearly two o'clock now; do you want to start today or wait until in the morning?"

Mummering broke out in the group, the whole team chomping at the bit to get to it. Blake and I led the way to the original site about half a mile up a small grade. "Here it is," I said.

Adaline and her crew walked around and looked at my work. "I can see why you picked this spot," Adaline said. "I'm with you about this being a good place to start. I must say, I'm a little nervous with the gun shots and assaults. Agent, how safe are we here?"

Blake pointed around and up. "First of all, Lexi won't be with you right now. She has to meet with the authorities at the headquarters they have set up near the entrance to the farm.

"So far, they have only shot at Dr. Ford. We think they are trying to scare her away. What they did instead is to bring more attention to the activities here.

"We have some snipers hidden in the trees. They will be able to see anyone who comes up from any direction.

"So long as you folks are here, someone will watch over you." His no nonsense, professional attitude seemed to calm the team's nerves.

Wade left and I stayed with the group to explain where I had dug and why. They were attentive but their demeanor and faces told me I should stop my explanation and let them get to it.

Within fifteen minutes I stood with Agent Wade and Chief Davis by a truck. It looked like something you would use in a war zone. They called it a Crime Scene Light Source. They planned to use it at night to light up the entire area around the dig site. It would turn on a random pattern and light up everything within half a mile making it difficult for anyone to sneak up on the officers guarding the site.

While I'd been gone, the area had filled up with onlookers, news cameras and news reporters. The ambulances were gone. CSI teams were in and on the police cruisers. A dog on a long lead sniffed around the area.

Indy whined at my side to go with her.

It all exhausted me. I needed to get away from the noise and chaos so my ears would stop ringing and I could think in peace. Too much had happened and I'd had no time to process any of it.

Rescue came when Blake leaned over and whispered in my ear. "Now would be a good time to go to town and pick up your Jeep."

He didn't have to ask me twice. When he turned toward his SUV, Indy and I were right behind him.

# Chapter 28

"We need to talk," Agent Blake Wade said as we drove away from Izzard farm.

"Okay, talk," I said.

"I'm afraid we'll get started and have to stop because we're ready to pick up your Jeep. Invite me to dinner."

What a strange request, I thought. Before I had time to answer him, he said, "I don't expect you to cook. I'll provide the entire dinner."

"Sorry, but I need to have dinner with the university crew. Besides, I think you're a nice guy and all, but the thought of eating another sandwich or a pizza for dinner kind of turns my stomach."

"I would offer to take you out somewhere but what we need to talk about can't be overheard."

Sounds ominous, I thought, but didn't say how I felt out loud.

He drove, never looked at me, and his hands remained at ten and two on the steering wheel. I wished I could have seen his eyes or expression better, but I couldn't.

"If you have a grill, I can pick up a couple of steaks, twice baked potatoes, a salad and ice cream."

"Sounds like a lot of trouble, I'm not up to. Johnny's Steak House in Strafford delivers. Let me see if I can beg off dinner tonight and take the crew to breakfast in the morning. If I can shift them to breakfast instead, we can have dinner."

A text came to my phone from Elly. *The professor's funeral is at noon tomorrow at the auditorium at Dorman. Burial will be at Benton Memorial Cemetery on East 12$^{th}$ Street, food will be provided by the Archeology Club and its sponsors directly after the internment.*

"The text was from a friend of mine," I explained, even though he hadn't asked. "The professor's funeral is tomorrow at noon, at the college. There is a luncheon after, also at the college. So I most likely won't be at the dig site until after two."

He didn't reply, just glanced down at his dashboard. The time read two-forty-five p.m.

"I'll order dinner at six, but please don't answer the door until I get there. I'm not sure who the target is, but the bullets are flying," Blake said.

When we pulled up to the mechanic's shop, I was both relieved to get out of his car and thrilled to see my Jeep. I wanted to go home, shower, and have some peace and quiet before Blake got to the house with dinner.

I got my wish. Finally, I was allowed to go home. A patrolman in a cruiser drove in front of my car and one behind me. Chief Davis wanted me to put the Jeep's top up but I couldn't because the hard top sat on sawhorses in my garage and the canvas top was still at the Auto Interior Shop having damage repaired from the winter before.

The drive home proved to be eventless, thank goodness. The first cop took my keys and cleared the entire place before he would let me enter my house when I got there. When he handed me my keys back, he smiled at me and wanted to know if I wanted him to stay with me.

"No, thanks. I won't open the door to anyone." I swear, it felt as though I was in a scene from CSI.

The two of them seemed reluctant to leave but I did my best to make them feel secure. Seemed as if they were more nervous than I was.

Before I could relax, I texted Dr. McGuire and changed our meal from dinner later tonight to breakfast tomorrow morning. I told them I would be at the Holiday Inn by eight a.m.

I took a shower, washed my hair, and rested on my bed. I needed to get dressed and go downstairs. Blake and the food would be there any minute. How I wished I'd said I didn't want to have dinner with him. I had too much drama in my life already to want to add whatever he wanted to talk about to it.

For him to say, we needed to talk, only served to further rattle my fragile nerves.

I chose long blue jean shorts and one of my branded shirts, in pink with the logo in maroon. After I brushed my hair, I put it in a low ponytail and headed down to the kitchen. It wouldn't hurt to have the table set; it would cut down on the time I would have to be with someone in the house.

It was six-forty-five and Blake hadn't arrived yet. I went to my office and turned on the computer.

When the search bar began to blink at me, I typed in Blake Wade, FBI.

The article that popped up didn't say much, only that Agent Blake Wade was assigned to the St. Louis office. He'd been with the agency for seven years and was considered skilled at his job. To reach Agent Wade, call the St. Louis office at (314) 555-55501. Short and sweet, I thought, but nonetheless, he held the job he said he did.

---

I looked up Barclay Simmons in Missouri Case Net. It was a cool website. All one had to do was pick a court. I left it on all courts after the stories about Simmons' varied interests. Next, I filled out his name, Simmons, Barclay. His name came up. As a matter of fact, he covered three pages. The cases included,

Executor of the estate of Minie Izzard
State of New Jersey vs Barclay Simmons
State of Virginia vs Barclay Simmons
Morgan Rentals vs Barclay Simmons
Corporation papers for a Delaware corporation by the name of Simmons Holdings, Inc.

The doorbell rang just as I started skimming the first case. I shut down my computer. Then wondered who got to the door first, Blake or Johnny's?

The food got there first.

I hesitated for a second. I had no intention of living my life in fear. The car in front of the house clearly said Johnny's Steak House, Catering, Eat in, Delivery. I opened the door.

"It's paid for, ma'am." Before I could ask, the young delivery boy stepped in, sat the bags on the floor, and handed me a receipt. He politely told me to have a nice evening and left.

If FBI Agent and protector, Blake Wade, wanted me not to open the door, he should have arrived before the food. The time was ten after seven. I'd already given him an extra hour.

Twenty minutes passed before the doorbell rang a second time, Blake. He began to speak before I had the door opened wide enough for him to step in. "Sorry. I stopped to help a teenage girl with a flat tire."

"Well, aren't you the gentleman. It's a shame your cell phone didn't work," I said as I turned on my heel and headed for the kitchen.

Without warning Indy jumped up from his bed under the microwave cabinet and ran toward the back door. Blake pulled his gun from the shoulder holster he wore and walked up to stand behind the dog. "Let her out," I said. "If there is anyone around, he'll scare them away."

"I know your dog is the smartest I've ever seen, but he is no match for a gun."

*A good point*, I thought.

Blake went to the front door, turned off the outside lights and started around the house to the back. Indy watched him go for a few minutes and then went back to her station at the back door. She growled.

I'm not an alarmist but I took a seat where I couldn't be seen from the window in the back door. The hair stood up on Indy's neck and all the way down his back. Whatever stood or crawled on the other side of the door, had his attention.

Someone tapped softly on the back door. Indy sat and the hair on her back laid down. "Blake, is it you?"

"Yes," he said through the back door.

I opened the door. He held a .9mm semi-automatic with his thumb and forefinger. "Does this look familiar to you?"

"I know what it is. Where did you find it?"

"On the back porch, near the stairs. There was definitely someone out there a few minutes ago." He looked at Indy who walked over and sat in front of him. Today was the first time the dog paid any attention to the agent.

"Do you have any large zip lock bags? I don't have anything with me, and I'll like to have the lab check the gun for fingerprints."

I'd put the food on the table before he arrived. So much for our talk.

We ate in silence.

## CHAPTER 29

Silence was not my strong suit. Once we were finished with our meal, I could hardly choke down, I poured us each a glass of wine. I set Blake's glass on the kitchen table and carried mine to the living room. I chose a chair away from the front picture window. After a sip, I sat the glass on the end table.

Blake came in a second or two behind me. He took a seat at the end of the couch nearest to me.

"I thought you wanted to talk," I said.

"I do, but you have been rather unapproachable since I arrived."

Usually when I'm caught off guard, I try not to show emotion. Now I felt a slow burn redden my face. My breaths became more shallow. One would have to be blind not to see my anger. "This conversation was your idea. You said you needed to talk to me alone so we won't be overheard. Yet you have been here for over an hour and haven't said anything.

"What is this secret subject you want me to hear?"

"Wow," he said. "I'm one of the good guys. I wanted to talk to you about Officer Anthony Asbury."

"What about Tony?" I asked.

"Tony left the second dig site. I'm not sure why. But I heard you call for him and he didn't answer. Later he told you he heard a noise and it ended up being a covey of quail.

"When is the last time you saw a quail around here or heard a bob-white?"

I didn't think he wanted an answer, and I wanted to see where he was headed with this line of thinking.

"Tony was left alone to guard the bones and jewelry," continued Blake. "Someone hit him on the head with a rock but poisoned the others? Why did he volunteer to guard you?"

"Are you suggesting Tony hit himself on the head and stole the items I dug up? It sounds a little far-fetched to me. I would need a why?

"That's exactly what I'm saying. Bill told me Tony showed up here about six months ago with a certificate from NYPD saying he'd passed his training.

"There are over thirty-five thousand police officers in New York City. He found someone with a name he liked, borrowed name and accomplishments."

"What makes you think he would do something like this?" I asked.

He got up. "I'll be right back," he said as he walked out the front door.

I got up to follow him, but he was back in the house before I crossed the threshold.

He carried a bright red duffle bag which he set on the coffee table and then unzipped it. "This is why," he said. Blake began to take the items out of the bag one at a time. Each item had a white towel wrapped around it. He opened the towel, but left the item cradled in it.

First came the finger bones and then the bones and trinket I'd found the day before. Everything that had supposedly been taken by the two people who'd attacked Tony.

"Why would he do that? You think he killed the professor?" I asked. "Who is he?"

"I'm not sure, but I'll have to arrest him." He smiled grimly at me. "I'm hoping when Bill and I go to arrest him, we find out more about what really happened."

"Unbelievable," I said. "Where did you find the duffle bag?"

"The bag was hidden behind the hickory tree, in the tall weeds about twenty feet from where he sat to guard you."

"Could someone else have put it there?" I couldn't wrap my mind around this new revelation and the possibility that Tony was in on what had been happening.

"Bill said Asbury's fingerprints are all over it. I'm sure he didn't expect anyone to find it, so he didn't bother to be careful about leaving evidence."

"My head is spinning. He is such a nice, polite, helpful guy. He doesn't look like a criminal," I said.

Wade looked at me. "Ted Bundy also looked like someone you would invite to Sunday dinner."

The office called on my way here. Appears the Chief called the governor and asked for help here. Eighteen National Guard are being sent here to help out and keep your crew safe while they search the Izzard farm for anything else that might be there."

I shook my head in confusion. "Why would they do that?"

"My dear, whether you want to admit it or not, you're now a celebrity. Professor Thompson was one of the foremost experts on antiquities in the world. Bill told them he thought we had a potential killing field here. Plus, the Trail of Tears is a diplomatic powder keg and can cause the government a lot of trouble if we mess up a burial ground or come across a sacred artifact.

"And between me and you, the professor was indeed working for the CIA and many artifacts from other countries that should have gone through his hands have disappeared. This has been going on long before I was called in.

"Although we're all on the same team, the initial groups don't work well together. Sometimes it's like being at war." While he looked frustrated, all I could do was stare at him in shock.

The most surprising element of this entire mess I was in, is the fact it was now being talked about in every newspaper, scholarly journal, NBC, ABC and CBS, as well as PBS. They were even airing old documentaries of some of the professor's exploits in the field from over the years. A huge special with the old footage of me when I found the money in the field behind my house was even being aired alongside the documentaries. Boy did I look young back then.

And through it all, there had been no word from Barclay Simmons, the man who should have been the most interested in what was happening on his newly acquired property.

SUSAN KEENE

# Chapter 30

I didn't have much to say. To believe Tony had killed the professor didn't jive at all with the story Blake had laid out earlier. He originally told me several men killed Thompson. in the middle of the night.

With a description like that, the murderer could be anyone of millions of people.

It all gave me a headache.

Tony Asbury didn't have a scratch on him. Had it not been for the bones, I would not have believed a word of it.

Agent Wade's phone rang and interrupted my train of thought. I could only hear his side of the conversation. It consisted of a bunch of grunts, undecipherable sounds and a "goodbye, keep me posted."

The look on his face was one I had yet to see from him. His face had paled. He moved to a chair and nearly fell into it.

"What happened?" I asked.

"Officer Asbury is out of the hospital. When Captain Davis couldn't raise him on his cell phone, he sent someone to Asbury's apartment.

"They found him hanging from a rope. They know Asbury didn't kill himself because he had bruises all over his body. It certainly makes my entire theory of the crime wrong, doesn't it?"

I stared at him. After I ran through everything he'd said, I sat down across from him. He didn't look up.

When the silence became so loud, I could no longer stand it, I said, "Are you upset it wasn't Tony?"

He looked me straight in the eye. "Of course not. I don't know where to go from here. Davis and I went through the entire scenario. Tony's real name is Nathan Rhodes. He flunked out of the NYPD Police Academy. He stole the papers of Anthony Michael Asbury and came here to work.

"You told me he'd only been here for a few months. He told me he'd been here for three years.

Now I believe he got caught up in something over his head and someone killed him because of it," Blake said looking thoughtful.

"Do you mind if I use your computer to report this all to my office? I don't want to take the time to go back to my motel."

"Sure, I have it set up in my office. Through those doors."

He sat another minute or two, staring straight out in front of him, when his phone rang again, he jumped before he answered it. "Yep, it's me. What's up Wayne?"

I couldn't hear the other end of the conversation, again.

"You have got to be kidding! How long has he been gone? Okay, let me know when you have more information."

He had the same look on his face as he'd had earlier. "Barclay Simmons is gone. They lost contact with him two days ago.

"His gardener is one of our guys. We know Simmons liked to drive himself to and from his appointments. He's been under investigation for nearly five years. His patterns haven't change much in the time we've been surveilling him.

"He was supposed to have dinner with a woman but never showed up. The valet said he parked the Lincoln in the lot. The kid said he always remembered him because Simmons was a big tipper.

"When the restaurant closed, the car was gone. The kid got busy and didn't get Simmons' car for him if Simmons had indeed left. The other two guys there, also young, either in high school or newly graduated, said they didn't see him leave either.

"They found his car in long term parking at Lambert Field, at the St. Louis Airport. He either left on his own or someone forced him to leave. He didn't buy a ticket in his own name.

"As we speak, they are combing through videos at the airport. So far, nothing."

"I'm beginning to feel as if I am in a movie. First the professor is killed, we don't know why. Now Tony is killed, and we don't know why. I'm not easily frightened, but this is scary," I looked at him intently. "Can I ask you a question?"

"Sure."

"You told me you knew who killed the professor. You said you could pick him up any time. Why did you lie to me?"

"Because at that time, we didn't know in what way you were involved. You went to his house the day before his murder. The next day you went back and found the body. But you stayed in the house forty-five minutes after you found him, and you didn't tell anyone.

"I thought if I told you we knew who the murderer was and you were involved, you would let your guard down and we could figure out what you were up to. Now we know you are not involved, but I didn't know how to bring it up. Let's face it, most of the time you would be happier if I wasn't around."

I didn't know how to answer him and since he didn't phrase it as a question, I remained quiet.

"I don't want you alone until this is over. You have clearly become a target for a reason, even if we aren't aware of what that reason is. If you don't want me to stay here, I'll bring some agents in from the office. We have no idea why Tony or the professor were killed or why Simmons is missing. And I don't want the next one to be you."

He walked toward the office. I followed him, I didn't want to be alone right then any more than he wanted me to be.

# Chapter 31

"Did you find anything out about the case?" I asked.

"Not much. They told me I was the Primary Agent on the job. It was another way to tell me if I screwed this up, I'd have to answer for it. The entire crime takes off in a whole new direction if a law officer is killed, even if he turns out not to have been legit. Maybe even more so because of that.

"I wouldn't want to be in the killer's shoes when we catch him," he added.

We drank our wine as we tracked Barclay Simmons back to Ozark, Missouri, with the help of the FBI surveillance database, the traffic cams and a hundred other tabs he pushed on the computer. He hadn't been in the area for well over two years. And the signature on the land deed had been sent electronically.

The FBI's resources were amazing. Blake led me to digital resources I couldn't get to on my own as a civilian.

"The deed says he bought the property for one dollar from Imogene Rathbone."

With the help of Ancestry.com, we found out Imogene Rathbone was the niece of Judith Izzard and the last of the Izzard clan. We might never know how she happened upon Barclay Simmons or vice-versa. No one is forthcoming with any information, and there was no cause of death on the death certificate.

He got up from the computer and motioned for me to sit in the seat he had just vacated. "Look up case net, I want to see the court notes. Maybe we can find more out about the farm."

"What a mess," I said. "I think the court has the name wrong on the site. Imogene Rathbone is the only name. on the deed. Things like that happened a lot back then. Nicknames went on generation to generation and after a while, the nicknames were mistaken for real names.

"Minie Izzard could very well be Imogene Rathbone. A nickname and a maiden name can make people hard to find," he said.

"Anyway, it doesn't matter, I have a copy of the deed of trust right here. For some reason, the Rathbone woman signed the deed over to Simmons. Whether he scammed her or stole it or what, it doesn't really matter. She is dead and he is missing.

"I'm not sure how it works," Blake said. "But if he comes up dead instead of missing and there is no will, seems like the different states would end up with the businesses If you die with no relatives the state can take your property.

"Knowing what we know now, I say it's all about two murders, the murder of Judith Izzard and the death of the girl we haven't identified as yet. If there is another girl.

"It must be the murderer trying to cover his tracks. The murders of three people are enough to get you the death penalty. Once you add Tony's murder, you have a serial killer," Blake said.

I picked up the wine bottle and looked at the contents. It had less than a glass in it, so I put the bottle straight to my lips and drank. "Let me get this straight." I looked behind me to make sure a chair was there before sitting. "Someone found out Barclay Simmons bought the old Izzard farm and was going to have it searched. Whoever it was most likely killed the girl whose finger bones I found earlier and left with the professor. They were too young to have killed Judith. Right now they would be at least 112.

"When they saw me go to the property to check for artifacts, they knew where the fingers were, saw me take them and followed me to Professor Jonah Thompson's house.

"Somehow, they found out I left them with Thompson. When he wouldn't hand the bones over, they killed him, but didn't find the bones or what they were looking for.

"They followed and watched as I found more artifacts that pointed to murder. So they killed the cop. That's where I get lost, why kill the policeman? Even if he was helping them?"

Blake stood up. "Do you have any more wine, or maybe something stronger?"

"I didn't think law enforcement could drink while on duty," I said.

He smiled the first time all evening. "If I waited until I was off duty while I had a case, I'd never get to partake."

"Good point," I said as I got up to get another bottle. "Do you prefer red or white?"

"Pick what you want. Do you have any food?"

"Didn't we just eat?"

"Look at your watch," he said. "We ate at seven-thirty. It is now close to three a.m. I'm a growing boy."

"How about a ham and cheese sandwich with chips?" I offered.

"Perfect, I'll make them," Blake said.

"None for me," I said, "late night meals give me nightmares and I'm already living one."

I took the lead as we walked to the kitchen. "I'll make you a sandwich, I'm the hostess here. By the way, my dad had some bourbon in the hutch in the den. You are free to drink it."

He went off to the other room in search of the stronger drink. I took sliced ham, white American cheese, iceberg lettuce, a tomato and mayo out of the refrigerator and set them on the counter. By the time he came back, I had the sandwich on a paper plate, and it sat on the kitchen table waiting for him.

Blake took a bite of the sandwich, held it up to me so I would know what he was talking about and said, "Do you always do this well in the kitchen? You are quite a good cook."

Neither one of us had anything else to say. It was a pleasant silence. I sat down and watched him. His sandy blond hair was long enough to fall into his eyes. He had a superhero square jaw line, and light-colored eyes. I would have had to get closer to get the full effect of them. The thought sent a shiver through me. Whether it was a good sign or a bad sign, I wasn't really sure. I still wrestled with the fact he had already been in the area when the first murder had occurred.

Once he finished his sandwich, Blake looked up, "What?" he said.

The blood rushed to my face. I didn't realize how intently I'd been going over his looks. "Nothing. I was lost in thought." Okay, it wasn't a total lie, I had been lost in thought. I was under no obligation to tell him the subject.

"I received a call while you were making the sandwiches," he said. "I'm going to fly to Newark and look into the disappearance of Barclay Simmons.

"The Agency has had an investigation going on him for a long while. I'm going up to see what I can find out about his disappearance. Those guys who have been surveilling him for five plus years like him. He seems to be good to his employees and friends. I believe I'll be the first person to look at it objectively."

"Do you think it's connected to what's going on down here, or is it a separate case altogether?" Then before he could answer, I asked, "When are you leaving?"

As soon as I figure how to keep you safe while I'm gone."

I chuckled. "I have managed to take care of myself for years. I don't need a babysitter. Indiana Jones won't let anything happen to me."

"I know you love your dog but let me point out he has no defense against bullets. I might not have his acute hearing, but I can fight equally and Indy can't"

When the dog heard his name, he got out of his bed, walked over to me and leaned against my leg.

"I've been around you long enough to know you think you're unstoppable, but I'll tell you right now, no one is." Blake looked deadly serious.

"Let me tell you about this from my point of view. I think we found a bone yard. It is just a matter of time before we find more bones. I have a job. I need to do it, and it makes no matter to me if he is missing or not. He paid me to do a job and I'm going to do it."

Blake was seated on the couch with his back relaxed against the cushion. When I finished speaking, he leaned forward and rested his elbows on his knees. "I asked Captain Davis if he could assign an officer to guard you. He can't. He's already lost a man out of an eight man force and has two more down. Though he doesn't think the other two will be out for long. They may come back as soon as tomorrow."

"Go, do your job. I asked for a crew from the school and they're here. It costs the college a small fortune to keep them here. I need to be with them." I looked at my watch, "As a matter of fact, If I'm going to meet them for breakfast, I need to get some sleep. Go, go to New Jersey."

"You have plenty of room, why not have Dr. McGuire and her people stay here?" Blake countered. "You can put the three males down here. Anyone would not only have to go through Indy to get you, they would also have to go through those young, strong and smart post graduate students."

He didn't say anything else. He picked up his jacket and briefcase and walked to the front door. Blake stopped with his hand on the doorknob and turned around to face me. "I have no choice but to leave. Keep your head in the game. Watch your surroundings. Make sure your outdoor lights are on and your doors are locked." With that, he opened the door and walked out.

I wasn't touched like I probably should have been. Instead, the thought that popped into my mind was, *How dramatic.*

While I cleaned up our plates and put the food away, my mind raced from event to event. The body of the dead fake police officer who I worked hard to keep out of my mind, floated into my thoughts over and over again.

The information I had so far told me the man had done nothing to deserve to be hanged. Purely a senseless act. It was possible that fake Officer Tony Asbury had killed the young unidentified girl, but who had killed Tony? Tony could not have killed the professor. The man who killed Professor Thompson left the professor's house with a wound. A wound big enough to leave two massive puddles of blood behind.

A thought occurred to me. The person who killed the professor potentially kidnapped Simmons, poisoned the cops and hanged Tony, might have you in his scope.

I intended to find out what it was.

# Chapter 32

I decided the best place to think, after the warning from Blake, was my bedroom. As I walked towards the front door to set the alarm, I noticed the newspapers I had stacked on the small hall table. For the last few days, I'd picked the local newspaper off the front porch and laid it on the table on my way by.

There were now four of them. I vaguely remembered I looked at the newspaper the day after the professor's murder. I picked them all up and took them with me upstairs to my room. Indy obediently followed behind me.

We both lay on my bed. I petted him and he put his head on my thigh. I opened the first paper.

*World famous Dr. Jonah Thompson, a professor emeritus at Dorman College, was found dead in his home on the Dorman Campus. Preliminary reports lead the authorities to believe his death to be a homicide.*

*Authorities are tight lipped as to the details of the professor's death but promise more information as it becomes available.*

*Professor Thompson was born January 11, 1951, and died May 30, 2025. It is not known if the professor had any close living relatives.*

*Professor Thompson received his doctorate in Archeological Studies from Oxford University.*

The second paper had speculation as to why the professor had ended up dead. It went through some of his most famous digs, a jug from 82 B.C. in Egypt, a sword from Lebanon said to be dated 556 and several digs resulting in the closure of a crime. Most everything reported happened overseas. The article ended with the statement. *Most of the expertise he provided lately was done at his home on the Dorman Campus.*

The third paper delved into Professor Thompson's family. It didn't mention a wife or an x-wife. He was proceeded in death by his father, Senator Michael Thompson, and his mother Theresa.

I closed my eyes and from memory I scanned the wall of his office. There were no people in those photos I couldn't recognize. Definitely, no children were pictured and no family photos. I reminded myself that until his death, I'd never seen the inside of the entire house.

The third paper also mentioned the time and place of the funeral as noon on June 3, in the auditorium on the Dorman campus.

It was tomorrow and I intended to go.

The article went on to say the crime scene tape had been taken down at his house and it had been cleaned so the visiting alumni could use it to receive mourners after the funeral.

I jumped up, put on a pair of dark sweatpants, a dark tee shirt and a gray hooded sweatshirt. I grabbed my flashlight.

Before I left the house. I text Dr. McGuire and extended an invitation for her and the young men to stay at my place instead of the hotel. Her reply came back nearly immediately, *I'm guessing you don't know it is four-thirty in the morning. Personally, I would love to take you up on the offer, but I need to talk to the guys first. We will let you know at breakfast.*

Indy and I went out the back door and headed to Thompson's home. I didn't put Indy on a lead. On the way over to the campus, we stayed in the shadows. If we ran into anyone who walked their dog or came by in a car, we would hide between the sidewalk and the nearest tree. I would turn my head to signal and Indy would lay down. It was the plan anyway, but at four-thirty in the morning, no one was around.

I knew what I intended to do was illegal, but I also knew if anything in that house pertained to the ruby ring or the property in Seymour, I was more likely to recognize it than the police or FBI.

Besides, I had my doubts about a couple of things. First, Agent Blake Wade happened to be in Benton at the precise moment the professor met his demise. Second, that anyone in their right mind would want to spend the night in a home where a murder was committed less than ten days before. And last, if someone did stay there, there was no way they would not look around. I didn't want to take the chance someone would take an item I wanted.

If people were at the house, I didn't know what I would do.

The only plus I could see about being in the inside circle of the law was the knowledge of where the cameras were on the property and on the streets around it. There might be more benefits later, but now, I couldn't imagine what they could be.

I took so many precautions not to appear on camera, or be seen on the street that the forty-five-minute walk took us over an hour. The sultry night had left me soaked with sweat.

On a hunch, I reached up and let my fingers slide across the top of the back door. Sure enough, there was a key.

The electric panel had been built into the wall inside the back door. I pulled the switch, turned off any power inside the house and took my flashlight out of my back pocket. I held the light so it only lit the area in front of me. The drapes were already pulled shut in the kitchen. They were as dark and dense as the ones I'd seen in the other rooms I'd been in.

"Indy, stay by the door. If I need you, I'll whistle. Bark once if you hear something." People who heard the way I talked to my dog smiled as if I didn't have my entire brain. It didn't matter to me. I knew for a fact the dog understood every word I uttered.

I took the sweatshirt off and laid it on the floor for Indy to lay on. He did.

After I looked through every drawer and cabinet in the kitchen, I stood in the doorway and had one more look. It seemed as if the wall space didn't match on both sides of the room. On the longest side, I began to tap along the wall. Adjacent to a floor cabinet the sound changed.

When I shined the light at different angles, I saw a slight line I knew didn't belong. I got a knife out of the silverware drawer, poked the point into the slit and pried it open. A packet fell onto the floor. I didn't take the time to open it. It looked like it would be a formidable job.

The packet, made from a manilla envelope, folded over and taped with at least a half roll of clear packing tape was heavy. I walked over and laid the packet near Indy. He rested his head on it.

"I won't be long," I said.

There were two rooms off the kitchen I'd never been in. The layout of the house reminded me of a hotel. A long hall ran from the front door to the kitchen. There were five rooms on each side. Each door remained closed.

Tentatively, I put my hand on the doorknob, turned it and pushed the door inward. Inside a queen size bed sat against the far wall. The bed had a green chenille bedspread with the pillows tucked under the top like I had seen my mother do years ago.

Throw pillows were placed casually around the head of the bed. On the left a tall chest with several pictures on top caught my attention. They were pictures of a beautiful dark-haired woman in a dress, standing with an arm around two children, one on each side of her.

Since one of the children was a girl, the other a boy, I guessed it was the professor and possibly a sister. The other pictures were of the kids on a set of swings with a young Jonah and the woman sitting on a blanket.

I guess you really never know anyone.

It took another hour for me to go through the house. I didn't find anything exciting until I went into the office I was so familiar with. The pictures on the wall were like old friends, I could have recited their place and who the participants were without looking.

The bookshelves were a different story. They were not like average bookcases along the walls. They were set up like a library, back-to-back. In order to see the books I'd never seen before, I was forced to go behind the front set of shelves to see the ones on the opposite side.

I used the flashlight a little more liberally knowing no one could see it from the outside or even if they had been in the same room with me. The first two shelves were over my head. I stepped back to the wall behind me and used the light to read the titles.

At the top were books about every country arranged in alphabetical order. The second shelf held textbooks. I recognized most of them from my time in college and grad school.

The next shelf gave me more insight into my dead friend. He had books like *Animal Farm*, *Prince of Tides*, *1984*, *Hawaii*, *The Old Man and The Sea*, *Grapes of Wrath*, *Lord of the Rings*, and dozens more.

On the next shelf sat a book with no title looking lonely by itself.

I turned off my light and took the book over to the desk. When I opened it, I took a deep breath. The book was one of those hollow books people use for decoration or to hide objects. So many papers were in it that they began to float off the top. At the same time, I heard voices outside. I pushed the chair away from the desk and scooted down so I couldn't be seen. I prayed Indy would hold her place and not bark.

The voices faded and I realized the people were talking on the sidewalk outside. I wanted to look through the book but decided it would be best to take the items with me and leave the professor's house.

# CHAPTER 33

The naturalists have said for years that Bradford Pear trees were invasive. There must have been several hundred of them between my house and the professor's. They ran alongside every sidewalk on the campus and ran up and down both sides of all the driveways. They had already bloomed but were bushy and full. Indy and I used them for cover on our way home.

We walked around our house to the back door and went in from there. My phone rang as I turned around to lock the door. "Lexi, it's me, Bill. The patrolman I've had cruise by your house twice tonight said all the lights were off and he didn't see any movement. Are you okay?"

What I wanted to say was *thank goodness*. What I actually said was, "I was in my room upstairs. I decided to watch a movie and I fell asleep. I'm fine."

"Be careful. Too many people have been hurt already. Until we find out who's doing it and why, we need to watch our own backs and each other's," he said.

I could hear a baby crying in the background. "I'm fine. Heading for the shower and then to meet my university crew for breakfast. The doors are locked and the alarm is set. Enjoy your family. I'm going to Professor Thompson's funeral at noon, so don't worry if I'm late."

After a lull, he said, "Take care," and hung up.

Maybe breaking and entering made me hungry. I poured a bowl of dog food for Indy and made a turkey and dressing TV dinner for myself. I forced myself to wait until I was in my room with the drapes pulled until I opened the hollow book again.

I looked from the packet to the book. The book seemed to be the path of least resistance. The cover had flowers of muted colors with a fake title, *Flowers of the Southwest*, printed on it. When I opened it, I saw the papers inside were yellowed with age. The one on top had a date of August 11, 1928. The headline read, *Famous ring comes to Seymour. A rare Fortner ring once owned by Queen Katherine V will be on display at the First National Bank on Third Street during business hours for the next two weeks.*

Three things came to mind. First, who in their right mind would put an article in the newspaper broadcasting the ownership of a ten-thousand-dollar ring. A ring at that price in 1928 would be worth ten million dollars today.

Secondly, did they leave the ring at the bank after the showing? If not, were people really that much different then and it was safe to have it in your home?

Third, why did Jonah Thompson have an original article about the ring? I could understand if it were a copy or a reprinted article he had used for research.

The contents only got stranger from there.

I noted at least forty-five photos of the ring. All from stories in newspapers and magazines of the era, all cut from the original sources.

In an article dated December 1928, a picture showed Jacob, his wife Mini, and Judith on their way to a holiday party. Jacob was dressed in a waist coat and top hat. Mini and Judith were decked out in formal dresses. Judith's gown had sequins from top to bottom. It was modestly cut in a scoop neck style and looked to be less than an inch from dragging on the floor. In a later picture Judith wore a fox stoll. Those were the days where the fashion was to have the tail of the fox wrapped around and latched into the mouth of the fox.

Mini's gown was more understated. Although it showed way too much cleavage for my taste, it showed her to be in line with the times. Since the photos were black and white, I couldn't tell the colors.

The ring stood out prominently on Mini's finger, as if she posed to help it catch the light from the camera's flash. In one of the photos, she wore a full-length mink coat.

The stories continued. There were at least twelve about the disappearance of Judith dated from June 1929 to 1942.

I studied the pictures of Judith over the years. A beautiful young woman with what I thought was red flowing hair, high cheekbones, and a slim figure. All of the photos after her disappearance mentioned the ring and how her father hadn't wanted her to wear it, but her mother had seen no reason she couldn't. Personally, I always thought the ring and the ring alone had been what caused Judith's disappearance.

Once I felt I knew most of what the book contained, I went downstairs and made a cup of coffee before returning upstairs to continue going through the stack of papers.

Boy, was I wrong. August 12, 1929, a young man named Morgan Thompson was arrested for the kidnapping and murder of Judith Izzard. Morgan, aged 25, the last person to see Judith alive on the day she disappeared, was arrested and charged with first degree murder. It didn't quite get into the details such as why he was suspected of Judith's murder, or how the two young people were connected.

Morgan Thompson. Surely, he wasn't a part of Jonah's family. I needed to pay another visit to my computer. Or maybe what I needed would be in the packet I found hidden in the kitchen.

Another article from the book said Morgan Thompson was found hanged from a tree near the James River. Nowhere did it say why he was released from jail, if he had a trial, nor did it mention her murderer again.

Either way, I had to put the stack of papers down. The crew would be ready for breakfast in less than an hour. Then there was the funeral and the lunch. I had to get some sleep, or embarrass myself by falling asleep at one of the three events.

I laid the papers down, picked up my cup, leaned back against the headboard and mulled over all the reasons I could think of why the young man, Morgan Thompson, was never mentioned again in all of the years I'd been following the Izzard family saga.

Although, I knew the boy had most likely killed Judith from the phantom visions I'd had while holding the ring.

I don't remember falling asleep. The next thing I was aware of my alarm was blaring in my ears. As much as I wanted to turn over and go back to sleep, Indy would have no part of it. He wanted food.

# CHAPTER 34

There was no desk in my room, although I had bought an old wicker dressing table with a circular mirror on the back, and a drawer on each side to put in there. My computer sat on the dressing table most of the time. I moved off my bed and went to sit in front of it.

Google flashed open on the computer screen and I typed in the name Morgan J. Thompson into the search bar. Eighteen thousand answers in .0016 seconds. It always amazed me; I'd have hated it to be the last one on the list.

*Morgan Johnathan Thompson was the one and only known suspect in the disappearance of Judith Izzard, Seymour, Missouri, in June of 1929. According to records at the time, Thompson was found drunk and disoriented on the Izzard farm the night Miss Izzard disappeared.*

*Earlier in the evening Judith Izzard, the daughter of Jacob and Mini Izzard, left her home to attend a graduation party at the main ballroom of the Bailey House in Springfield. The Izzard's driver took Judith to the hotel and left her there. She was to meet him after the party inside the hotel foyer.*

*Miss Izzard wore her mother's ruby ring, once owned by Queen Catherine V of France. When the driver, Jackson Weston, arrived Miss Izzard was not at the hotel. None of the guests remembered seeing her leave the venue. The nineteen-year-old was never seen again.*

*Young Morgan Thompson, son of Senator Michael Thompson was found hanged near the James River.*

*It was never determined why the Thompson boy, who was older than the Izzard girl was a suspect. Many thought the carriage driver should have been investigated.*

*Young Morgan was twenty-five when he was hanged by unknown assailants. Morgan's brother was away at college when he received the news of his brother's death.*

*The Senator spent the remainder of his life trying to keep his son's name out of the newspapers and to silence the rumors that his son might have done harm to the Izzard girl.*

I couldn't believe it. Senator Thompson. Jonah had to be involved. His uncle had been hanged for the crime without proof. His grandfather, the first Senator Thompson, had lived with the unanswered questions until his death in 2003 at the age of 93.

It explained why Professor Thompson had all of the articles as well as his interest in the ring when he saw it. With that realization, I hid the papers and the packet I'd yet to open in the bottom of my linen closet and went on with my day.

# Chapter 35

I had forgotten how much I liked Adaline McGuire. She and I had taken several classes together when our schedule and schools permitted it. I was reminded when I realized how much I was looking forward to working with her to uncover the mysteries of the Izzard farm.

When I walked into the restaurant, all four of the team members, the three undergrads and Adaline, had been seated long enough to have coffee in front of them.

"Where's your puppy?" One of the guys asked.

"He's outside the door. Everyone is not a dog lover, especially if food is on the table."

Adaline stood and hugged me. Her long silky blond hair bounced when she got up and again when she sat down. She couldn't have been over five-feet-two, and one hundred pounds or less. "I hope you're going to fill us in on what's going on and why we are digging in a war zone," she said.

I smiled and sat down. "I'll do my best. I'm not sure why all the bloodshed is going on, but I can tell you what I think. Introduce me to your crew again." I directed that last to McGuire.

"Sure," she said pointing to each one in turn. "This is John Wilson, Terrill Jones and George Drake.

They each nodded to me as she said their names.

We stopped talking when the waitress came to the table. I ordered a Denver Omelet, ham, cheese, green peppers, onions, mushrooms and eggs. It came with sides. I chose a short stack of buttermilk pancakes and hashbrowns. I needed food to make up for the lack of sleep and the long day I had ahead of me.

Adaline said to me, "I'd forgotten how much you can eat and never gain a pound."

I smiled at her. "Seems to me you could hold your own in a food eating contest."

Once the food came and the coffee refills were poured, I began my dissertation. "You heard some of this yesterday. If I repeat myself, I apologize. A man from New Jersey hired me to go over a fifty-acre farm when he bought it and found out it was on the Old Wire Road and the Trail of Tears ran through the middle of it."

George, a good-looking young man, tall with green eyes and an inviting smile interrupted. "I'm excited about the dig, but a little worried about the amount of killing going on."

"No one will bother you. I'm 99.9 % sure of it. I think it's all related. Their goal, in my opinion, was to scare me off. There's something on that farm they don't want me to find. I believe with all of us and the equipment we can find what they're hiding. There's no reason for trying to run us off. Right now, it is the biggest story in the news, and I heard it came up on national news as well due to speculation we might find the Izzard girl's ring because we are on her farm. "

Adaline looked me up and down. "You're a little dressed up for a dig, aren't you? And please, call me Addy."

"Sure, I'm going to drop by Professor Thompson's memorial service. I shouldn't be long. Meanwhile, we have an entire fifty acres to dig. I suggest you start at my original site where I found the fingers.

"I don't think I've had time to tell you. The man who hired me, Barclay Simmons, has apparently been missing for three days now. He's a tycoon and has his hand in several high profile enterprises.

"Agent Blake, you met him yesterday, flew to New Jersey to follow up on the investigation. He is the lead on this case and Simmons' disappearance became a part of it when he went missing.

"I shouldn't be long at the service. But I want to hang around and go to the dinner so I can see who's there. Lots of people go to the dinner who don't go to the funeral. "

"Before you go," Addy said, "I know the name Barclay Simmons. I'm not sure why, but I'll have time to think about it. Maybe I'll remember before you get back."

On our way to the funeral home, I asked Indy what he thought about Dr. Maguire knowing the name Barclay Simmons. He barked once. It wasn't the first time I talked to my dog like he was human. I didn't think it would be the last.

The funeral home sat two blocks to the south of the Dorman Campus. There were few cars in the lot. I parked and told Indy to stay. I knew he would even though the top was off the Jeep.

I was surprised when I walked into the building, nearly every seat was full. Apparently, judging from the age of the crowd, a lot of the attendees were the professor's students and had walked over from the college.

No one sat in the first two pews. Instantly, I realized how horrible it would be to have no one close enough to you to sit in the front rows of your funeral. More tears escaped when I realized I didn't have much family myself.

There was Aunt Sharon from Agusta, Maine, Mom's sister, Aunt Linda from Little Rock, Dad's sister and four cousins. Each time we met we swore we would keep in touch, but lives, distance, kids and jobs kept it from happening. Every year I still receive a letter from Aunt Linda's clan. One of those boring epitaphs of the passing year. But that's it.

My thoughts were interrupted by a priest who went to the lectern and welcomed us all. He began by saying family did not have to mean related by blood. He said he could see from the packed church Jonah was a popular man.

I felt someone slide in beside me, it was Emmy. She squeezed my hand and then gave her full attention to the service.

The clergyman gave a resounding eulogy touting all of Jonah's accomplishments. He must have known the professor well because his recitation was filled with anecdotes only a friend would know. At times laughter rang through the crowd.

He dismissed us about a half hour later with an announcement of the lunch. He also added, Professor Jonah Thompson's ashes would be spread over the campus when the time was right.

# Chapter 36

Emmy walked beside me down the steps and to my car. She didn't say anything. She looked springy in a light beige suit that set off her natural amber colored hair. It hung to her shoulders. The straightest hair I'd ever seen.

"I didn't expect to see you here," I said. "Where are the kids?"

"Roger is working from home today. It's one of the perks of owning your own business. Actually, one of the only perks."

Roger and Emmy's restaurant was a happening place. They had established a huge clientele, they had hired a manager who was a chef in his own right. They seemed happier since they had hired him. Emmy and I had become fast friends in high school and remained friends all of the years since. I loved seeing her happy.

"Are you going to the luncheon?" I asked.

"No. Roger's in a golf tournament this afternoon. It's put on by the Lion's Club. He needs to go. I wanted to drop by and make sure you were alright. "

"I'm fine. Lots of good memories with the professor and one event I'll never forget. By the way, when all of this is over with the job I have to finish, we need to get together. Do I have a story for you."

She smiled. By this time, we were next to the Jeep. Indy jumped out and insinuated himself between me and Emmy. He wanted her to say hello. They had a five minute love fest and Indy jumped into the front seat again.

Emmy gave me a quick hug and off she went. At least I'd have one seat filled in the family section if I died.

My Fitbit said it was nearly time for the luncheon. Indy and I drove over to the auditorium and were amazed at the number of people milling around.

I thought about running Indy home or letting him lie outside the door of the building.

He made up my mind for me when he jumped into the backseat and snuggled in for a nap. "I won't stay long," I told him.

Imagine my surprise when I ran into a group of girls who were there to see me. A gaggle of fifteen girls decked out in FORD shirts, pants and headbands. I had no choice but to stop and say hi.

They all had pictures and wanted them autographed. I stayed long enough to find out they were a treasure hunting club from Springfield called Trinkets and Treasures. I smiled and told them I needed to go on inside to the memorial lunch. They scurried away.

The place was packed with students. I guessed the entire student body had come. Silently, I hoped it wasn't only for the free food. I'd spent many years at institutions of higher learning and knew for a fact free food was a big draw.

I walked in the front door where a young man took me by the elbow. "Miss Ford, there are special seats for Professor Thompson's friends. I am here to take you to yours."

We were student and teacher, colleagues, partners in some digs, but I didn't think the professor had ever thought of me as a friend. I followed the man down the stairs to the spit shined gym floor to a section where six tables were situated, one at each end and two down each side, making a rectangle.

Four people were already seated. One I knew to be an attorney, and three professors from Dorman. Out of the other people seated there, one was the governor, another the Mayor of Springfield and a national politician I knew from sight, but not by name. Thank goodness they seated at least five women I recognized.

It took another twenty minutes before anyone official climbed the stairs and began to talk. "I want to thank you all for coming. Professor Jonah Thompson taught here at Dorman College for thirty-seven years

"Sometimes he was gone for many months to exotic places and found treasures we wished we had found. Dr. Thompson was a member of Mensa, a Fellow in the National Archaeological Society and dozens more organizations pertaining to his occupation. Dr. Thompson was a private man. We have seated some of the people who knew him best, down here." She pointed to the group of us down and in front of her.

"At this time, if anyone seated down here on the floor would like to share anything with us about the professor, the mic is open to you."

For the next hour, men and women walked to the stage and sang the praises of Thompson. I couldn't really think of anything, especially knowing the entire crowd knew I had found his dead body.

I glanced at the time, two fifteen. I had expected to be back at the dig by two and we had yet to have lunch.

After the last person spoke, the original speaker, who I'd hadn't seen until two hours before came back to the microphone. "Those of you seated at the tables in front of me, there is a buffet set up at the far end of the gym. Feel free to have this wonderful lunch provided for you by the Dorman College Archeology Club and its sponsors.

"Students, thank you for coming to say farewell to our illustrious teacher. You are all dismissed."

Students began to file out in an orderly fashion. The people seated near me, began to rise and walk to the end of the gym. I didn't get out of my chair.

I sat, wondering how I could get out of the gym? All the doors were filled with students making a hasty retreat.

A little light came on in my mind as I remembered a back entrance. With as little disruption as possible, I walked behind the stage, through the girls' locker rooms and out a back door which was, thankfully, not locked.

All I could do was open and close my eyes to try to see in the bright sunshine after the darkness of the auditorium. A crack of a breaking twig behind me caught my attention. I whirled around to see behind me.

A man dressed all in black with a hood over his face stood close to me. More dark cloth obscured any skin I should have been able to see from under the hood. "Dr. Ford, I'm here to warn you to stop digging on the Izzard farm. You've opened a can of worms and alerted people you don't want to upset. This is your last warning."

"Who are you?" I asked.

"Only a messenger," he said as he turned on his heel to leave.

He didn't get two feet before I heard galloping feet behind me. Indy jumped in the air and came down on the man. They wrestled and I thought Indy had the best of him until he was able to reach into his pocket and brought out a short thin knife and began to slice it down toward my dog.

Until then, I had been standing like a zombie. I guessed it was the shock of what happened and how quickly. I strode to the man and kicked him in the side of the head. Indy backed up out of reach of the knife. The man scrambled to his feet and ran around the gym in the direction of the parking lot, Indy close on his heels.

I trailed the dog by at least five feet, not fast enough to keep up with them, when I heard it. Indy let out a cry of anguish. I knew he was hurt. I flew to his side as he lay panting in the grass. I grabbed my phone and dialed 9 1 1, ignoring the man as he disappeared around the gym, in my panic over Indy.

I didn't know what to do. Paramedics were not going to treat my dog. He needed a vet. I couldn't leave him and go for the car. Anything could happen while I retrieved the Jeep. I couldn't believe I'd parked it so far away.

I heard sirens.

Bill Davis came around the building at a dead run. He said nothing, just knelt down beside Indy and stroked his head. Indy whined. The sheriff keyed a radio he wore on his collar and called for help. "I need a vet. I don't care which one. Dr. Ford's dog has been badly hurt. Go to the closest office, Dr. Strang, I think. Pick him up, or better yet, escort him here so he will have his truck and supplies with him. And hurry."

Indy had calmed down some. His back leg had been sliced from the top down to his paw. The bleeding had slowed, but not stopped. He lay with his head down. While Bill called for help, I'd sat down near Indy's head, and he'd raised up enough to lay it on my leg.

I knew how sensitive he was to my moods, so I did my best not to let him see or feel how scared I actually was.

When the deputy came, he drove around the building, down the embankment and parked on the grass near us. Dr. Strang did the same thing. He jumped out of his truck before it stopped. He looked Indy over and then ran back to his truck, opened the back and came back with a duffle bag full of medicines and bandages.

"Lexi, I need to sedate the dog to stop the bleeding. Please help him to look away."

Indy didn't move. The doctor administered the shot and my dog closed his eyes.

Stang looked at me. "I don't think there is any irreversible damage here. The cut is mostly superficial. What I mean is I don't believe any tendons or muscles are beyond repair. I need to clean the wound, stitch it and immobilize it until the stitches can be removed. That might be as much as ten days from now."

I said nothing. I did my best to keep my tears from flowing.

"While doc is doing his job, tell me exactly what happened," the chief said.

"I went to the professor's funeral. The event here ran long," I said trying to focus on the chief's request. "I was expected at the dig around two. When people began to line up for the buffet, I slipped out the back door to escape the crowds and so I could head for the site. I heard someone behind me. This man got right in my face and told me this was my last warning that I was to stop digging at the farm."

I took a deep breath before continuing, "Indy came around the corner and jumped on the man knocking him down. They fought and somehow the man came up with a knife. I kicked him and then he ran, and Indy chased him. I lost sight of them for a minute. He must have cut Indy and took off running."

"What did he look like?"

"Hard to tell, he was taller than I am because I had to look up at him. He wore black clothing and a black ski mask with a hood pulled down low over it. When I realized Indy was hurt, I stopped chasing him. He must have used that time to run around the gym, the same direction you came from."

"Did he have an accent? Did you notice any scars or tattoos? Fat or skinny? Voice high or low?" Bill calmly asked. His voice helped keep me focused.

"I didn't detect an accent. He was too covered up to see if he had any marks on him. His voice was low. Sorry, that's all I have." I turned my attention back to my dog.

The vet had cleaned the wound, put twenty-six stitches in it and had put an ace bandage over a gauze wrap underneath.

"Keep him quiet," Dr. Strang directed. "No running for the next couple of days. No stairs until the stitches are out. Call the office and make an appointment. I need to take a look at it in a couple of days to make sure nothing bad is happening under there." He pointed to Indy's leg. "Where's your car?"

"In the back lot."

"He can't walk that far. As a matter of fact, don't let him exercise except to go out to do his business."

Deputy Anton, who had stood quietly while the doc fixed the dog, offered to get the Jeep for me. I gave him the keys.

"I need to get back to the office," Dr. Strang said.

"Thank you for coming so quickly."

He nodded his head at me and walked over to his truck. He used the concrete apron near the door to make a three point turn around and left.

The deputy came back with the Jeep and he and Bill gently put Indy in the back.

"I need to go to the dig site. Think it is okay for Indy to go?"

"Truthfully, I would take him home. Deputy Anton will go with you and carry him into the house. I'll go to Seymour and tell your crew what happened.

"Dr. Maquire and her students said they are spending the rest of their time here at your house. I'm relieved. I talked to Wade today. He called me to check on you because he said you didn't answer your phone. He is also thrilled you'll have house guests."

"There will be people around and now you'll have three strong young men to help with Indy."

I didn't have anything more to say. I took my dog and drove home. Once he was inside and in his bed in the kitchen, I laid on the floor next to him.

# CHAPTER 37

I must have fallen asleep, because the next thing I knew, my text alert chimed and I jerked awake. I looked over at Indy. I put my hand on his side and followed his even breaths, up and down, up and down before looking at the text. The text was from Addy. *Heard what a horrible day you had. Hope the dog is better. The guys and I are on the way over. I assume you still live at 330 Rosedale Court? We will bring supper. See you in a few. Addy.*

The clothes I wore to the funeral were wrinkled and full of blood from Indy's cut. I tried to get up without moving his leg and went upstairs. The bloody top, I threw down the stairs. I would soak it in the washer later. The skirt, I tossed in the dirty clothes hamper in the hall.

After I looked around at my things, I decided to go with the most comfortable clothes I could find. I put on a long sleeve tee with Queen on it and a pair of sweatpants with no elastic around the ankles. The Queen shirt had been red but now, was a cross between pink and nearly white. The sweatpants were gray.

I'd worn my hair down to the events earlier in the day. Now I brushed it and pulled it back into a low ponytail. I put on white crew socks and no shoes.

Before I made it back downstairs, the text notification on my phone went off again. This time it was Blake Wade. *Bill let me know about the events of the day. Glad Indy will be okay. Happy the folks from the university are bunking there. I should be back tomorrow. The local cops in Oklahoma City found a body. They believe it's Barclay Simmons. A camera on the Will Roger's Turnpike flashed a picture of him early yesterday morning. There were three others in the car. None of the others have been identified. Simmons was identified using a tattoo of a red ribbon on his forearm. Most of the body was beyond recognition. Waiting for dental records. It was found in Little Rock*

The next text read, *Will tell you the rest when I see you. Try to stay out of trouble. Blake*

It blew my theory out of the water. I thought for sure the entire mystery revolved around Simmons. He could not have threatened me today if he was dead yesterday.

The doorbell rang and I went downstairs. For the first time since it all started, I was leery to open the door. I went into the living room and pulled back the curtain enough to see the car in the driveway was a rental and there were at least four people on the stoop.

I walked over to the door and for the one hundredth time in the last two weeks, I wished I had a peep hole. "Who's there?"

"Dinner," Addy said in a happy voice. "I hope you are hungry."

I opened the door, and they flooded in. Addy and Terrill had bags of food. George and John had the luggage and odds and ends.

Indy woke up and I could hear his tail hitting the floor as he wagged it in greeting. When I got to him, he hadn't tried to sit up but still enthusiastically wagged his greeting. With Blake's warnings ringing in my ears, I went back to the door and locked it before I guided the group to the kitchen.

They all went over to Indy one at a time, they talked to him and told him how sorry they were. His tail never stopped.

"I can only tell you to set your stuff over by the stairs because I haven't had a chance to figure out the sleeping arrangements yet," I said apologetically.

George smiled and patted John on the back. "We are used to sleeping where ever we can. Even the floor is good. We'll go with the easiest for you. Although we think our mentor most likely requires a bed."

"Let's eat first," I said. "I haven't eaten since breakfast with you guys and it seems like three days ago."

I didn't have to guess what was for dinner. A large bucket of Kentucky Fried Chicken, lots of mashed potatoes and gravy, coleslaw and rolls along with a gallon of ice cream they must have stopped at the store for along with several toppings.

Within a moment or two, Indy stood next to me in the kitchen, leaning against my leg. He walked over to the doggy door and whined. He knew he couldn't get through it without it hurting. All three guys jumped up to help. I opened the backdoor and John helped him down the steps.

I stayed outside with him while he did his business. Poor guy.

We all ate like it was our last meal. Indy ate bits of chicken and licked up some mashed potatoes and gravy. I would feed him his regular dinner later. Tonight, he deserved a special treat.

They had also brought a twelve pack of beer and a bottle of a local Missouri peach wine. It was only available in the years when a good peach crop had come in, which wasn't often.

After dinner, we went to the living room where the TV was and settled down. The guys each had a beer. Addy and I each drank a glass of peach wine.

"Here's my idea. I need to stay down here with Indy. Addy, you can have my room. Two of you," I pointed to the men, "can have the two other bedrooms upstairs. There is another bathroom at the end of the hall.

"One of you can stay in the extra room off the laundry room. There are two small bedrooms down here. Indy and I will take the one closest to the back door and one of you can have the other. They share a Jack and Jill bathroom, so be sure to lock and then unlock the other door in case the other person needs it. Is that okay with everyone?"

"Sure," Addy said, "but they all don't mind sleeping on the floor if it's easier."

"No problem at all. I don't mean to be a drag, but it has been a long day for me and Indy. I think we'd like to go to our room soon. But first, what did you find today?"

"I'll give you a hint," Addy said. "We've renamed the Izzard farm the *killing fields*. We haven't taken the time to put the bones together into bodies, but we do have five skulls and seven pelvic bones."

"Any more personal items?" I asked.

"Several, plus a few Civil War buttons, a cap and ball pistol and two cannon balls."

"Wow."

"Yes," John said. "The power of machines. We were able to go deeper and wider than you could by hand. The worst thing was people tried to sneak in and see what we were doing."

Addy took up the thread of the recap of the day's events. "Tomorrow the National Guard will be here. Oh, yes, and the national news media. When they couldn't find you today, they called the university who gave them my name. I think it will be a circus if we aren't careful. The more people we can keep away from the dig site the better."

"Amen," I said.

# CHAPTER 38

I went upstairs, packed some clothes for the next day, my toiletries, my laptop, phone charger and other items I might need to get through tonight and next day. I also retrieved the book and the packet I'd taken from Professor Thompson's home and headed back down.

"Will it bother you if we watch a movie?" George asked as he picked up the TV remote.

"Heaven's no. Listen, guys, feel free to eat anything, drink anything and use what you need to make your stay here pleasant. There isn't much food in the house but there is popcorn in the cabinet near the sink on the left and the popper is next to it.

"I'm a little paranoid right now, so please do me a favor and don't go outside anymore tonight. I know the doors are locked and I'll sleep better knowing they'll stay that way."

They all mumbled their agreement and put their attention on an old Tom Cruise movie .Addy had already gone up to my room by the time I went up to pack my things. Normally I would have stayed, had another glass of wine and visited with her. However, the events of the day had worn me out. I didn't want to leave Indy downstairs without me either. After all, he got hurt while he tried to save my life.

Once I was ready for bed, I propped the pillows behind my head and pulled out the hollow book I brought from the professor's house. I found it absolutely fascinating. He had every article I believe ever written about the disappearance of Judith Izzard as well as dozens and dozens of photos of Judith, the farm land, the old farm house and hand drawn maps of the route she must have taken from the farm to the dance at Madison Hall, inside the Bailey House.

The handwritten notes on the map even had times and distances as to how long it would have taken to go from one place to the other.

Next came notes about Morgan Thompson. Born June of 1904 and died June of 1929.

I heard Indy whine when he jumped up onto the bed. "Indy, you aren't supposed to jump or run or do anything to open your wound," I told him sternly He came up and laid his head on my chest and I melted. "Okay, you can stay, but don't get off the bed without my help. Got it?"

He yipped once, got comfortable at the end of the bed and within a minute or two he was snoring softly and breathing evenly. I had to smile. I'd never heard him snore, but I was sure the pain medicine caused it.

Once he settled, I laid the book aside and opened Ancestry.com to finish the search I'd started previously. I looked up Morgan Thompson. This explained why Thompson's interest in Judith's case was so intense. Morgan was his uncle, the son of Senator Michael Thompson, the first, and the brother of the second Senator Michael Thompson, who had fathered both Jonah and Jonah's brother Mark.

I closed and set aside the laptop and the book and opened the packet. It contained the birth and death certificates of each person mentioned on Ancestry.com and also another man who would be in his thirties. Had he been trying to clear his family name all these years?

There was a racket, the noise was so different, it made me jump. It was the ring. I'd laid it on the night table near the bed. I can only explain it as, the ring buzzed and moved around the table as if it were a cell phone with a super vibration setting.

I picked it up. It was like I had briefly touched a hot pan. As soon as my brain registered the sensation, the ring calmed down and lay still on the table. I quickly tapped my finger on it and found it had cooled down. I was still looking at the ring when

Judith made her ghostly appearance, as if she hovered over the bed.

She didn't speak to me. Her brilliant eyes locked onto my face. *I thought you were going to help me.*

Her lips didn't move, but I knew exactly what she said. I felt tethered to her. Judith's voice went on, *I need to get out of the limbo I'm in. Maybe it is a purgatory, maybe my soul was troubled, but I want to go on now, where ever that may be.*

*It is a constant worry and uneasiness in my mind. I need to move on. Why aren't you helping me?*

"I am helping," I answered aloud earnestly. "I know who murdered you, and I know why. Isn't that a start?"

*You don't understand. You need to find me and set me free. Morgan and I are trapped together. He haunts me day and night. He says his death is my fault, I must go. Speaking to you like this from the beyond wares me out. Find me. I don't know how much longer I can do this; yet, I see no other eternity for me.*

This time, she faded. Both of her arms were straight out toward me as if beckoning me to free her from whatever realm she was held in.

How could any of this be real? I couldn't tell anyone about it, they would put me away. I sat up, suddenly. My lack of sleep slipped away, driven by a desire to help Judith, and I went back through the information I had. My only clues so far were that Morgan Thompson had killed Judith Izzard. She'd been gone for nearly a hundred years, and she told me before she was underground. It made me think she couldn't tell me where either because she herself didn't know or something was preventing her. The last time I had seen the room or basement she had most likely died in, it looked like a cellar, possibly under a house.

Once I calmed down, I went back to the professor's papers.

There were blanks. The professor mentioned a man named Neal and his son Neal Junior. There wasn't any other information about them. There was a birthdate and date of death for every one of his relatives, except Neal and Neal Jr.

I must have gone back to sleep because I had the strangest dream. I could see Judith Izzard in her long emerald dress with its sequined bodice and empire waist. She was a small-boned girl with dark red, wavy hair which hung loose around her face and down her back, almost brushing her waist.

The dress brought out the color in her eyes. She sat in a carriage behind a man on a high bench seat as he drove her to her destination. She held her hand near her face and admired the ring on the fourth finger of her right hand.

A horrible sad and foreboding feeling overwhelmed me. I sat up, breaking the hold the dream had on me, and looked around the room. Beginnings of morning light peeked through the windowpane. I had to blink several times to try to clear my head. I would have bet my last dollar I had just witnessed Judith Izzard's last ride on the way to the dance.

Yet it couldn't be. Was lack of sleep making me hallucinate? Everything that had been happening could definitely impact my dreams, but what about Judith's ghost?

I got up, took a shower and put on a pink pair of Rosie overall shorts over a short sleeved white tee. My hair was still wet so I brushed it back and twisted it around my hand and clipped it in place with a long silver barrette. I was more relaxed now, yet I could not get over the realness of my dream, or the conversation with Judith – real or otherwise.

Nothing like it had ever happened before. I remember for months after Mom died, I would look up at a store or the library or even along the street and think I had seen her. It happened to me again when Father died.

This situation resembled those happenings in no way. When I saw visions of Judith, I could feel the breeze, see the color of the horse and see the color of Judith's eyes. I thought about when she talked to me through the ring and I realized I could smell dirt. Dirt isn't the right word. I could smell an earthy, damp smell.

I looked up and said to the air, "I will find you; you have my word."

My attention was suddenly focused on Indy. Before I could help him, he lithely jumped from the bed and limped toward the back door at a fast clip. He didn't even try to use the doggie door but waited for me to catch up. I opened the back door for him. The air was cool and the humidity low. I decided the back porch would be the perfect place to have breakfast.

I didn't cook much although I could cook when I wanted too. I drained a small can of mushrooms, chopped an onion, sliced a red bell pepper in long strips and set it all aside.

The house began to come alive. George and John came down the stairs. I could tell they were trying to be quiet. Their shushing of each other was louder than their conversation. On my way to the back door to let Indy back inside I met Terrill as he came out of his room, his black, curly hair shining in the sunlight.

"Hey guys, how about you go out and make sure the table on the back porch is clean enough to eat off of. I'll start scrambled eggs, toast and bacon. We can eat out there. The coffee is ready. Mugs are in the cabinet right above the coffee pot. Cream and sugar are on the table."

They all agreed outside would be great. Terrill and John went out to tidy up the table and chairs. George made toast and buttered it as it came out of the toaster. Addy came down as we were taking the last of the food outside.

"Looks like I overslept," she said.

"Hi, not really. I got up early. Indy needed to go outside. The morning is so nice, I thought we'd have breakfast alfresco."

"Great idea. Can I do anything?"

"No, go on out. I'm going to melt cheese in these eggs and bring them out. Grab a mug of coffee on your way."

No one said much else as they sat and gobbled down the breakfast I made.

After we ate and everyone had a fresh cup of coffee in front of them, we began to talk about the dig. "How long has the farm been empty?" Addy asked.

"I'm not sure," I said. "At least for the last twenty or more years. After almost all of the Izzard family had died off, no one wanted to farm it and the old lady didn't want to sell the house. Finally, they separated the house and the fifty acres we are working on from the other four or five hundred acres which went to a cattle and land management company."

Terrill asked, "Do you think there is a serial killer around? That's a lot of bodies to be from just the Indian Relocation."

John added, "We'll know soon enough. A courier took some of the bones to the university yesterday. We'll be able to tell a lot more once the lab has a look at them. Who knows, it might just have been a convenient place to dump bodies over the years."

I'm not sure that made any of us feel any better.

# CHAPTER 39

Addy was dressed in white cotton coveralls with long sleeves. She wore brown ankle high Nike boots. Her blond hair hung down her back. As the heat of the day built, I bet she'd eventually put it up. I'd known her for years, great gal.

We worked until lunch. Small groups of bones were sifted up with the dirt. Scattered among the remains were feathers, beads, and hammered silver trinkets and jewelry. We began to think it was a boneyard rather than a killing field.

Seymour is a quaint little town. There are two separate Amish settlements. As the crow flies, they are only about five miles apart but remain totally independent of one another. Like most of the towns in the area, every store, café and specialty shop wanted to be on the square.

As the area grew, the restaurants and fast-food joints began to spill out onto the highway. Nine out of ten towns in the Ozarks had their Sheriff's Department and City Hall on a square. In Seymour, there were hitching posts for the Amish to hobble or tie their horses and buggies. Since the three grad students and Addy had been in town, they hadn't seen anything of the actual town itself. I took them to a small restaurant on the square where one could order breakfast, lunch or dinner for our midday break.

One reason we wanted to go to town was because we ran out of water in our hand washing station and none of us wanted to wash our hands with a wet wipe one more time. It didn't take long for a film of dust and dirt to cake our hands and make them itch.

Once we were seated and the waitress came by with menus, we took turns using the bathroom. Addy went first, I waited outside the door. When it was my turn, I used my time to pee and wash my hands and face. When I leaned over the sink, I could feel the red velvet pouch in my pocket. I removed the bag and stepped back and away from the sink before I took the ring out. I didn't want to take a chance of dropping it down the drain.

The ring fascinated me.

The style reflected the ring's age. No one bought dinner rings anymore. I held it up to the light. As I did, I glanced in the mirror to see Judith Izzard's face staring back at me. She smiled a sad smile.

*You are my last hope.* She gave a half smile again and faded away. I took it as a reminder of what she told me in the middle of the night.

Someone knocked on the door. They did it loudly as if I should have known whoever it was.

When I opened the door, a large, short, not too clean lady with a moo-moo dress of bright green, swished past me. She almost caused me to lose my balance.

"Nothing like camping out in a public restroom like you are the only one in the entire town," she said before slamming and locking the bathroom door before I could say I was sorry. My hand still held the ring. The heat from it now radiating up my arm. It was almost unbearable to touch.

I slipped the ring into a pocket in my overalls and walked back to the table. The waitress came over immediately. Everyone else had ordered. In spite of the air conditioning, I could feel a drop of sweat as it ran down my forehead. Maybe I really was going crazy, because in my mind, I knew what I kept seeing had to be real. I'd been sleep deprived before and this had never happened.

All I had seen were pictures of Judith, yet, I knew the spirit I kept seeing was her even though photos from the 1920s were less than optimal.

John reached over and touched my arm. "Are you okay? You look flushed."

"I'm fine," I answered. "I think I got upset when I locked myself in the bathroom and couldn't get out."

Addy gave me a strange look but said nothing. She knew the lock only a hook and eye and wasn't capable of holding me hostage.

"Miss, did you want to order?" the waitress asked again impatiently enough that I realized I must have missed her first question.

"Sure, I'll take a patty melt well done, fries, a glass of ice water and a diet Pepsi."

She took the menu from me and went back to the kitchen.

We talked about the dig while waiting for our food. The general consensus was that a past event caused the death of many people. Due to all of the Native American items we found today, some of the bones had to be Native American. They might all be. Thousands of people were lost during the removal. Nobody wanted to take the time to see if they could find any history on it with our phones. We decided we would look it up on a computer to dig more into it when we got back to the house.

The ring in my pocket was cooler yet still felt uncomfortable against my leg. I heard a loud noise. When I looked at the others, I could tell they hadn't heard it. I followed the noise with my eyes. There stood Judith with a man I recognized as Morgan Thompson. He had one hand on each of her shoulders and appeared to shake her. It was as if that side of the restaurant had faded away leaving this scene from the past to play out before my eyes.

I could see they stood in semi-darkness. To the left I saw stairs. Judith and Morgan appeared to go up, meaning the two of them had been in the downstairs of somewhere. There were shelves with jars of canned food and hams hung on a rafter. Morgan shook Judith again. When he let go, she fell onto what appeared to be a dirt floor. He turned toward the stairs. Judith lay still on the floor.

I had seen this before, but now it was much more detailed.

"Lexi." Addy's voice cut in mirroring John's earlier worried tone, "Are you okay?"

Momentarily I was stunned. The vision faded away leaving me blinking to clear away the last remnants of that underground room. Where was I? What was I doing? I looked Addy straight in the eye and said nothing, knowing I should say something, anything, to end these visions. I looked down. My food sat in front of me. The others were eating. I put my hand on top of it; it was still hot. The food hadn't been on the table for long.

"I'm sorry," I said, thinking quickly. "I thought I heard Indy. Leaving him in the car with his leg the way it is, worries me."

George laughed. "I don't think he's still in the car. He looks pretty comfy laying near the door."

I looked over to the restaurant's entrance to see Indy laying calmly, sleeping to the left of it. I smiled at George and then at the dog. When I was alone, I would go over the strange series of events unfolding in my mind, scene by scene.

My phone rang. I checked the caller ID before I answered it: Blake Wade. "Hi," he said in a cheerful voice. "I'm at the airport. Should be back by tonight. Mind if I drop by? I have lots to tell you."

"It would be okay. If you get in after nine, why don't you come to the dig tomorrow. Adaline and her team are staying with me. We're all pretty wiped out after a day in the sun."

He said nothing until I said, "Blake, are you there?"

The cheer had gone out of his voice. "I forgot about them. Okay, I'll see you tomorrow."

He hung up. It gave me a strange feeling, as if we were a couple or something and I had just put him off.

I shrugged my shoulders. Oh, well. We weren't a couple, and I didn't owe him anything. I went back to my lunch and the conversation.

"I've been thinking," I said. "We should move up to the house. Looks like no one's been there for years. The windows aren't broken, and the doors are shut so we shouldn't run into any big wildlife. Maybe a few rats, mice, spiders, and snakes."

"Why the change?" Terrill asked.

I couldn't tell them I had visions of Judith Izzard and I thought the ring in my pocket was trying to give me the answer to everything. And I thought, maybe Judith hadn't left on her own. Maybe she still remained on the land.

"I've been thinking. We're all assuming the family is innocent and played no part in Judith Izzard's disappearance. What if they were'? What if this ties into Professor Thompson's death? I went into his house the night after his funeral. There were two items I took.

"One is a packet of birth and death certificates and some tin types of the era. I'm not sure we are looking in the right place."

Addy said, "It depends on whether you want to look for artifacts of historical significance or want to find a murderer."

"Can't we do both?" John asked.

There was a lull in the conversation. The waitress came to clear the dishes, refill drinks and suggest dessert.

"We make all of our pies fresh daily. Can I interest you folks in a piece?" She didn't wait for an answer. "We have pumpkin, cherry, blackberry cobbler, peach cobbler, chocolate and lemon today. We also have vanilla cheesecake with or without strawberries and a three-layer fudge cake with real homemade fudge icing."

They all ordered pie or cobbler. I chose the cake. Today required chocolate.

"If we are going to hunt near the house, let's use the thermo-imager. I doubt we would find heat signatures, but the settings also change if there is something else, such as a large bulk of matter in the same place, under the ground. I don't really want to fall into a cistern, an old well or an underground food storage space without any inkling it's there."

George added, "I brought a handheld sonar gun and we have some powerful metal detectors in our equipment."

"Okay, here is my idea," I said, "we use the afternoon to pick up all of the bones, fragments of bones and other goodies we've found so far, put them in the panel truck and start this tomorrow. I would like to have time for all of you to see the information I have at home.

"I'll give you a little teaser. What I have compiled identifies a relative of Professor Thompson's as a man who was hanged back in 1929 for the murder of Judith Izzard. And I don't think anyone has ever proven there was a murder."

I didn't add, *If you believe in the supernatural and the power of one's soul, then I know who killed Judith.* But I sure thought it.

# CHAPTER 40

No one wanted supper later that night when we finished wrapping up the dig site so we could head back to my house. We'd already eaten ten thousand calories at lunch. We put the last of the artifacts into the van and locked it around four o'clock. Addy drove it down to the guard station the sheriff had set up at the bottom of the hill. The sheriff's men ran it like a well-oiled machine. Men came and went according to a schedule.

There had been no trouble at night since the light source had arrived and been set up. We were ready to leave when Terrill said, "Why don't you two," gesturing to Addy and me, "go on to the house. We'd like to stop by the store, get some beer and snacks. We know we'll want something later."

"Sure, "Addy said, and tossed the keys to him. "We'll see you at the house. You might pick up a pizza at Papa Murphy's. They're great and we can bake it later when we finally get hungry again."

George said, "This shouldn't take long. We saw an Amish grocery store in town and there's a Papa Murphy's on the way.'

"Later," John said as they prepared to drive away.

Addy and I made a make-shift work area out of the kitchen table when we got back home. Seated across from one another, we set up our laptops, paper and everything else we might need to begin digging into the pile of papers. We discussed it and decided the guys could work wherever they wanted when they returned.

I opened the fake book and sat it between us. First item, *Morgan Thompson, son of Senator Michael Thompson was born 1904 and hanged in 1929 for the murder of Judith Izzard of Seymour, Missouri. As no body or motive was ever discovered, why the boy, aged 25, was a suspect remains unknown at this time.*

I told Addy, "The handwriting is Professor Jonah Thompson's. I recognize it from all of the notes he made on my papers. He always broke his cursive letters in a word." I pointed to the word *suspect* where the *sus-* was separate from the *-pect,* but close enough to know it is the same word.

Addy looked where I pointed and nodded. "It is unusual, but his penmanship is neat and easy to read. If we read anything written by another person, we should put it aside and try to identify who wrote it."

"Agreed," I said.

Indy began to bark at the front door. I looked out the window to see Addy's three grad students. Each carried a brown grocery bag. As I approached the door, Indy moved away and began to wag his tail.

They came in and walked on through to the kitchen, placing the bags, not too gently, on the counter. John looked around. "Looks like the two of you have made a dent in our research already."

"Not really," Addy said. "We're only spread out to appear productive. When you fellas are ready to work, let me know. I have a couple of things I'd like you to look up for us."

"Sure."

"Absolutely."

And "Right away," were the answers.

"Terrill, I'd like for you to research the ring. Why would a man in the tiny town of Seymour, Missouri think to buy his wife a ring once belonging to a queen? How would he even know about such a ring?"

"I've seen many pictures of it and seems to me you could buy one made recently in the US for a third of the money, even all those years ago. I wish I could see it and touch it. I'd like to know what's so exciting about it that someone would seek it out?"

The ring was warm as it pressed against my leg through my pocket. The thought occurred to me to take it out and let them all see what I had. In a voice much lower and quieter than I usually used I said, "Could it have secret powers and revealed things to the owner others couldn't see?"

They all chuckled. They thought I was joking. I knew it was true, the ring did indeed have power, and it was a little scary.

By the time we read through all of the notes and read all of the articles, most from the archives of newspapers of the time it all happened, we had a lineage.

Working backwards, Professor Jonah Thomson's father was the second Senator Michael Thompson. Michael was the son of the first Senator Michael Thompson. Senior had had two sons, Morgan and Michael, who they called Mike to keep the two Michaels straight. Of course there were other men mentioned in the family tree. Michael, the second, had three sons, Albert, James, Jonah. There were as many as twenty years between them and none of them had the same mother.

To make a long story short, Morgan was Jonah's uncle.

"Lexi," George said, "sorry I made fun of you when you asked if the ring could have superpowers. The ring has lots of folklore attached to it. Seems as if everyone who owned it came to some sort of calamity. The ring is from the 1600s. When the stories became more strange, someone put the Fortner mark on it to try to help it shake the stigma created by the rumors. George read from his computer screen where he had been researching the ring.

*The ring came to America in 1858 in the pocket of a well-known thief by the name of Sir Phillipe Raynaud. According to the lore, Raynaud had an appointment to sell the ring at Sotheby's. Samuel Baker, who started the auction house in London, had stations in some major cities by 1805.*

*Raynaud sold the ring at auction for $8000 but was later robbed and killed as he left the auction house with his ill-gotten earnings. This further enhanced the stories saying the ring had special powers or was possibly cursed. The ring was recovered and eventually, Sotheby's sold the ring to Reginald Brick, a jewelry broker in St. Louis. The next registered owner of the ring was Jacob Izzard, who bought it for his wife as a $25^{th}$ wedding anniversary gift.*

*The ring stayed with the Izzard family until 1929 when Izzard's daughter wore it to a party. The ring and the girl have never been seen again.*

A visible chill ran through me. My mind spun around what I heard. Supernatural powers, the owners or wearers came to a bad end. I wanted two things, for the ring to lead me to the body of Judith Izzard and to guide me as to how to get her out of wherever she is trapped and give her peace. I hoped I could find out all of what I needed to know and get rid of the ring before I succumbed to an unforeseen and hurtful end.

Addy reached over and put her hand on my shoulder. "Are you okay?"

"Yes, I don't know what brought that on. I don't and never have believed in inanimate objects having mystic powers." I also hoped a small, white lie wouldn't lead me to a sudden and gruesome end.

# Chapter 41

"Why do you think someone killed the professor?" Addy asked.

"I don't know. Agent Wade said Professor Thompson was helping the FBI track down and return items taken during World War I and II and return them to their rightful owners. They believe he was murdered because someone connected to Barclay Simmons found out about the rare artifacts and came to steal them.

"There are a couple of things wrong with that scenario so far as I can see. They didn't take anything. They definitely wanted the professor dead, because they shot him twice, execution style.

And no one still knows who the killer or killers are. "I have no doubt, one day the ring will show up."

"Interesting," George said. "Maybe we'll find it while we're here."

I said nothing more. It was the best I could do without telling them I had palmed the ring the first chance I had gotten and put it in my pocket.

We next talked about the farm itself. Everyone agreed the Indian artifacts we kept finding were important but would not help us in solving the two murders as well as the murder of the man impersonating a policeman found hanged in his apartment. And at this point, solving the murders had become our priority.

I had an arial view of the farm Barcley Simmons had originally sent me when he hired me to search it. It showed a farmhouse, two barns, a chicken coup, a small green house, and had two x's marking structures no longer there.

We were in the middle of trying to decide where we would start when the doorbell rang. Indy ran to the front door and growled. I looked out. Standing outside the front door with a couple of pizza boxes was Agent Blake Wade.

Before I opened the door, I said, "Let's table this discussion for tonight."

Addy gathered the papers we'd been looking at and the boys turned off their computers and turned on the TV. It was eleven o'clock.

"Hi, I drove by and saw your light on. Thought I'd stop," Blake said.

"With two pizzas," I said incredulously.

"Sure, I know young men are always hungry."

"But it's late. I thought we said not after nine."

He gave me a look I didn't quite understand and stepped around me. "Anyone hungry?"

After a long moment's pause, they all muttered yes in a different way, and everyone walked into the kitchen. I swept up my computer and Addy did the same with hers, clearing the table for the pizzas.

"I'm not hungry. If you don't mind, I'm going to go upstairs and take a shower, get my things for tomorrow and I'll be back down. I only grabbed enough stuff for one day and night yesterday."

"Sure, "Addy said, "go ahead."

"Indy, you stay down here. I'll be right back."

Blake leaned down to pat Indy's head, but my dog moved out of his way. I doubted anyone noticed but me. The dog always picked up on my moods and echoed them as his own. He clearly had been warming to Agent Wade earlier, but not so much now.

Back upstairs, I carefully took the ring out of my pocket, opened the pouch and peered in at it. I didn't take it out of the pouch. I was rattled enough with the history of the ring and stymied by the unbelievability of all that had happened.

With a deft eye, I looked around my familiar room for a place to put the pouch while I showered. I decided it would be best to keep it with me. I opened the linen closet door and took out a clean towel and wash cloth. I picked up the basket I kept my makeup in and put the pouch under it, then thought better of it. I picked up all of the towels on the bottom shelf and put the pouch under them.

For one thing, I would be in the bathroom. If anyone came in, they would have to pass Blake Wade, the grad students and Addy. It would be safe under the towels. I took the hottest shower I could stand, washed my hair. and stayed in long enough to put a conditioning aid on my hair that took four minutes.

I exited the shower rejuvenated.

After I folded my dirty clothes and put on a pair of long shorts and a big tee shirt, I gathered what I'd need for the dig tomorrow and went downstairs. They'd eaten all the pizza and were sitting around talking about sports, mostly about who liked football and who preferred baseball.

Addy sat on the couch with an *Architectural Digest* and a glass of wine.

The clock in the hall struck midnight.

"We'd better think about getting some sleep, "Addy said. "We have a lot to do tomorrow."

"Let me take you all to breakfast in the morning," Blake said.

"Nah," Terrill answered. "We found out the McDonald's here serves biscuits and gravy. We are going to stop there. But thanks anyway."

"I'm heading upstairs," Addy said as she turned and took hold of the banister.

The rest stayed with me until Blake left. "Guess I'll see you at the dig tomorrow," Blake said as he walked to the door. Then he looked to me. "I have a lot to tell you about what I found out on my trip. I'll catch you up tomorrow."

Indy came up and stood between us.

"Well, I'd better go," he said after a slightly awkward pause before he walked out the door.

The ring warmed against my leg. I turned the deadbolt on the door and turned around to lean against it. I wished I could put my finger on why he made me nervous. Maybe it was because the stories he told me had contradicted each other and he had admitted he'd made some of it up to catch me in a lie.

"I'm going to take Indy out back," I said to Terrill, the only one downstairs with me by then.

"I'd feel better if I went with you. Hope you don't mind the company."

"Of course not. With all that's gone on since I took this job, I'd be glad to have you out there with me."

# CHAPTER 42

Everyone seemed subdued the next morning. They were going to McDonald's for breakfast, and I needed to take Indy to the vet for his check-up.

We had gone over the plan for the day the night before. Addy's team would go to the site and grid off the area going 500 yards in all directions from the main house. Since an acre is 4840 squares yards, we knew our area would be too small to encompass everything, but it was a start. I'd meet them there after Indy's vet visit.

Dr. Bruce Wagner, Indy's regular vet, said the wound looked good. He gave Indy a shot to calm him down so he wouldn't jerk and hurt himself as the doctor pulled the bandage off to check the healing progress.

"Alexa, I can't guarantee hair will grow back along the line of the injury. Put triple antibiotic ointment on it several times a day to keep it moist and we'll hope for the best. Indy may have himself a battle scar."

"Did they ever figure out who attacked you?" Dr. Wagner asked as he continued to look over Indy's injury.

"No," they didn't." Not wanting to offer an explanation, I said, "There are lots of crazies out there. I'm glad Indy sensed something amiss and ran down to where I was. If not, there might've been a completely different outcome."

"I believe the leg will be fine and it appears to be healing nicely. The cut didn't go deep enough to cut muscle or tendon. He is one lucky pup."

Indy barked in agreement and wiggled impatiently.

"Come back in about a week and we will take those stitches out. I guess the shot has worn off. You two be careful out there."

Indy, who hadn't acted as if he were hurt in the first place since arriving at the vet's, jumped into the front seat of the Jeep and off we went to Izzard farm.

By the time we arrived on site, the crew had placed a marker every fifty yards along the perimeter of our working space. We decided to begin inside the house and go from there. It was quite the home in its day. A wraparound porch circled the entire house. Inside, a hall ran from the front entrance all the way back to the kitchen. On the left side of the hallway were the entrances to the living room and dining room, on the right was a den followed by a sitting room. At the end of the hall was a kitchen to the left and a maid's quarters to the right.

A spiral staircase ran up from the front foyer to a second-floor landing. Another set of plain stairs went up to a smaller landing on the other end of a wide upstairs hallway. It boasted four bedrooms, two on one side and two on the other.

By 1950, indoor plumbing had become a constant in most homes. Since the Izzard house was built in the early about 1850, I could tell where they had cut into closets and rooms to add the two bathrooms. One on each side of the hall.

Downstairs a bathroom had been built between the living room and dining room. All of the pipes were run on the outside of the walls and painted or wallpapered to blend in.

Everyone had a basement, usually used for food storage and to house the furnace. This house didn't appear to ever have had central heat or air. A fireplace had been installed in every room and of course they had servants to keep the home fires going at all times in chilly and cold weather.

Addy and I said we would take the upstairs. George and John took the downstairs and Terrill, the basement. We hoped to finish the entire inside of the house in one day. Time would tell.

The plan we made said if we found something exciting, we would bang on a pipe and the others would join us. We were going to skip lunch because everyone else had had a large breakfast. I had my yogurt with me and some cheese. I'd dropped by Starbucks and got a chai tea and a scone. Indy had a bone to keep him occupied and would be fine.

Our plans were interrupted when we heard a car drive up right outside our flags and honk. I didn't make any attempt to see who it was. It reminded me of what my parents said when a boy I went out with for the first time drove up in front of the house and honked.

My dad had said, *If he wants to take you out, he can show some respect and come to the door and pick you up.* I had to smile when I thought about the guy. He turned out to be a jerk in many more ways than not coming to the door.

Finally, a door slammed, and someone walked up onto the porch. "Anyone here?"

It was Agent Wade.

"Geez," I said, loud enough Addy must have heard me. She came out of the room she'd been going over.

"You don't like him, do you?" she asked.

"I like him. but there's so much going on. He acts like I'm twelve and need his advice before I make a move. He's annoying is all I think it is."

"I think it is a matter of a bossy male and strong independent woman."

"No, George or John can talk to him. They're downstairs anyway."

She smiled at me and said, "Ouch."

A few minutes later John yelled up to us, "Agent Wade is here. He brought us Subway sandwiches. Come on down."

"See my point," I said. "He doesn't care what we're doing. It doesn't override what he has planned."

She patted me on the shoulder. "Whether or not he's messed up our lunch plans, I need to get out in the fresh air."

I shook my head and followed her downstairs.

# CHAPTER 43

It took two full days to finish the house. We found only a few things worth our time. I found a roll of pennies in the corner of a closet. Addy found a postcard dated June 1, 1919, from New York City. *Having a great time. See you in a week. Sarah,* read the back. Terrill found a pair of shackles in an old coal bin. George and John found a gold ring and a silver hat pin with a pearl end on it.

We were exhausted by the time we left. We ended up being glad the agent had stopped by. None of us wanted to go out to eat and fortunately, we still had pizzas from the night before we hadn't baked courtesy of our friendly FBI agent bringing some over.

Ordinarily, I wouldn't be in the mood for pizza two nights in a row, but I was too tired to care. If I didn't have to cook it, it was fine by me.

We were all disappointed with the items we took out of the farmhouse. The old postcard and the roll of pennies were the best finds of the lot. No one wanted to unwrap them for a closer look tonight. We figured they'd be worth just as much in the morning.

In the morning, we intended to tackle all the land to the west of the main house. George had the thermo-imager and John had the sonar gun. The rest of us intended to use metal detectors to see what we could find.

Once home, the guys decided to bake the pizzas, watch National Treasure for the umpteenth time and go to bed. The guys didn't even want a beer. Each was on his third or fourth bottle of water.

"I'm going to take Indy for a walk. It's a habit we've been inconsistent with while he was supposed to rest. We can't walk as far as we usually do, but is be good for him."

"Want company?" Addy asked, "I've seen that movie at least ten times and a walk in the cool evening air sounds good."

Who could say no to that?

"This is a great place. Was it your parents?" Addy asked as we headed down the front walkway to the sidewalk.

"Yes. I could sell it but it's a great home base and I've lived here all my life. I travel enough that I don't get tired of it."

Indy walked ahead. He had a slight limp but I knew he was happy to be out again.

We walked around the block taking the long way since each lot was at least three acres across from house to house in this direction.

It occurred to me I hadn't been so relaxed since the job came my way. "Did I tell you they think Barclay Simmons is dead? It's why Wade went to New Jersey. The FBI found what they think was his body in Little Rock."

"Is it? His body, I mean?"

"I don't know. Wade always wants to talk to me alone to tell me anything. I find it annoying."

"Maybe he has the hots for you," Addy suggested.

I laughed. "I think I rub him the same way he rubs me. But we've been thrown together until this mystery is over, so we might as well get along."

Indy, who was at least two houses ahead of us came back and ran circles around us, stopping our progress. He growled and yipped.

"Are you tired, boy? Ready to go back?"

The first shot rang out. Indy immediately herded us behind an old tree with a wide trunk. He laid down, nearly flattening himself to the ground. Two more shots sounded. One hit a tree to the left of us. The other hit the tree we were behind.

I turned around so my back was to the tree, pulled out my phone and dialed 9 1 1.

"9 1 1 what is your emergency?"

"Someone is shooting at us. Please send someone. We are at the corner of Elmhurst and Magnolia."

Only seconds passed before I heard sirens. The shooter must have heard them too because a door slammed, an engine started and the bullets stopped.

Addy started to move away from the tree. "No," I said. "Indy is still on his belly. He'd be up if the danger was over." Addy crouched back down again.

Much sooner than I expected, two police cruisers pulled up in front of us. One came from the south and one from the north.

A patrolman got out of each car. They knew me. More importantly, I knew them.

"Are you okay?" said the younger of the two, Officer Clayton.

"Just scared to death," Addy said.

I added, "It's been days since anyone tried to harm me. I thought it was over."

"Whoever it was is long gone." The other officer, named Reed said as he looked around for remnants of bullets.

"I know one hit the tree we were behind and another hit the big hickory over there." I pointed in the direction of the tree.

"Let's get you home. On the way we'll call CSI and have them dig the bullets out. We might ruin them if we try to do it now."

When we got to the house the two officers got out and checked the property's perimeter. Instead of going to the back door we left by, I rang the doorbell. When Terrill answered, Addy and I both thanked the officers and went inside.

"Would one of you go lock the back door and the doggy door?" I didn't say it to anyone in particular. I sat down hard on the couch, as did Addy, with Indy between us.

"What happened," the three asked almost in unison.

"Someone shot at us," I said, "but not like before. I think this time whoever it was intended to hurt us."

Addy reached over and petted Indy. "If it weren't for him, we would surely have been hit."

"So much for a relaxing walk around the neighborhood," Terrill said.

"Should we call the FBI agent?" Addy asked.

"No. Chief Davis will hear about it soon enough and hopefully they'll dig the bullets out of the tree and there will finally be some evidence against whoever it is." I stood. "I'm going to my room. Feel free to stay up and finish your movie. I need to rest."

I heard whispering voices and in five minutes the house became quiet. Everyone must have taken my lead and gone their separate ways.

A thought came to my mind. Bad things were said to happen to those in possession of the ring. I didn't want to believe it to be anything more than folklore. But, could the ring be to blame for getting shot at?

I took the ring out of my pocket and pouch and held it up to the light.

Nothing happened for a long time. Then a faint blurry scene unfolded in front of me. A saw a man lean down and take something out of the pocket of a man who appeared to be dead, lying near a river. The man on the ground had a rope around his neck.

The man who went through the pockets found something he held up to the light.

I could clearly see it was the same ring I now held in my hand.

What could it mean?

Before I changed into shorts and a tee to sleep in, I opened a small notebook I kept in the nightstand and wrote down my vision as I had done the others that came before.

I put the pouch under my pillow and did my best to go to sleep.

# CHAPTER 44

I'm the kind of person who dreams. The thing is, I know I dream but for the life of me, I can never remember them. This night was different.

A dark space became the backdrop of my dream. The man who had shaken Judith earlier now tried to calmly talk to her.

"How unfortunate you were in the wrong place at the wrong time. I can't ruin my life over something that happened in a fit of temper. I need to finish law school in the fall. I want you to know how sorry I am for what I'm about to do." His voice didn't sound sorry at all.

"It is not what I want either," Judith said in a pleading voice. "I promise, I'll never tell anyone I saw the fights."

"I can't take the chance. Give me your hand."

She raised her left hand.

"The other one you stupid cow."

He jerked the ruby ring off her finger so violently, it broke her ring finger and she screamed. With one hand he held the ring and with the other hand slapped her so hard Judith's head snapped to the side.

"There is no reason to put this off," said Morgan Thompson thoughtfully. He slipped the ring in his pocket, put both hands around her tiny neck and squeezed until he finally let go and Judith fell to the floor.

Indy sat straight up in bed bringing me abruptly out of the dream and back into my bedroom. "What's wrong," I asked.

More and more I was certain the legend of the ring's powers was real.

I wanted to stay awake and go over the story I'd seen in my dream, but I couldn't. Before I fell back asleep, I made sure the ring remained in the pouch. The heat of it had subsided. I moved it over to the bedside table. I opened the drawer and put the pouch in the covering it with a copy of the *New Testament* I found there.

I quickly went back to sleep. This time, I didn't remember what I dreamed.

I woke up and looked at the clock. It blinked nine-thirty back at me. I couldn't believe it. I sat up, opened the drawer in the nightstand, moved the *New Testament* and picked up the bag. It was room temperature.

I put on the clothes I had brought down from my room the night before and slipped the ring in my pocket.

The thought I could not get out of my mind was, if the events I had seen in my dream or vision or whatever, were true, how could I prove it?

I wished for a day alone so I could read up on magic and mystic powers and such without making everyone helping me think I was losing my mind.

"There she is," Addy said as I walked out into the kitchen.

"I'm sorry. You guys should have gone on with your day. "

"No, we need to talk to you about that. The dean called this morning. I don't have any classes to teach this semester, but these three have missed a few classes and tests. They need to go back and catch up. Had they known they were going to be able to go to a dig this summer, they wouldn't have signed up for classes.

"If they work their butts off. They could catch up by the end of next week. I have about two days' worth of work I need to be at the college to finish. The bottom line is, we need to leave today so we can sign in before five. We will be back soon; me on Monday and the guys a week from Monday.

"We hate to leave you under these circumstances but have no choice." Addy looked apologetic.

"What can I say? I will miss your help and company and I'm not sure how much I'll get done on my own, but I'll carry on. Truth is, I work alone nearly all of the time."

In case they needed it, I added reassurances, "Do what you have to do. I'll be fine. I'll have the chief move a couple of his men closer to me as guards. He'll be okay with it."

I got ready to go to the dig as they got ready to leave. Terrill handed me the sonar wand. "Do you know how to use this?"

"Sure, it's been a while, but I know."

George held up the imager, "Add this."

"Definitely that," I said.

"Okay, we are leaving it all for you," Addy said. "I'll call you for sure on Sunday night."

I walked them to their car and they all hugged me, which I didn't expect.

They honked and waved as they pulled away.

Well, I got my wish, didn't I?

# Chapter 45

I decided to take my time going to the old farm. I'd enjoyed my time with Adaline and the grad students. But to have my room back for a few days and not have to live with what I remembered to gather every evening to get me through the next day was a great relief. Especially since Indy would no longer have trouble getting up on my bed.

The bedding on all of the beds needed to go into the laundry. Also, I'd put my clothes, including the bloody shirt from Indy's injury, in the laundry room for days and I needed to wash them too.

I bounded down the stairs and reached the front door at the same time someone rang the bell. My spirits sank. The last thing I needed was for someone else to shoot at me or to have Agent Wade visit. I'll say it again. At my age and with my experience, I don't like *someone looking out for me*.

Wade had said he wanted to tell me what happened in New Jersey. Two days had passed, and I hadn't sat down and listened to his story yet. If it wasn't him at the door, I decided I would make it a point to call him later and meet him to hear what he had to say.

I hope it didn't mean I had to stop my search at the farm. If Simmons was dead, my permission to search died with him.

I dropped the bedding in a pile a few feet from the door and walked to the window to have a peek. The bell rang again. A U.S.

Mail truck sat in front of the house and a mailman stood at my door.

"Hi," I said as I opened the door.

He was a man of about fifty, fit and well-groomed with longer brown hair and brown eyes. He didn't have a nametag and held a letter in his hand.

"Are you Alexa Ann Ford?"

"I am."

"I have a letter for you sent Registered Mail with a return receipt requested." He held out a pen and the letter. It had a yellow card stock ticket on the front with a line for my signature and the carrier's initials. I signed it. He tore the card off the front and handed me the letter.

"Have a good day, miss," he said as he turned to walk back to his truck.

The letter addressed to Alexa Ann was odd in itself. I looked at the front and back of the envelope after closing the front door behind me. I held it up to the light. The return address read Edward Jones D. Michaels, Esquire with an address in Springfield.

A tingle ran through me, not a chill. It was more like I had touched a piece of metal after walking across a carpet barefoot. I went into the kitchen, got a bottle of water out of the refrigerator and sat at the kitchen table.

I chose to sit in the chair with the wall behind me so I could see the entire area, including the back door, the hallway and the edge of the front door. *My goodness*, I told myself, *it's only a letter.* I took a knife out of the silverware drawer and used it to slit the envelope across the top. I opened it and read the contents aloud feeling my confusion rise.

*Dear Alexa Ford*

*This letter is to inform you that the final will and testament of Professor Jonah Thompson will be read on June 6, 2025 at nine A.M. in my office, located at the address listed above.*

*As a beneficiary of the gentleman's will, your presence is requested at the reading. If you cannot make the meeting at the time and place mentioned above, please notify us immediately.*

*Signed,*
*Edward D. Michaels*

His name had been stamped on the letter with the initials of, who I believed must be his secretary, written below.

I took out my phone and pulled up my calendar. The meeting was the next day. First, I didn't understand why I was in his will or what on earth he would leave me. The house reverted back to Dorman College, and I knew he left his money to them also.

Of course, I would go, but it would bug me until I knew why.

With no way of answering my immediate questions, I went back to the laundry. Indy dogged my every step. We went for two uneventful walks. One walk took us all the way to the professor's house. The lawn had been mowed, the windows washed and as far as I could tell, the drapes had been taken down.

There were no signs in the yard or on the door. I walked up onto the porch, made a sun blocker out of my hands and looked inside. The house was empty. The pictures were not on the walls, the rooms had been painted, and the rugs looked freshly steamed.

Indy and I walked around to the back of the house. All of the windows along the sides of the house were too high for me to look into even if I stood on my tiptoes.

I could, however, see into the kitchen through the window at the top of the door. It was the same as the view from the front. The floors were clean. There were no appliances on the counters. It didn't take a genius to figure out every item that had made the house Jonah's home, was gone.

Since I was a small child, I have compartmentalized. So, when the only thing on my mind was Jonah's house I didn't think about the fact someone might shoot at me. If I had thought about it, I might have thought since I hadn't gone to the farm today, maybe the shooter thought he scared me away last night and would now leave me alone.

Three blocks from my house I heard a big engine. By big engine I mean a diesel truck or a motor home. Whatever it was, it drove slowly down the road behind me. Indy barked at it. Not a good sign. I realized it was possible I had overestimated the safety of going for a walk on our own.

I glanced back to see a Winnebago gaining on me. A foreboding feeling enveloped me. Did someone want to get me in the motorhome?

*Paranoid,* I told myself until Indy began to bark his head off and we ran, cutting between property lines. By now I was only a couple of houses down from my house. My next-door neighbor, Max Long, had his lawn mower out and was tinkering with it near the sidewalk.

I walked up to him, trying to appear casual and began a conversation. The Winnebago hung back a minute or two and finally passed by us. It didn't have any license plates. The windows were tinted so dark it was impossible to tell if the driver was male or female.

Once Indy and I were safe inside our house and I double checked all the locks, I called the police. "Bill, this is Lexi. Did you hear about the shots fired at me last night?"

"Yes, and I have been trying to get over to talk to you all day. The two officers who responded and made sure you were home safely, went back to the scene to find evidence someone had already dug the bullets out of the trees and picked up any spent shells."

"Amazing. To me that says the shooter expected the police to come back for anything they'd left behind."

"It's been quite a day. Some kids stole a motorhome in St. Louis and now they're joyriding down here somewhere. Of course we get to look for it."

"Thank goodness." I felt tension leave my shoulders.

"That's an odd response. I see nothing good about it." His voice had gone up a couple of octaves in annoyed frustration.

"I didn't say what I meant there. A Winnebago motor home followed Indy and me as we came home from a walk. Scared me, it's why I called. I was afraid it was trying to grab me or kidnap me."

"I can see how you would think that after being shot at." He sighed. "Help me out here. Where did you last see the vehicle?"

"It passed by the house about five minutes ago. It hasn't come back by and there is no other way out of the neighborhood."

"We'll be right there."

I could hear him key his mike and put out a call for all cars to head to Cali Heights. Three police cruisers flew by a minute or two later followed by Bill in his SUV.

One less thing for everyone to worry about.

# BURIED IN TIME

# Chapter 46

The next day I found myself in front of a small office building with Edward D. Michael, Esq. emblazoned on the window, where there were three parking places reserved for his clients. I chose the one closest to the building and left Indy in the Jeep, as always.

I had to laugh. Indy sat in the driver's seat and watched people walk up and down the busy sidewalk. He didn't bark. He didn't growl. But every person moved to the opposite side of the walk and tried not to look him in the eye.

If they only knew.

The front of the office was a small waiting room. The carpet, chairs and tables were top quality. There wasn't a speck of dust or dirt anywhere. A short lady sat behind a tall semi-circular desk. I knew she was short because the top of her head didn't clear the top of the desk. She had to get up to greet me.

I guessed the woman to be in her early thirties. She wore a beige tailored suit. As she walked around the desk to meet me, I noticed she wore four-inch, spike heels. Thank goodness it wasn't me. I wore heels only when absolutely necessary. Today I wore my Finn, black Mary Janes, a gray skirt, and a bright red short-sleeve silk blouse.

She reached her hand out to greet me. "I'm Mrs. Jolly. Mr. Michaels is waiting for you. Shall we go in?" She turned left and began to walk down a hallway clearly expecting me to follow. I followed.

Mr. Michaels sat behind a cluttered pecan desk and stood when I entered the room. He reached over and held out his hand. "Dr. Ford, so nice to meet you."

"Call me Alexa," I said, shaking his hand.

"Of course, have a seat."

Mr. Michaels, Esq. looked more like a biker than a lawyer. The hand he had extended to me had a tattoo of a rose that climbed up and under his cufflinked, long sleeve white shirt. He had jet black hair and a mild manner. His piercing blue eyes didn't match the rest of his coloring.

"Alexa, I called you here today because Professor Thompson left you something in his will. I will read the part of the document pertaining to you."

He picked a paper up off his desk and read from it, *I leave my, library, all of my personal notes, correspondence and research to Alexa Ann Ford. Whoever cleans out my possessions upon my death should see she gets every book and sliver of paper found in my house. She will know what to do with it.*

"I tried several times to get him to be more specific, and his answer was always, 'How could I be more specific than to say everything?'"

I sat dumbfounded. Why me? "How long ago did he make this will?" I asked.

"The majority of the will was drafted nearly ten years ago. The addendum pertaining to you, he added a mere two weeks ago. He seemed to think you would know his reasoning.

"He did say, more than once, you were an 'exceptional friend and extremely smart'."

"May I ask where his work is being stored?"

"Of course. All of your items are in a rented and locked storage trailer in a locked garage. It isn't as much as you think. Well, the books and the photographs take up a few totes. His personal notes and research fill one tote. I can have it all delivered and unloaded wherever you would like."

I gave him my address and asked him to have the items delivered to my home.

We shook hands again and I left. I knew Professor Thompson wouldn't have left me his things if he didn't have a specific reason. Going by the two items I already had, I thought I could probably solve the murder of Judith Izzard

He did, after all, state in the other items that his family was deeply involved.

# Chapter 47

At eight A.M. the next morning my phone rang. I didn't recognize the number and the ID read *unknown caller*.

I answered it in hopes it meant my bequest was going to be delivered soon. It did.

A box truck pulled up out front before noon. I went out through the garage and asked the driver and his helper to unload the boxes into my garage and stack them on the side I didn't use.

I don't know what I expected. There were two totes of photos in frames, the ones that had hung from the professor's walls. Six more totes were books. The last three were marked *Personal*. I had the men put those on top. I assumed the rest of the boxes pertained to his travel and teaching and the one's marked personal could be family history so I started with those.

They were professional and polite. It took less than ten minutes for them to unload and stack everything. They were not even out of the driveway before I closed the door and began to inspect the totes. Each one not only had a label on the top, but they had a list of contents for each.

Of the three marked *Personal*, one also said *Research*, one said *Notes* and the third, *Family*.

I opened the one marked *Family*, took as many folders as I could carry and went into the living room. The house seemed eerily quiet after having had guests for days. I turned on the TV and sat on the couch. I had no idea if the folders were in any particular order, but I decided to start at the top and work my way through to the bottom.

A thought occurred to me. I hadn't seen or heard from Agent Wade since he brought food to me and the gang at the farmhouse. Strange, since he had let me know more than once he wanted to tell me what happened in New Jersey. I thought sure he would call once he heard about the last shooting. I had said that I would contact him, but right now I was more interested in what the professor had left me.

Before long, my mind was so engaged with the wealth of information in the first folders I had brought in, I decided to bring in a lap desk and put my notes directly onto a word document.

I'd been back to the garage three times. Each time I brought back another treasure trove of information about Thompson and his ancestors. For me to obtain his family background and all they had accomplished would have taken me years.

The phone rang, Agent Blake Wade. "Hello," I said before he had a chance to speak. "I thought maybe you had resigned and were no longer here."

His voice came out low and serious. "I've been trying to find a time to sit down with you to fill you in on the happenings in New Jersey and find out about your progress here. Have you had dinner yet?"

"It's much too early for dinner," I answered.

"You must be busy. It is nearly seven-thirty."

I couldn't believe it. It meant I'd been sitting on the couch with the weight of the desk and laptop on me for nearly seven hours. Except for a trip to the bathroom and several trips to the garage to bring in more papers, I'd worked steadily all that time.

A glance at my document showed I'd written five thousand words of notes spanning fifty-six pages.

I looked down at Indy. "You must be hungry." He stood and put his head on the edge of the desk. What a great friend. He would have stayed with me until I stopped what I was doing, and not complained once.

"Lexi, are you there?"

"Yes, come to think about it, I'm starving. My problem is I can't stand the thought of another pizza or sub sandwich and I don't feel like cleaning up to go out."

"I'll spring for dinner. Tell me what you're hungry for, anything, and I'll bring it to you."

"Lobster fest is going on at Red Lobster. Lobster and crab legs are my favorite foods in the world I won't ask you to pay though. I hear it's pretty expensive."

"Lobster it is. Can you do one thing? Call in the order. I'll pick it up on my way to your house. I'm in Springfield right now. Order anything and everything you want and then order the same thing for me. Even if you do that, it will take me at least an hour to get there. Does that work for you?"

"Sure, I'll call it in to the one in Rogersville. I think they do a better job there. See you in about an hour."

I asked my phone to dial Red Lobster. There was a time when you had to either look the number up or call 4 1 1 for directory assistance. Things had sure changed in the past fifteen years. Sometimes technology was great.

I fed my poor dog, who ate like he had missed two or three meals instead of just being late for one. My neighbor, Zeb, the great deer hunter, always cut and skinned deer leg bones for Indy. I had at least ten in the freezer. I took one out and put it in the sink with hot water to defrost. Indy definitely deserved a treat.

My most important task, other than Indy, was to put all the papers I'd gone through out of the way so Wade wouldn't see them. I had an empty plastic tote with a lid upstairs in my closet. I got it, put the papers, my computer and the lap desk inside, put the lid on it and took it out to stack with the others in the garage.

Again, I went back upstairs, two steps at a time. I washed my face and hands, put on a little blush and lipstick, changed into clean jeans and a Dorman tee. One thing about working outside all year was what it did to my skin. Even through the sunscreen and lotions I wore, by the end of summer, my tan was so dark it carried a slight red glow. Make up is something I rarely had to use to even out my skin tone. I looked at myself in the mirror and realized I hadn't brushed my hair out from the night before. I added a little mascara and took the first step downstairs as the doorbell rang. I moved to the side of the door and reached back to open it.

"Hi," I said, "want some help?"

"If you can handle these bags, I'll go get the rest."

"Get the rest? Did you add something to my order?"

"Everything on the Lobster Fest menu."

I had nothing to say. I just smiled at him.

As I took the bags into the kitchen and set them on the table, I heard him come back in and lock the door behind him.

"Have a seat," he said. "I'll put everything out."

I leaned back against the chair and put my hands in my lap. He really was handsome to look at. Even as he moved to arrange our dishes on the table, he maintained a military stance. A lock of his dark blond hair kept falling into his eyes. He wore tailored jeans, a white shirt with a button-down collar and a dark grey sport coat and Sperry Topsiders.

He looked up at me as he took a bottle of Marcus Negri Moscato d'Asti out of a bag and held it up for me to see. I was amazed he remembered me mentioning how much I liked it.

I began to stand, ready to go fetch some wine glasses when he said, "Don't worry, I know where they are."

I considered being annoyed that he had made himself at home, but the food looked marvelous. I took a lobster tail, a helping of snow crab legs and a Cheddar Bay biscuit. He did the same but added some sort of lobster pasta to his haul.

"Don't you like this?" He pointed to the lobster dish.

"I like it, but I can only eat so much and I'm not going to waste my appetite on pasta." Once we had both eaten a lobster tail, he put another on my plate.

I said, "Are you trying to fatten me up?"

"Not possible," he answered with a wink.

I blushed in spite of myself.

"I've wanted to talk to you for days, but between your house guests and your work and mine, it hasn't been possible."

I took another piece of lobster, dipped it in butter and put it in my mouth, chewed and swallowed. "Company is gone for a few days, and we are both here so go ahead."

"When I went to New Jersey to see about Simmons, it wasn't him. With the damage done in the accident, no one would be able to identify him through facial recognition. We ran his fingerprints and used dental records to find out his identity. His name was

Johnny Rushing, a member of a motorcycle gang called Renegades who ran in the area. We couldn't tie him, or his gang, to Simmons or any of his companies.

"Later, as we were wrapping up the paperwork for Rushing's death, the Arkansas State Police contacted us about a burnt car outside of Little Rock they had found. This time we were able to positively identify one of the bodies as Simmons' along with two more members of the Renegades. The current thought is, Simmons was kidnapped irrelevant of Judith Izzard, the farm or the death of the professor.

"We've been forced to conclude someone took Barclay Simmons for ransom before realizing he was a man without a past or family to ransom him. While transporting him to some location, they hit a semi carrying propane and all were killed but the semi driver. So that part of our mystery is over.

"What happens to the dig?" I asked anxiously, thinking about Judith's ghost. "He already paid me a great deal of money. We have so far found an Indian Burial Ground, several articles from the 1800s and early 1900s. We uncovered evidence of a recent murder."

"Mr. Simmons had a will. He didn't leave any money or land to any individuals. He did, however, leave any property he owned that were near a college or university to those schools. He left every business to the managers who ran them for him."

"The farm now belongs to Dorman College," he said, smiling at my obvious relief. "The general consensus is that the college will let you finish the project and then add the land to their agricultural program.

"What they do with the artifacts depends on what you and your people find. You can't dig the burial ground, right?"

"Right," I confirmed emphatically. "We have already marked off the burial ground. A fence and a plaque will be affixed to the area along with no trespassing signs. Addy called the Bureau of Indian Affairs. They are sending someone to make sure the sacred ground is handled properly."

"Where are the artifacts you found so far?"

"I'm not in charge of any of it. The University of Missouri has a panel truck near the site. Every night they put every item inside. They are labeled and catalogued daily. Then the truck is taken to the police impound and left there overnight where it is guarded. A few items were sent back to the university as well for dating in the lab."

He stopped the conversation long enough to pour us both another glass of wine. "Do you know where the diamond and ruby ring is? It's evidence in a murder case."

I tried my best not to change my breathing or voice and keep my inflection the same. I didn't feel right not telling him I had it in my pocket, that I'd actually had it this whole time, but now that I had interacted with it, I couldn't let the ring go. Not until I had done what Judith had asked of me.

"I really don't know. I assume it is in the van with the rest of the artifacts. Adaline will be back in a day or two and I can ask her then."

"We haven't managed to identify who the finger bones you found belong to. Scuttlebutt has it, Chief Davis is going to put a missing person alert on TV and see what becomes of it."

Despite feeling low grade panic over this line of questioning, I yawned. I tried not to, but I couldn't help it. Two Cheddar Bay biscuits, two lobster tails, a helping of snow crabs and an order of shrimp scampi coupled with poor quality sleep was doing me in. It was a wonder I could even move.

"I'll get out of here in a minute. I hear you were shot at. Again. Anything happening about that?" Blake had his serious face back on as he looked steadily at me.

"Not really. So long as they don't hit me, I'll be fine."

"Doesn't it scare you?" He sounded exasperated.

"Not like the first couple of times. I am pretty sure now they don't want to kill me. I was surprised about this one because now that what we are doing is public, there is no stopping the farm from being excavated. I believe they keep at it because I'm difficult to scare."

"I'm afraid I need to go." He got up to clean off the table, but I stopped him.

"I can do that," I insisted, stifling another yawn.

He smiled at me showing snow white, perfect teeth and flashing small dimples on each cheek.

I walked him to the door. He leaned against it, but I didn't stop in time in my sleepiness and ran into him. He rested his arms lightly on my shoulders, steadying me. He leaned down and kissed me. He pulled back and when I stayed where I was, stunned, and kissed me again.

My leg began to hurt and I realized the ring in my pocket had turned ice cold.

# CHAPTER 48

After Agent Blake Wade left, I let Indy out for the last time until morning. I locked the doggy door and checked all the downstairs windows. Even though I knew I had locked the front door behind the FBI agent, I checked it again to be sure.

Lying had never been easy for me. As a child I quickly learned I wouldn't get much of a punishment even after some of the pranks I pulled, as long as I told the truth when I got caught. Even the time Alice Sweeny, Mark Donalds and I let the air out of one tire on every car in the neighborhood. As a result, I had an overdeveloped sense of honesty.

When I had lied to Blake about the ring, I prayed he wouldn't see it in my eyes. He kissed me goodnight and after a moment, I kissed him back. Another mystery I needed to figure out because I didn't think of him as a romantic interest. I tried to tell myself he caught me off guard, but that wasn't it. And I'd found myself enjoying the kiss.

No one had any idea the ring lived either in my pocket or under my pillow. When Blake gave the bones back to me after the professor's murder, I had put them back where I found them. The ring, I'd kept.

In my heart, considering the apparitions and visions I'd thus far witnessed, I knew the ring would help me solve Judith's case. To give the possibility of closure for Judith up at this point seemed totally wrong. But telling anyone what I experienced and how I interacted with the ring would make me look like a nut.

Blake and I had finished dinner around nine thirty. He had left about ten thirty. Indy stood next to me wanting to go upstairs and go to bed. I wanted to research everything I could about Queen Cathrine V's ring. Thank goodness for the Internet and laptops.

With all the famous Queen Cathrine's over the years it was difficult to find the one I wanted. I stopped searching for the name and began to search for the ring itself instead. Kathrine of Belmonte had reigned over a small island in the Pacific from 1785 to 1835 at which time she left the island and went to Hawaii.

There she met a man by the name of Sir Hamilton George who married her and brought her to America. They settled in Seattle. Sir George wanted Kathrine by his side all of the time. He lavished gifts on her. One of the gifts was a four-carat ruby encased in two circles of half carat diamonds.

The story went like this, a diamond mine in South Africa got robbed. The men with the diamonds were decapitated. No one would buy the stones, but Sir George who referred to the stories of them being haunted and cursed as rubbish. He wanted his wife to have a ring made of the stones. He thought she was the most beautiful woman in the world.

The photos in the articles showed her to be portly with a bulbus nose and crooked teeth. One writers said he was sure *beauty is in the eye of the beholder* had to have come from those people who saw how Sir George worshiped his Kathrine.

The first incident came when Sir George fell off a boat in the ocean and was nearly immediately eaten by a shark, in front of Kathrine and the crew.

It was then the stories about the ring's power became news. No one believed them.

For years, the tales stopped and news of the ring faded away. In 1921 a human interest story was printed in the Miami Herald about a twelve-year-old girl and her mother who were walking along the beach in Key West when the girl, age 15 found a ruby and diamond ring.

As the two stood by the ocean watching the tide come in, a rogue wave came in and washed the mother out to sea, never to be seen again. The girl swore the ring turned hot in her hand, the wave enveloped her but when it rolled out, her mother couldn't be found and the girl was left unharmed.

Of course no one believed the child. But it was when the first picture of the ring had been taken in years. The only images of it before were from the jeweler who fashioned it and some reproduced from memory along the way.

The story soon faded from the spotlight. The story I read on the internet said the girl's father pawned it for a few hundred dollars. In other words he was cheated by the pawnbroker who took it to a New York auction where it went for thousands of dollars.

Before the auction house sold the ring they researched its beginnings, thus the story of Queen Kathrine. Many stories about the ability of the ring to warn people of danger and lead others to their death, multiplied.

A paper trail says Jacob Izzard went out East on business, saw the ring advertised by the auction house and bought it. If the ring had mystic powers, they were not mentioned from then on.

One thing I knew to be true was the ring did react in certain instances.

I looked up mystic powers of inanimate objects. I did this mainly for myself to assure myself I wasn't going mad. Article after article popped up about objects said to have mystic powers. After I read at least ten of them, I made up my mind to suspend my disbeliefs and let the ring guide me to the truth.

There was at least ninety years between Judith's death and the girl the finger bones belonged to, so there had to be more than one killer. The possibility also came to my mind that Judith Izzard lived somewhere to a ripe old age but for some unknown reason had left home never to return.

The clock in the hall announced midnight, yet I had no desire to sleep. I wanted to glean as much information as I could out of the professor's personal papers before the folks from the University returned in two days.

Some of the reading was mundane, Aunt Sally married Uncle Fred and such. When I reached the two weeks leading up to the day Judith had gone missing, the notes read like a bestseller. I couldn't put it down and hardly took notes myself, knowing I would never forget what I read.

According to what the professor had collected, the Izzard family owned a lumber yard and saw mill on the outskirts of Seymour. Men and boys were always around delivering logs and poles they cut to sell at the mill by the foot to Jacob Izzard.

Jacob, according to what I read, had the personality of a wet rag, the morals of an alley cat and an attitude of entitlement.

Some of the men, not of the same manner and social class of the Izzards, flirted, made off color remarks and harassed both Jacob's wife and daughter. One such young man, Morgan Thompson, son of the then Senator Michael Thompson had asked Jacob permission for Judith to accompany him to the graduation dance. Not knowing, nor caring who the man was, Jacob had given a firm no to the very idea.

The time came closer and closer for the graduation dance, but no matter how much Judith had wanted to go with the Senator's son, or how many times Morgan had asked, the answer always been, "No."

To make sure his only daughter didn't disobey him, Jacob had sent his coach driver to take his daughter to the dance and made arrangements for the man to pick her up exactly four hours later.

To appease Judith, Jacob and Minie had let her wear her mother's ring which Jacob had purchased for Minie for their twentieth-fifth wedding anniversary.

That night, the coachman had taken Judith to the hotel where the dance was. At least fifty people reported having seen her arrive, no one remembered seeing her leave. Most importantly, no one ever saw Judith Izzard again.

I jerked myself out of the trance like state reading the papers put me in. I realized I'd taken the notes the professor left, added my own twist and made up a story about the young girl's disappearance. I shook my head and admonished myself. Judith and the ring were real. I needed to stop second guessing myself. But I knew I didn't have to worry because Judith would eventually show me what happened. I was sure of it.

Although it might not have been exactly as the notes indicated. It was certainly feasible.

When the clock chimed three, I knew I needed to give it up. Two things, however, stayed with me. When I saw Judith the first time in the vision she had smiled and looked happy. The next time

I'd had a vision, she had somehow gotten wet, dirty and tear stained. Some of that happened before she came into contact with Morgan Thompson and the rest had to be after he threw her to the ground, stepped on her fingers and stole the ring.

What about the two men she'd seen in the woods in another vision? One had been on the ground, unmoving and one had taken the ring out of the dead man's pocket. Who could they have been?

Last but not least, why did the ring nearly freeze in my pocket when Blake and I kissed at the door, yet turned warm, actually down-right hot, before I had a vision.

Maybe I *had* lost my mind.

Then I remembered all of the inanimate objects with mystic powers I had read about. My main question then became, *why me?*

## Chapter 49

The sunshine hit my face and I had to close my eyes and turn the other way. Sunshine on my face could only mean one thing, I'd slept past noon.

I reached under my pillow and felt for the pouch. Right then I decided I intended to keep the ring, no matter what I had to say or had to do to accomplish it. I had no idea how I would pull it off. My best bet was to carry it in the pouch somewhere on my person until the case was over and the killers identified.

Blake would leave, Adaline and her group would go back to the University. And I had managed to keep the ring a secret.

If I ever had to refer to it, I would call it the Queen's ring. The phone rang and brought me back to the present. "Hello."

"Hi, Lexi, It's me, Addy. I wanted to catch you up on our schedule."

"Great. Are the guys through with their testing?"

"Yes, and they all did well. John won't be coming back with us. He's joining an expedition in Peru. He said to tell you it was nothing personal."

"I understand. Peru is way more exotic than Missouri. When will you be here?"

"The day after tomorrow, Wednesday. If you're tired of us, we can go back to the hotel."

"Nonsense, I like having you all here," I replied, realizing it was true. The house had felt too quiet after they'd left.

"Okay then, we are leaving here at six so we should be there by noon." We said our good-byes and hung up.

My stomach growled. "Indy, what do you say, before we get started, we go to Five Guys and get a burger. We can sit outside, enjoy the day, and then come back and get to work."

Indy jumped off the bed, ran downstairs and came bounding back up with his collar and lead.

"Does that mean you're okay walking in the heat of the day?" He barked and ran around in circles. This was the price I would pay for not keeping my regular schedule.

I dressed in knee length shorts, Nike tennis shoes, and a Cardinal's tee. I let my hair flow free. The weather said it would only climb into the eighties.

When we were ready to go, I got a feeling of dread. I ran back upstairs, put my Ruger LCP II in a small holster and shoved it in the lower zipper compartment of my shorts. I was tired of people shooting at me. Maybe if I shot back, just once, they would stop.

I coiled the lead and put it over my shoulder like soldiers do in parade dress, grabbed money and my house key, and away we went. A slight breeze and the shade from the trees that lined sidewalks took care of the heat. Indy ran ahead and chased squirrels up trees. After the first mile, he came back and walked beside me.

As we turned a corner close to town, someone honked at us. The sound came from a Black SUV with Missouri plates. A thought ran through my mind wondering why Agent Wade didn't have a government ID on the license. The thought went away as quickly as it came when Agent Blake Wade, pulled over, put the window down on our side and said, "Hi, want a ride?"

"Oh, no thanks. We're out for a walk, we are getting fat and lazy."

"I doubt that would ever happen. Where are you going?"

"On our way to Five Guys."

"Yummy, can I meet you there?" Sure, you can leave your car and walk with us if you like."

"I would but I don't think my suit would hold up to this heat. I'll go ahead and get us a table. He started to drive away but before he did, he said, "Is that a gun in your pocket?"

"Yes, it is. I have a carry permit."

"That wasn't my worry. Are you so scared you believe you need a gun?"

"In truth, I'm tired of getting shot at. If someone shoots at me today, I might shoot back."

He shook his head and gave me a hard, unfriendly look. "Not a good idea."

"Depends on if you are the one being shot at."

A long minute passed. He looked at me, then hit the palm of his hand on the steering wheel. "See you," he said as he drove away.

It took Indy and me another fifteen minutes to arrive at the restaurant. The black SUV sat neatly in front of the place with a placard in the window reading *FBI, official business.*

I shook my head when I saw no less than four open places he could have parked closer than where he sat, double parked. When I looked around once inside the restaurant, I didn't see him. I picked a table outside and told Indy to save it, but *be nice.*

Finally I spotted Blake standing in line inside and when he saw me, he motioned me to cut in front of him. I did, but I said, *I'm sorry* to everyone I passed.

When it was our turn to order he asked me what I wanted. "I'll order my own, thanks."

He gave me a look I didn't quite understand and ordered himself the biggest burger they had, a coke and fries.

I ordered three of the biggest burgers they had, two plain and one loaded, a bottle of water and a diet Pepsi. I took the number the man gave me and told him we were eating outside.

Indy was thrilled to see me return to our table, but was standoffish with Blake. I knew it to be a vibe he got from me. I sat with my back to the front window, Indy beside me which put Blake in a chair with his back to the street.

Indy scarfed down both triple burgers and drank the water out of the bottle as I held it up for him. "Smart dog," Blake said.

"The smartest."

"You haven't been to the dig site for three days. Isn't it costing the police a pretty penny to keep it guarded?"

"Bill said not to worry about it. All of the expense will be covered by the University now. They have a man clearing the sod off of the ground for five acres around the farmhouse. If he comes up with nothing, they will remove another six inches of soil. It will go like that until they begin to find artifacts and then they will stop digging down.

"Addy and her crew, sans John, will be here Wednesday and we'll get started again."

"Aren't you bored?

"Goodness no. I had a life, jobs and research before this entire Judith Izzard, Barclay Simmons ordeal came up. I've been busy every minute trying to catch up on other things. Thus, our walk to the restaurant today. Indy needs to exercise his leg and I could use a change of scenery from my computer screen."

"I understand Professor Thompson left you all of his personal papers and research."

"Where did you get that information?"

"I'm an FBI agent." He grinned at me.

"I'm sorry, Blake. That's not a good enough reason. It's my personal life. It has nothing to do with Judith Izzard or the ring."

He put his hand on top of mine and two things happened. The ring in my pocket almost froze my leg and a chill went up my spine for a totally different reason. I moved my hand and stood up. Half my burger remained on a plate in front of me. "Come on, Indy, we're leaving."

He stood also, "Alexa. You are being unreasonable."

I turned toward home and walked off.

"Wait."

"I don't know if that's an order or not. If it is an order, arrest me. If not, leave me alone."

# Chapter 50

The two and a half mile walk home did little to ease my temper. It did, however, convince me I needed to lock up the material I received from the professor's will. And I needed to lock it in a place difficult to find and more difficult to get to.

My house had an attic. I could pull the ladder down and put the material upstairs except for what I needed in my immediate research.

In the meantime, I intended to move my workspace to my bedroom. It took me three trips to shift everything, but I knew I was safer upstairs. Then I did something I had not done since I was thirteen and Mom and Dad had left me alone for the first time while they went to a movie. I took a kitchen chair, wedged the back under the doorknob and pushed it as tight as possible. I did the same thing to the back door and the door to the garage, which happened to be the only entry to my office behind the garage.

Then I called the lawyer's office. "Do I have to show the papers I inherited to the police or FBI?

"No, Dr. Ford. The reason everyone knows about the papers is it was posted in several places as it had to be according to probate laws."

"Professor Thompson left me all of his research papers and all of his personal papers including his family history. Agent Wade today, asked me about them."

"My opinion is what is yours is yours. It would be different if you were a suspect in the professor's murder, but you're not and never have been." She said.

"To be perfectly honest, since the professor was murdered, I wonder about my safety." I said.

"I can see why you would be leery., dear, but I don't believe a professor's notes on his classes or life's work would be something to kill over. Besides, all of his important work has been printed and reprinted. Anyone can have access to it at the library and on the internet.

"The rest of those papers are his family tree. I doubt anyone would commit a crime to get those either."

I heard a phone ring in her office. "Have a great day, Dr. Ford and don't worry about this."

Chief Davis called. "Lexi. Don't take Indy for a walk tonight. Lock your back gate while I'm on the phone. Indy can go outside within the confines of the yard. I'll stay on the phone."

I chill went up my back. "Why?"

He paused a long moment. "This may sound silly, but it is just a feeling I have."

" I will, but Bill, you don't need to stay on the phone while I check the lock on the gate."

"I want to."

I put the phone in my pocket, took the chair from under the door, turned off the porch light and the backyard light. Indy went with me, and we locked both locks on the gate. When I got back inside and had the door safely locked behind me, I said, "Okay, it's done. Thanks."

"No problem. I'll get someone to drive by your house a few times tonight. The people in your area are still on edge about the motor home the other day. I'll have them use the spotlight around your place when they patrol. Talk tomorrow."

As fast as I could, I put the chair under the door once again. After I finished, I closed all of the drapes downstairs. I considered turning off the back lights and then thought better of it. To appease myself, I stopped at the front door and turned on not only the porch light but also the lantern by the street and the sidewalk lights.

Had the lights been colored, the house would have looked like it was lit up for Christmas.

Stress does different things to different people. It makes me extremely tired and my stomach rolls. To help my stomach, I put on my PJ's and lay in the fetal position on my bed. To help my exhaustion, I closed my eyes and tried to relax.

I left the ring in the pocket of my PJ shorts. A thought came to me, if I bought a chain, I could make it long enough to wear the ring around my neck. No one would be able to see it and I wouldn't have to worry about whether I lost it or not. If I lost the ring, how could I help Judith or solve the mystery around her disappearance once and for all?

After I calmed my nerves, I could put the ring under my pillow. I must have fallen asleep. Indy's sound of alarm woke me up as did the sensation someone had hold of my hand. I sat up, jerked my arm and bent my elbow so my hand rested near my face.

The velvet pouch laid open on the bed, the ring on my finger. I looked around the room. All the papers were on the end of the bed where I left them. The tee I'd had on lay on top of the shorts and the shorts were on the floor where I remembered leaving them as well.

But the ring had somehow moved from the pouch to my finger while I slept. I told myself I must have woken and put it on myself. Intellectually it had to have happened like that. In my heart, I knew the ring had gotten on my finger through more inexplicable means.

But why put the ring on my finger?

I left the ring where it was, got up, stacked the papers on my makeup table, washed my face, brushed my teeth and hair. As I went through my routine, I stopped every so often and just looked at the ring. Once I got back to bed, I turned on my table side lamp and took the ring off.

Although I'd seen it a hundred times, I looked closely at the ring one more time. The setting, so exquisite, the stones so bright and the ring fit me. The first time I had tried to put it on, it wouldn't go past my knuckle. Now it fit perfectly, not so big it would slip off or so small as to be uncomfortable.

My mind made up that something supernatural had caused the ring to somehow get itself on my finger and size itself to fit, I somehow felt more at ease.

I turned over and went to sleep. I slept a deep, dreamless sleep until morning.

## Chapter 51

I didn't think about it until the next morning when I woke up in a good mood at six a.m. I'd slept nearly twelve hours straight. I poked Indy, "Get up sleepy head. Time to face the day."

After a stop by the bathroom, we both bounded down the stairs. I unlocked the doggy door for my buddy and he went out. I took the time to walk around the inside of the house, opening drapes and turning off outside lights.

Sunlight flowed in through the eastern windows and made the house instantly bright and friendly.

When I reached up to grab the drapes in the den, the ring on my finger caught the sun and I stared at it. I could hardly take my eyes off of it. But in the daylight, the thought of the ring magically taking itself out of the velvet pouch and onto my finger seemed unbelievable again. I, who didn't even like scary movies might not been a good choice for Judith to rely on. Right then, I promised myself I would solve this mystery and get the ring back where it belonged. I just needed to survive all this supernatural vision stuff first.

The Hope Diamond came to mind. I went to my favorite chair in the den and tried to recall what I knew of it. At the present, my mind cleared, and I remembered the entire story. Much like I could recite the Preamble to the Constitution I'd learned in third grade.

In one of my college classes, I had spent an entire semester learning about artifacts, their worth and how some of them impacted history. One of them was the Hope Diamond. It didn't begin with that name but ended up with it.

A gem dealer stole the diamond out of a Hindu shrine where it had been part of a statue. Before its theft the diamond had served as one of the statue deity's eyes. At that time, it was the size of a man's fist. I don't remember all the names the diamond had had, but I do remember King Louis XIV of France ended up with it at one point. He had at least a dozen children but only one lived past childhood. The King suffered from headaches, boils, fainting spells and diabetes. He died of gangrene at age 77. Was it the curse of the stolen diamond?

King Louis XV inherited everything including the throne, he was five. He grew up to be a weak womanizer who lost the Seven Years War. He lived a pretty long life but died a very hated man. The curse in action?

Next in line was Louis XVI, whose fate was to be hung and his wife Marie Antoinette, beheaded and her head put on a pole for all to see. It marked the end of the French monarchy. Was that part of the curse?

The diamond ended up with people whose names I wouldn't forget; Henry Hope owned it in 1830 and it became known as the Hope diamond. The name stuck. In America, Pierrie Cartier and Henry Winston had each owned it for a time. During those years it was cut for a second time and at that point was the size of a large walnut. It still was today.

Harry Winston donated the Hope Diamond to the Smithsonian in 1958. Contrary to popular belief, Elizabeth Taylor never owned the Hope Diamond. The rumor started because Harry Winston also cut the diamond Richard Burton had her ring made from.

My phone rang and pulled me out of my thoughts. I looked at the caller ID for a long time hoping the caller would hang up. He finally did.

After three cups of coffee, (I like the cream better than the coffee), two pieces of rye toast with organic peanut butter on it and a Greek Yogurt, I filled my water jug, grabbed a chew for Indy and we headed back upstairs.

Even though the day was what is referred to as a Chamber of Commerce Day, I would get more done upstairs where no one could tell if I was home or not.

Indy went downstairs a couple of times to go outside, but I didn't get done with my work until after seven p.m. And what a job I'd done. Once I put it all together, I realized the entire mystery had nothing to do with Judith Izzard and everything to do with the ring on my finger.

Have you ever stared at a picture so long, you saw another image in it? It happened to me as I stared at everything the professor had known and I now knew. I sat on my bed and looked out the window.

As I did, an ash tree down the street came into focus. In front of it , superimposed over the trunk, stood Judith. Again I had the feeling of being underground. I knew that feeling wasn't mine, but Judith's. Her image became clearer.

She faced me and the man with his hands on her shoulders slapped her in the face. She looked at me and it all faded away.

Okay,

The phone rang again. This time I answered it. "Yes? What do you want?"

"I don't want hard feelings between us. I'm just doing my job."

"Listen Blake, I know you will most likely be here until the dig is over. And I like having you around. But sometimes your over-protection suffocates me."

"I would like to know if there is anything in the professor's papers that could shed some light on his case."

I let my voice get colder and more impersonal, if it possible. "It has been eight days since Jonah's killing. All of that time, the papers were in his house. You had every opportunity to get a warrant, or whatever you needed to look at them. But you didn't. Now they are in my possession and if you want to see them you will need a court order."

Neither one of us said another word. I counted to ten and disconnected the call when he said nothing else.

I looked at the clock. It wouldn't be dark for a while longer. "Indy, let's go."

He ran and got his leash but didn't know whether to go to the front door, back door or garage. He whined. "Garage," I said. He ran toward it.

I had taken my gun upstairs with me the night before. I retrieved it, took a handful of extra bullets, stuck them in my pocket and took my dad's 22 rifle from behind the desk in the office. I looked out the garage windows before I opened the door and we left.

In case Blake actually did follow me, I cut through the field at the end of the street which took me down a rarely used farm road to the highway. I was in Seymour, at the site in less than ten minutes.

One of the patrolmen on watch, Adam Lane, walked up to the car. "We were wondering if you were ever coming back."

"I just had some work to catch up with. The college staff will be back tomorrow and we'll get back to it. I came to take a look around and see how much dirt has been removed. I won't be long."

"You want one of us to go with you?"

"No, I'll be fine. Looks like the show's over for the day. No one is hanging around now."

I had put the rifle on the floor of the car so it couldn't be seen. When I looked down on it, I considered that maybe I had gotten paranoid. But then again, I'd been shot at three times and two men were dead. So, maybe I wasn't paranoid enough.

Wow, it looked so different. They had the dirt down about six inches. I didn't see anything but dirt. It surprised me how close the workers were able to get to the buildings. I walked up the stairs to the house. I wanted to go to the basement. Indy followed, carrying his bone, saliva running out both sides of his mouth.

When we got to the basement door, he hesitated to go down the steps. "You can stay here and chew on your bone. I want to look around." He must have thought it was a good idea because he sat and started chewing contentedly.

I had my Mag Light which I turned on as I stepped on the first step. I saw the shackles one of the grad students had noted when we had spread out to search the house previously. Spiders as big around as my thumb didn't bother to move when I passed them. First, I took the small hammer I had in my pack and tapped the walls gently all the way around the room. There were no changes in sound.

Maybe this wasn't the room I had seen in my visions. I told myself not to get depressed. I had only begun. There were four more structures on the property that might have underground structures. I went to sit on the stairs. I hoped I could walk around the room, stomp around it, and not have to get down on my hands and knees to see if there was anything underneath it.

Then I saw it. A section of the northwest corner was at least three inches lower than the rest of the room. I put my backpack down and knelt on it. I couldn't do anything with my hands with how packed the dirt floor had become over the years. I got the trowel out of my tools and used it to try to see more.

When I had dug out a space about two feet by two feet, I heard Indy begin to bark and smelled smoke start to filter down into the basement. Within a minute, the basement had filled with smoke. There were no windows. Indy started down the stairs.

"No, Indy, go get help," I yelled.

He kept coming down. His bark changed and I knew he couldn't get enough air. For the first time in his life, I yelled at him. "Indiana Jones! Up those stairs! Get help!" I stamped my foot. I heard the sounds of him scrambling back up the stairs.

I knew I needed to get out of the basement and out of the house. I also knew the lower I stayed to the floor, the better chance I had to get a little air. I knew also, in ten minutes it wouldn't matter if I was up or down. I'd be dead of smoke inhalation.

I laid down where I had dug the hole. There was enough room for me to put my nose to the damp ground. I had to get out of there. Suddenly, I didn't feel alone anymore. I looked up and Judith hovered over me. She moved her left arm in a large circle, faster and faster. She helped me off the floor and helped me to the stairs going up to the upstairs hallway, or at least her presence did.

The next thing I remember I was laying on a stretcher. Blake Wade held my right hand, and oxygen went into my nose from a tube attached to a tank on my other side. I couldn't see the house, but I could still smell the smoke. My left hand was so cold. The ring was gone.

It wasn't on my finger. I tried to talk but the words wouldn't come. I withdrew my hand from Blake's with what little strength I had. When I could, I tried to sit up. An EMT behind me lifted the stretcher head up and locked it in a sitting position. Instantly, I felt better.

"I think you should go to the hospital," Blake said.

"No, I can't. Where is Indy?"

I heard him bark. He appeared at my side with both front feet on the stretcher. I petted him and told him he saved my life, knowing full well, some way, somehow, Judith Izzard had helped me out of the fire.

"Is the fire out?" I asked.

Blake said," Yes but the house is a total loss. As old and dry as the wood was, it went up like paper."

I shook my head. "How did the fire start?"

"It hasn't been determined, but considering your past, I'd think it's possible someone didn't want you in that house."

I reached down to adjust the oxygen tube and realized the ring laid beside me on the cart.

I took my thumb and used it to push the ring up and over to me and then under the sheet. From there I, with great effort, slipped it into my pocket.

Chief Bill Davis walked over. He'd been with the firemen at the house. "How are you doing?"

"I'm fine. I would like to get up and as a next step, I'd like to go see the house, go home, shower and call it a day."

One of the paramedics came over. "I sent all your vitals to the hospital. They okayed you to go home. If your chests begins to hurt, you get a bad sore throat or have any breathing problems, call in. You having your trusty dog to lead you out of the flames and smoke likely saved your life."

I said, thanks, Bill nodded his head and Blake took my hand and squeezed it a little too hard.

# Chapter 52

I had to be downright sharp with Blake to keep him from following me home. First, he wanted to drive me. "And strand me at home with no car," I said.

Every time he stood close to me, the ring turned cold. In a gemology class I took years before, I remembered reading diamonds signified wealth, status, and familial connections. Rubies, were associated with heart chakra and related to family lineage. Love, passion and prosperity.

Not sure how much stock I put into any of it. I had read numerous books over the years where a stone or crystal meant life or death to the central character of the story. But this wasn't a story, it was my life.

After I showered to get the first layer of dirt off me, I ran a tub full of hot water, added milk and honey Epsom salts and climbed in to relax. I closed my eyes and sunk down as far as I could. Only my head and neck were above water level.

Once I was clean, I made arrangements to drop Indy off at the groomer's since he, too, reeked of smoke and ash. He threw a fit when I tried to leave him, so I put him in the shower and bathed him myself.

I was nearly asleep when my phone buzzed. Agent Blake Wade. I didn't answer. The man had something to do with the professor's death, the harassment of me, and the death of Officer Tony

Asbury. I had no idea what it was, but my interior alarm went off and I always listened to it.

The phone rang again. I almost didn't pick it up but I'm glad I did because it was Emily. Before I had a chance to say a word I heard, "Good lord, girl! Are you out to get yourself killed? They broke into the show I had on to announce the big fire out at the farm where you're working.

"My heart nearly stopped when they went on to say you had been inside when the fire started!"

"I'm fine. The house is gone though. This is really getting to be a dangerous undertaking."

"Bill was on camera and said they would be doing a thorough investigation because of the death of one of his officers, the four times you have been shot at and, oh, the man from New Jersey who hired you was found burned to death in a car in Little Rock."

When I didn't say anything, she went on.

"I wish you would give this up. Didn't a man ask you to help him dig in some ruins in Colorado? Or was it an old silver mine or gold mine? Either is safer than this!"

I took a deep breath. "Emily, if whoever shot at me wanted to kill me, I'd be dead. For some reason there is a person or persons out there who don't want the grounds searched. I'm not a detective, but I do believe it has something to do with the murder of that young lady, the Izzard girl, almost a hundred years ago.

"I'm safe. I must admit, the fire today scared me, but the Fire Chief said they thought it was caused by the sun shining on a piece of paper or metal or something working like a magnifying glass. It hasn't rained but once in several weeks and the house is over two hundred years old. It went up like a gas-soaked rag. Please don't worry."

"Well, don't go out there by yourself again."

"Yes, Mother," I said and laughed. "The people from the college will be back tomorrow. Not only will they be with me at the dig, but they will also be staying with me here at the house. "

"Good to know."

"Bye." I said before she had time to start on a new subject.

I still wasn't hungry, which I assumed was from the stress of the fire. Wine didn't sound good. I went down to the kitchen, refilled my water bottle and grabbed a treat for Indy.

My goal was to finish the rest of the papers which would finish my timeline. I already had a pretty good idea of who wanted to stop me. In the back of my mind, I even had an inkling of why.

At this point, I knew I should be afraid, yet I wasn't. I was excited.

# Chapter 53

Indy and I followed our regular morning routine. He seemed quite proud of his grooming I had done for him yesterday. He strutted around more than usual with me telling him how beautiful he was.

I packed my bag, including a pair of knee pads. My goal was to have the backhoe remove debris from the area of the basement, if the Fire Chief cleared it, where I'd been digging and have them help me see what lay below.

Since the group from the university wouldn't be around until noon, I headed to Crown's Jewelry store to buy the chain I'd been contemplating putting the ring on. I wanted the ring where I could get the full effect of its change in temperature. In the back of my mind, I knew the ring could do much more than change from hot to cold. I thought because of the confinement of my pocket I might be missing all of what it could actually tell me.

The store sat on a corner inside the mall. The openness of it made it appear so much larger than it actually was. A perky young lady with a jet black bob, thousand dollar bobbles in her ears and a couple of dinner rings on her fingers greeted me.

I wondered if she picked out different pieces of jewelry daily to show off the inventory. An older woman and gentlemen sat farther back in the store. He held a loop to his eye and she animatedly told a story, her arms flailing in emphasis.

Obviously, based on her volume the lady didn't care if the story she told was overheard. I'd bet my bottom dollar all of her showiness was a ploy to sell her items to the man for a larger price. She definitely had a story she wanted to share with the world.

The girl glanced back, "I'm sorry, let's move over here where I can hear you better." She pointed to a section of watches.

I looked at her name tag. "Amy," her name tag read Amy Feller, "I'm looking for a silver chain. I want a sturdy yet feminine one."

She began to walk to a case in the opposite direction she had first wanted to take me.

The selection seemed endless. When I told her 24 inches she said common sizes in a chain, not custom, generally were 25 or 28 inches.

"Twenty- eight would be my choice. I have an heirloom trinket I'd like to wear all the time, but it is so unique, I want it hidden under my clothing except on special occasions,"

"Do you see one you like?"

"Yes," I pointed to a serpentine chain with a hefty price tag. I shook my head but also knew I wanted a chain rugged enough for my kind of work.

"Would you like to put your pendant or the item you want to wear on the chain to check to see if it suits you?"

"Thanks, but I have given this a lot of thought. I know what I want."

Ten minutes later I walked out of the store with the chain. I moved the car to the edge of the parking lot where I could let Indy out to do his business and seeing him, no one would think anything of it.

I took the ring out of my pocket and the pouch. Once I had the ring around my neck, I was flooded by a sense of peace and empowerment.

We left and drove past a trash can where I stuffed the velvet pouch down toward the bottom and drove away.

By the time we reached the dig, Addy, Terrill and George were there. They walked through the debris of the fire. I drove my car all the way up the hill and beyond the point we intended to work and got out to meet them.

"My goodness," Addy said, "what happened. And don't say, *'There was a fire.'* "

Hum, those were going to be my next words.

"The Fire Chief said it was a matter of a 200-year-old house with no paint on it. Hot sun, no rain and the horrible wind just made it worse. He said it would only take a spark to set it off and it would burn like it was made of paper."

Terrill said, "I'm glad we were able to go through it before it burned then!"

"It brought up a new idea. I was in the basement when it happened."

Everyone murmured about how chilling it must have been.

"Enlightening too," I said, "while in the basement I found a section much lower than the rest of the floor. I was in the middle of trying to dig it up when the fire started.

"I would like to have the backhoe over here to scrape the debris off of the area and for us to see what is down there. I have a feeling it might be the key to everything," I said.

"What makes you think so?" Addy sounded interested.

"Because I don't think the fire was accidental. I believe until we open up whatever it is and get it out to the public, we are in danger."

"What is your reasoning?" Addy asked.

"A lot has happened since you left. It seems Professor Thompson left me all of his personal papers and files and all of his research papers.

"I haven't done anything but scan the research papers yet, but his personal papers were extremely enlightening. Seems the professor's uncle was the young man hanged for the killing of Judith Izzard. There was no body, and no evidence the boy, Morgan Thompson, was anywhere around."

I was the only one who knew for a fact Morgan Thompson was the killer, and I'm sure the professor had figured it out. He had papers and family history no one else had. I would imagine when the boy's father found him dead by the river, everyone suspected it was a lynching arranged by Judith's father. Knowing the kind of person her father was, I had no problem believing it.

But I couldn't just shout any of that out. I needed proof. The only way I knew to get closer to what had actually happened almost 100 years ago was to find Judith's body. Or keep going through the professor's papers in hopes of finding it in black and white.

"I found a birth certificate in the professor's papers. It has Professor Jonah Thompson listed as the father of a son. The mother of Professor Thompson's illegitimate son was a student by the name of Tamera Swan. I haven't researched her yet. So far, all I know is Swan died in childbirth and Jonah stepped up to take responsibility for the boy.

"I always wondered why a man with Thompson's education, expertise and fame stayed at little unknown Dorman college. After all I've read and studied, I believe it was because of Judith Izzard's disappearance and the unjust killing of his uncle. This illegitimate boy he fathered may be a factor also."

"This is amazing stuff! While I was back at the University, I got permission to make this dig part of the grad program. That means some of the students in the program will be able to come here, study, write their papers, and such until the location is closed," Addy said.

This was great news since it meant a whole team would constantly be on site.

"Wonderful," I said. "As I said, I'd like us to excavate the area where the basement is and see what's down there. I know it has a false floor. And at some point, I'd like to track down the professor's long-lost son. The birth certificate listed his name as Tyler Swan Thompson. He would be in his mid-thirties.

"When I first began working on all of this, I had no idea who the professor's killer was. Then after hours and hours of research, I thought the person causing all of the trouble was Barclay Simmons. It all makes sense except the part where Simmons hired me. If it was him trying to stop us from digging here, why hire me to do it in the first place?

"Then, Simmons was found dead in his car. Blows that theory out of the water."

Terrill said, "Let's get started on the basement. This is intriguing."

A man named Charlie Drum ran the backhoe. He worked leveling ground for new construction. He looked to be in his mid-sixties. He wore a Texas Titans baseball hat low on his head. To see us when we talked, he had to lift his head like he had on bifocals.

He couldn't have been over five feet three, and he scrambled up and down from the machine like a teenager. We told him what we wanted, and he went to work. He'd dug down over eighteen inches when he hit something hard and solid.

"We got something," he said. "Now what 'cha want?"

Addy was closest and answered him. "Go as far as you can toward the other side of the house. If the surface changes. Tell us. If you get all the way there with no change, can you turn around and come back making your track wider each time?"

"Sure 'nuf, miss." Drum got back to work.

He made four rows, which exposed about half the ceiling of whatever was down there and stopped. "Hey, over there." He gestured at what he meant with one hand.

We walked over. "The floor or ceiling here, depending on how you look at it is higher here. Not much, but about two feet by four feet. Want me to stop?"

It looks like the opening to whatever cave like feature we found had opened about a foot from where the basement steps used to be.

"Charlie, we can take it from here. How much notice do you need to come back if we need to do some more with the backhoe?" Terrell asked.

"Only a few hours, but I'm going to give you my bill for this work today. Every time I work for the school, they pay me but it takes them a while."

"Well, that won't happen this time. I have the authority and the money to pay you as we go."

He smiled. The man had perfect even white teeth.

While Addy took care of the financial end of things, the guys and I went to the van and grabbed shovels. There was no need to dig up the entire floor if we knew where the door was.

We had the entire door uncovered by five o'clock. Daylight savings time helped. If we desired, we would have about two more hours of daylight to work. We desired.

Terrill and George went to the van and came back with torches. They were battery operated, but they were still torches. I'd used them before at other digs, but I hadn't thought to pack any myself.

Addy had what looked like a huge leaf blower. We all went down wind of it, and she turned it on, using it to blow the residual dirt into a pile on the wayward side.

We discovered we had one more hurdle. The hinges on the trap door Addy uncovered were rusted shut. We tried WD40, graphite, white grease and brute force. They didn't move.

At twilight we gave up for the night. But we still had a problem. How to protect our site overnight?

I called Chief Bill Davis. "Bill, this is Lexi. I have a problem." I explained what we had. He remained quiet for a long time.

"I can't send my men out anymore. A judge stepped in and gave the search rights to the University of Missouri for sixty-days, or until they find someone who has a claim to the land. So you will have to hire private security. I can give you some names. You know me, Lexi, if I could, I would."

"I understand. Can you wait until I get a pen so I can write some numbers down?"

"I'll make it easy for you. When we hang up, I'll text you some numbers in the order of who I believe is best to worst."

We said our goodbyes and within a minute or two we had the numbers.

Terrill said, "I have an idea. Since the door won't open, why don't we park the van and the rental car right over the door and we can all ride home with Lexi."

We thrashed it around awhile and decided it was the best idea.

It was well after dark when we got home.

"I'm starving, "George said. "We passed a Panda Express and a Pasta Express on the way home."

"One plus of living in a college town is everyone delivers."

Two of us picked pasta, two picked Panda Express. No one said much until the food arrived. We ate in relative silence and were in bed an hour later, exhausted from all our hard work.

# Chapter 54

My phone rang. I must have been sleeping like the dead because I couldn't wake up enough to find it. As a matter of fact, I had forgotten I didn't sleep in my own room the night before. Whoever called finally gave up and hung up.

I don't know how much later they called back but at least I'd been alert enough to answer this time. "Hello."

"Hello, I'm looking for Alexa Ford."

"You found me. Who is this?"

"I'm Agent Blake Wade from the FBI field office in Chicago."

"Is this some kind of joke?"

"No joke Miss Ford. This is an official call. I'd like to know if I can come down to your area and talk to you."

The chain around my neck began to bounce up and down on my chest. I had no idea what it meant. This hadn't happened before. I sat up. "Is there some way I can verify who you really are? You could be calling me from anywhere and saying you're anybody. And what would the FBI want with me."

"Okay, here's what we will do. I'll hang up. You either get on your computer or look up the number of the Chicago FBI office. Call in, ask for me. Ask for the director, ask for anyone you want to. When you're done and you're sure I am who I say I am, hit redial on your phone to reach me. I must talk to you so please satisfy yourself and then call me back."

"I have a question."

"Sure, what?"

"Is your picture on the website for the Chicago office?"

"Heavens no. Would you work here if anyone and everyone could throw your image around whenever they wanted? It could get one of us killed fast. Not only that, but undercover work would be out of the question."

"Okay, give me time go do all this and I'll call back."

The first thing I did was to take Blake's card off the counter in the kitchen and call the number on it.

"Joplin, Missouri, FBI, how can I direct your call?"

"I'd like to speak to Agent Blake Wade."

"I'm sorry, Agent Wade is out of the office. I can give you his cell phone number or voice mail."

I hung up. I went to my phone and looked up Agent Blake Wade, FBI. Sure enough, Blake's picture came up nearly immediately. Though I'd never thought about it before, why would an agent want his picture prominently displayed on a website?

Then I Googled the FBI's number and dialed what came up. *For an emergency, please dial 4.* I hit the four button and a man's voice said, *listen closely to the following menu because some options have changed.*

Most of the options were the same. What it amounted to was, call 9 1 1 for immediate help. If the FBI needed to be involved the local authorities would inform them. Then da da da about how they didn't want to disregard you so please leave a message and someone will contact you as soon as possible.

Okay, said my Agent Blake was the furthest thing from an FBI agent I'd ever seen? I took a deep breath and told myself I wished the man stood in front of me so the ring, my helper, around my neck could do its thing.

I called the Chicago field office. "Is there any way I can talk to Agent Blake Wade?"

"Let me see. Yes, he has signed in and is in his office. I'll ring him for you."

After a long moment or a noise void, the man who called me earlier answered the phone. "Agent Blake Wade."

"It's me, Alexa Ford returning your call."

"Good because I think you may be in danger."

"I already knew that."

"Okay, today I am in the office. I had Chief Bill Davis of the Benton Police Department put a tail on your very own Agent Wade. The man is sharp and we lost him. Have you heard from him?"

"Yes, he called last night, but I didn't answer."

"I'm flying down tonight. I have a reservation near your exploration site at a place called, The Farm. I'll be in cabin nine. I will not be in a suit and do not address me as Agent or tell anyone I'm from the Agency.

"I understand you have three archeologists from the state university. I would like you to keep it from everyone because I don't want anyone to act differently around your imposter.

"You have no way of knowing this, but it is extremely rare for an agent to work alone. My partner's name is Eve Williams. We will both be at your dig site tomorrow. We are coming as helpers from the University of Illinois. I will text you William's phone number. She'll be in cabin 11 at the Farm.

"We believe you'll have to tell your partner Adaline Maguire about us. Tell her as little as possible. I will be using the name Adam Wright. Best of luck."

Wow, the Agent Blake Wade we knew wasn't an FBI agent and was silly enough to use the name of a real one. I thought a minute. I'd give him the benefit of the doubt. It could have been super smart or super dumb, depending on the outcome.

The smell of fresh coffee wafted down the hall when I opened the door. All three of my guests were up and George had bacon and eggs cooking. Terrill stood by the toaster and as a piece popped up, he buttered it and put it butter side down on a plate.

"You're just in time," George said. "By the time you get a cup of coffee your breakfast will be ready. Hope you like fried eggs."

I smiled at him and took a seat next to Addy. We ate with enthusiasm. Everyone eager to get to the dig. "I thought of something last night," I said. "I have a winch for my Jeep. We could use it if the hinges don't give today."

"Also," Addy added, "If you have a long enough pry bar, we might be able to unstick the door with that."

After we finished eating, I got the winch and pry bar. George rinsed the dishes and put them in the dishwasher. Terrill made us each a cup of coffee to go.

Indy mostly stayed out of the way although he begged for a piece of bacon if there was any left on a plate.

When we loaded up to head to the dig site, Indy sat in the back seat between the guys. He acted like a king.

I hadn't had the time or opportunity to talk to Addy. I'd have to do it soon. The Chicago agents could get there before we did if they were motivated enough. How they were going to pull off a vast knowledge of artifacts, I had no idea.

While the guys were unloading the equipment and attaching the winch to the Jeep, I walked over to the other side of the van and asked Addy to come with me. "Addy, I can't go into a lot of detail, so listen carefully. The man we know as Agent Blake Wade is a not an FBI agent. Right now, the FBI isn't sure of his identity. The real Agent Wade and his partner Eve Williams will be here this morning. They are coming as helpers from the University of Illinois.

"How they will pull it off or what their cover story will be is not clear. They don't want us to tell anyone else. We need to treat Blake the way we always do."

About that time George called out for us. "Hey Professor and Lexi, we have company."

Standing with the boys were a man and a woman. The man looked to be in his mid-thirties. Tall, fit and handsome with light brown hair and a popular two-day growth of beard.

I guessed Eve to be five feet six, athletic with natural blond shoulder length hair and bright blue eyes that danced in the sunlight.

The man reached out to shake everyone's hand. "I'm Adam Wright and this is Eve Williams. We're from the Southern Illinois Relic Collectors. It's a metal detecting and relic club near the University of Illinois. We were both on vacation when we heard about your finds and thought we'd come down and offer to give you folks a hand."

Eve chimed in. "We won't get in the way, but we can help dig and identify if you want or you can just use us for manual labor."

Before I could say anything, Addy stepped forward and shook each of their hands as did the boys. The three introduced themselves. "I'm Professor Adaline Maguire, call me Addy."

Eve looked at me, "I think I've read every article you have ever written on digging. I can't tell you how nice it is to meet you. You too Addy."

"We'd better get started."

We filled the couple in on what we'd done so far and what we intended to do. "Let's try the pry bar first."

George reached around and took the bar from the back of the Jeep. They had already moved the van and car out of the way. "Let's put it in the small groove opposite the hinges and use a fulcrum to see if we can muster enough strength to open it. If we can, then we can put the bar in further."

It took over an hour and three tries, but we finally moved the door up about an inch. The guys reinserted the bar in about four more inches and tried again. It opened but it took all three of them to lean it back far enough for it to fall open onto the ground.

It sounded like a sonic boom. Dust clouds bound up six feet at least and swirled around a minute or two before it settled again.

Once it did, I noticed we had company.

The noise had been too loud for us to hear Blake drive up. By the time everything settled down he was standing next to me.

"My goodness," he said, "looks like you all have been busy." He walked up and looked inside the deep pitch-black hole. "What is that?"

"We don't know yet," Adam answered. "We only just got it open." Then he reached forward and put his hand out to Blake.

"I'm Adam Wright. We came down from Illinois to help the crew here."

Blake went white. I thought he would faint. It looked like he would never let go of Adam's hand or say another word. After a long awkward silence, Blake said, "Agent Blake Wade, FBI."

Eve stepped up and went on to tell him about the relic club they were affiliated with. Blake smiled but none of the color had returned to his face.

"Who's got a torch," I asked, more than ready to see what the room contained.

I reached up and touched my neck before I realized why it felt uncomfortable. The cold emanating from the ring was nearly unbearable.

Everyone agreed that if not for me, no one would be there so I should go first into the room we found. I replied they were letting me go because they were chickens.

I laid down and held the torch as far into the hatch as I could. "This might be a difficult decent. There are no handrails on either side, and it's much deeper than I thought. I can't see the bottom from here with the torch."

"Maybe one of us should go with you," Addy said. "We would take a couple of lights so we can see when we get to the bottom."

"And let's put a rope on you, Lexi. When you get down. You can unhook and we'll send Addy down." Terrill said.

Indy began to howl. "Indy doesn't like this idea."

I assured him I'd be back and started down. I'd only gone two steps before I couldn't see anything beneath me and only the hole of light above me. Once in a while someone would tug on the rope and I would tug back.

n about twenty feet, I touched solid ground. The lack of light limited me to about two feet on all sides if I turned. The light from the door above looked more like a flashlight than sunlight.

"Can you hear me?" I called.

An echo came back to me, "Yes-yes yes."

I had remembered to take pen and paper with me. At first, I wondered why, now I knew what pushed me to bring them. I wrote, *Tie a couple of torches to this rope and send them down.*

I untied the rope from my waist and tugged on it. What little of the rope I could see, disappeared instantly.

In the time I waited I learned a lesson, where there is no light, time is not a factor. I could not have told you if the lights came back down in two minutes or two hours.

I turned the first torch on and held it out with one hand and the torch I already had out in the other. I now had my arms straight out from my sides and could see about four feet on each side of me. I noticed the floor was dirt so I stuck one torch into the ground, walked until I could barely see and then pushed another in the same way.

The ground, being as soft as it was, gave me pause. I'd been in enough ruins and cellars in my career to know the number of unimaginable critters able to live in this type of environment. Now that I could see a little I went back to the first light and yelled up at the opening. "Send Addy down and as many lights as you have. " My message echoed but they must have heard it because they pulled up the rope.

Once down, Addy needed a minute to adjust to the darkness even with the three lights I'd already staked out said, "We're going to have to take more of the top of this cellar off if we want to work down here."

"I know. I still can't tell you what's in here other than creepy crawlies and rats or mice. I'd imagine snakes too, although it's too cold for them to be moving around."

I don't know how long it took, but we finally had a circle of light laid out using the torches. It gave us a small section to study. "What do you think?" I asked once Addy had a chance to see what little she could.

"I believe," she said slowly, "we're standing in a room surrounded with World War II artifacts."

"I think so too."

"Let's go back up. We're going to get stuck down here with no lights. I guarantee the batteries will be gone soon. These torches are made for emergencies only."

Once we were back up the steps, I asked, "Anyone else want to go down?"

I felt the need to add a warning, "I'll tell you, you can't see much. There is shelf after shelf of antiques, so we'll be needing some real lighting down there."

Everyone but Blake said yes. His face turned a slight shade of pink. "I think I'll wait until tomorrow." He pointed to the three-piece suit he had on.

Adam and George went down next, followed by Eve and Terrill. We all had the same reaction. We had uncovered a treasure the entire world would be interested in.

"How are we going to keep this place safe?" I asked.

"Agent Wade," Adam said, "would the FBI send some men to help us."

He didn't waiver. "It would take too long. Everyone in my small office is on assignment. What did Bill Davis say?"

"Since it is no longer a crime scene, they can't use department funds and resources to protect it," I answered.

"The university gave us enough of a budget for a month down here. It included the hotel. Since we're staying with you, we can use that money for security," Addy said. She added, "If you can stand to have company for that long."

"Of course. The house is big enough for all of us. I called Chief Davis and I have the numbers of some companies he recommended," I said.

With Bill's help, we had four cops from the surrounding area who wanted to moonlight on their days off. They were going to guard the dig in pairs. They also liked our idea of parking vehicles over the opening which also provided extra protection from the weather.

We closed the latch, watched the men pull a Ford 350 Doolie with a camper shell over it and a Ram three=quarter ton, 4 by 4. They were both seasoned patrolmen. Dennis Sullivan, the youngest of the two, looked as if he spent all of his free time at the gym. His hair style was a military cut.

The other man, Elvin Moss, looked to be in his sixties. He had a bit of a belly and a deep voice. It looked like the length of his hair probably pushed the limits of police force guidelines. His hair had turned nearly all grey which made his soft blue-green eyes shine against his dark skin.

We would meet the other two guards when they came on duty the next evening.

Adam and Eve, it only then dawned on me what they had done in choosing aliases. The agent could have picked any name he wanted but he picked Adam. What a sense of humor. Now I would have to hope I didn't laugh when I talked to them in front of Agent Blake Wade.

Many problems needed to be solved before our team's next trip to the underground museum.

# CHAPTER 55

As we were all back at our cars discussing what would happen next, I suggested we order pizza and have it delivered to the house. George and Terrill said they would order it and pick both the pizza and some beer up on the way over.

Adam handed them a folded bill, as did Blake. Addy drove home with me. It was time I told her what was going on.

I wasn't sure how I would approach it until Adam came up to the driver's side of the Jeep and discreetly handed me a cell phone. "This is a Track phone. Use it if you want to talk to me or Eve. Our numbers are the only ones programed in it. Whatever you do, don't let your friendly FBI agent see it."

We drove a mile or so in silence before Addy said, "Are you going to tell me what's going on?"

"This is what I know. Adam Wright is the *real* Special Agent Blake Ward, Eve is another agent, Adam's partner. They came down to see what's going on and to expose Blake."

Addy shook her head. "How do you know he's any more real than our Blake?"

"This man is from the Chicago office. I called up there. They put me through to him. Two things about him are different from Blake. First, Blake's picture is on the website in St. Louis. Why would an agent, who might have to go undercover, put his picture on a website? Second, I've told you before, Blake acts nothing like an FBI agent," I explained.

"First of all, what does a *real* FBI agent act like? I'd bet my last dime our Blake acts the way he does partly because he likes you. Well, more than likes you. He's afraid something will happen to you. You are so damned independent. You won't let him protect you.

"And, look at other FBI websites. I bet there are pictures of some agents. Lexi, not everyone goes undercover. And lastly, if the case is so important, why didn't he show up when the professor was killed? Or during the last five years Blake's been here.

"I know he'd been on the case because I saw him up at our school last year. He's rather hard to forget. The man is gorgeous. I didn't meet him officially then, but he was in our director's office several days in a row.

"I don't think a person can pretend to be another person in a high-profile job for five years without getting caught. Personally, my loyalty stays with our Agent Wade."

By this time, I had pulled into a parking lot so I could hear her over the sound of the wind and the engine. "Did you see the look on his face when he saw Adam? He turned white and his color didn't come back for a long time."

"If the second Blake, Adam, is some kind of imposter, why didn't Blake call him on it?"

"Ask Adam," she said. "One more thing, the lab got back results on the first bones you found. They were dated at lease seventy or eighty years old. So one murder is solved. Those bones have a 99 percent chance of belonging to Judith Izzard."

I pulled back out onto the road. We didn't talk the rest of the way home, both too busy trying to figure out what was going on. Who was the *real* Blake Wade? I needed to think about it for a while. Maybe it was the mutual attraction that made me angry with him all the time. I had always thought men, at least the ones I went out with, wanted me to be interested in what they did, but not what I did. I'd had enough of one sided and shied away from boyfriends.

Once we were in the driveway, I told her, "It seems the only time I get shot at is when our Agent is not around. It makes Chief Davis think he is the culprit."

"That's not what you told me. You said the first time was when a delivery boy came and Blake had to pull the kid inside. He couldn't have shot at the house and been inside it at the same time."

That shut me up. And made my head hurt as I tried to resolve all the conflicting information.

No one else was at the house when we arrived. I asked Addy, "Why do you think the treasures are hidden at the old Izzard farm where the Thompson's didn't have access rather than a more convenient place?"

I took a bottle of water out of the refrigerator and held it up toward her. She nodded yes for the water. "First of all, I believe it's been over sixty years since the farmhouse was occupied. Then when this guy Barclay Simmons bought it, all of his signatures are internet signatures, so I don't think he's been here either."

"Okay, one more question," she said. "How are we going to make plans or work on this project if the fake Blake will be hanging around? If he knows our plans, he'll be one step ahead of us all the time."

"I'll also tell you I believe one of the Blake's killed the professor, the policeman Tony Asbury and the art dealer from New Jersey," I added.

"Okay, Lexi, what you're saying is we have hundreds of thousands of dollars' worth of artifacts, and a serial killer posing as an FBI agent?"

"Yep, that's what I'm telling you. Our goal is to not treat Blake any different than we did before we knew all of this. By the way, don't tell the guys. The more people who know the harder it will be to act normal."

"I'd bet my last dollar the guy from today, Adam, is the fake," Addy insisted stubbornly.

# Chapter 56

I was like a little kid on Christmas Eve. The only thing I wanted to do was go back down in the cellar and explore. My mind would not shut down. The problem I couldn't solve was why was the entrance to the space was three feet underground.

There had to be another entrance. An entrance a person could easily access without having to move a ton or two of dirt. An entrance one could go into without being seen.

My eyes were tired. I closed them knowing I could never go to sleep, but I think I must have. The dream started with Judith Izzard in what appeared to be a tunnel. Whoever was in it with her shook her. It was the same dream I'd had before. Just like before, the man took the ring off of her finger, slapped her so hard on the side of the head she fell down. Judith didn't move. He took a long board and began to hit the low ceiling with it. Gravel and silt began to fall.

The man backed down a narrow passageway. Dirt and debris fell in bigger globs until the entire roof of the passage collapsed. The image went blank.

Judith had been buried alive in a mine or a tunnel. I knew that was the moment she had died because her face disappeared and my chest grew icy cold. After that, my dreams were normal and I dropped into a deeper sleep.

In the morning, I got up and dressed by six. Indy and I went outside and sat on the back porch in the cool morning air. My thoughts were jumbled. Did I really know the fate of the Izzard girl from the dream?

Would the ring always be powerful or should I give it to Addy when the project was finished and let her add it to the other items?

But mostly, I wanted to find the tunnel I knew had to be on the farm. It couldn't be too far from the foundation of the house, yet it needed to be somewhat hidden so a person could come and go without too much trouble if they brought an item in or took one out.

I went inside, got my pack and took it back outside. I had aerial pictures of the entire property. They were in with the papers I got in the will.

By the time the smell of coffee made its way to the back porch, I had marked off three places I believed were viable to put a tunnel entrance.

One was fourteen feet away in a well house. It looked like a well house, but I'd never seen a pump handle anywhere near it. The second was inside the barn. It would have to be a longer tunnel, but the barn could be reached from the other end of the farm. No one would see you from the road or any of the fields. The third and most unlikely was under a small building on a knoll nearly fifty feet from the basement.

I decided not to mention it until everyone had a cup of coffee in their hands.

George addressed it before I had a chance. "I've been thinking," and I don't believe anyone used the entrance we found under the house. Somewhere there's a tunnel. I suggest we spend today looking for it."

"Since you brought it up," I said, "I have some aerial photos of the farm. Since great minds think alike, I had the same idea." I laid the picture on the table and pulled out the map I'd made with the measurements next to it.

I showed them all three locations I'd marked and they agreed we should look there first. No one wanted breakfast. Excitement was palpable in the room.

Adam and Eve were at the site when we got there. The guards told us except for the coyotes, the night had been quiet. I'd called

Charlie Drum on the way over. His truck pulled in directly behind us.

"My idea," said Charlie, "is we go down, set up lights. I can get my generator. Make sure you folks can see good and you can find the tunnel from the inside. It would save a lot of time.

Charlie paused and looked thoughtful before continuing, "Because of carbon monoxide, we will have to put the generator pretty far away. You folks go get some spotlights and three one-hundred-foot heavy duty extension cords and I will drive back to the house and pick up the generator.

"I have four five-gallon gas cans. I'll fill them up and bring them too. All I ask is that I get my money back for the gas."

"Charlie, that is a wonderful idea. Do you think the site will be safe until we get back?" I asked.

"I won't be more than ten minutes. I'll bring my shotgun when I come back."

"We don't all have to go. How many people could it take to get this stuff?" Adam looked at me. "Why don't you and Eve and Addy go. Me and the boys will stay here and have the generator set up by the time you get back."

Everyone agreed and we went to get the supplies.

By noon we had the buried room lit up like daylight. By then, since none of us had taken time to eat breakfast, Adam and Terrill made a much needed run to McDonalds. Even Indy had a double burger.

The number of items in what I decided to call *The Cave*, mostly because it reminded me of Aladdin's Cave of Wonders than any natural feature, would have intimidated any museum director. All of us looked at as much as we could. It was stacked to the ceiling on two sides and numerous wooden shelves held pottery, masks, flasks, bejeweled crowns. swords, and Egyptian artifacts were abundant.

One section of the west wall had nothing on it. A section about five feet wide remained bare. Adam went over with a hammer and began to tap the entire area. There wasn't a door. It looked like dirt and silt. The entire area was packed dirt.

Knowing it would take days to dig our way out, not to mention the difficulty of dirt removal from twenty feet underground, we decided to figure out the corresponding space outside.

Adam moved the hammer up above what appeared to be a doorframe. Once he hit a solid surface, he began to hit the wall harder, hoping we would hear it outside.

I counted off the number of steps it was from the entrance to the space where he stood. George and I climbed out of the cave and began to use our calculations to find the outside entrance.

We never did hear the tapping or pounding from down under. Then I heard a sound on top where Charlie had removed all the dirt to expose the metal ceiling. We knocked back. From there we stepped out to the edge of the foundation.

For better or worse, we were where we wanted to be. Charlie turned the bucket toward the backhoe and began to excavate from the outside wall to the bottom of the cave. We heard a horrible sound; dust began to bellow out of the entrance and people began to scramble up the ladder to fresh air. Adam, the last one out let us know, "The dirt came inward. There must be four feet of dirt that came down. It poured in. We ran out because we didn't know how much more would come in, plus, the dust hampered our breathing."

Indy ran from person to person, sniffing them and running in circles. Even he knew we almost had a catastrophe.

No one went back down. We all moved out of Charlie's way, but stayed close enough to watch him work. We didn't have to guess whether what we'd found was the entrance to a tunnel.

Before long, my curiosity got the best of me. I walked over to where Charlie dumped the dirt and began to look through the pile. It had grown to nearly five feet wide and five feet high. I noticed he had begun another pile.

It made it easier for me to study since the dirt didn't have to resettle with the next dropped load. Charlie dropped the bucket for me to inspect; he must have noticed something. Then I could see it, sticking out because of its color. It was about nine inches in length and looked like a piece of wood. I went over and gently picked it up.

In my hand I held a bone, a femur, that had once belonged to a human. I held it up to my leg. Whoever this person was, they were about four inches shorter than I. I could tell by holding the bone up to my own leg. It wasn't very scientific, but for now, it was close enough. Whoever it belonged to stood about five feet six inches, give or take. I waved my hand for Charlie to stop. Then I called, "There are human remains over here! We need to look through the pile and see if there are more!"

Everyone ran to get their favorite digging tool. We went to the back of the pile. Before we began to dig in earnest, Addy spread out a clean white tarp to lay our findings on.

Charlie wrapped up and left knowing this might take days and he wouldn't be needed for a while. He said to call when we needed him again. The rest of the afternoon and well into the evening we combed through both mounds of rock and dirt. By the end of the day, we'd found at least three-fourths of the body.

Also from the dirt piles, we found a gold ring, a silver hair barrette, a long strand of auburn hair and a piece of material heavily covered with pearls. We were all pretty certain we had found the body of Judith Izzard. The chain around my neck began to feel warm around and I had no qualms to identify it as Judith.

The two night guards showed up around seven P.M. "You won't be able to park over the site tonight. We opened the cave beneath the house and uncovered old artifacts. There is no way to cover it up."

"No problem. We'll see nothing happens to your dig site. Are those bones?"

"Yes, they are. We will roll up the finds and take them with us. We'll be here earlier tomorrow. You have my cell phone number, but if you need backup in a hurry, call 9 1 1."

I realized then, Blake had not called or showed up all day.

We all went home exhausted.

The guys grabbed a beer. Addy and I had a glass of wine each. Adam and Eve joined us for drinks after they had cleaned up back at their hotel. We all sat on the back porch and enjoyed the late evening, pondering everything from the day.

After a bit, I thought of something. I went to my office behind the garage and came back with a picture. "Look, I want to show you something." I passed around a picture of Judith from the newspaper. It showed her as she left for the party on the night she disappeared. "See the barrette, the pearls, the bracelet on her right wrist? And it is her house we're excavating."

"I believe when we get the tunnel cleared out, we'll find canned goods and staples like dried meat and beans." I saw it when I held the ring, but I couldn't tell them that part, so I needed a reason I thought that. "I bet anything the front of the room was a root cellar. Someone cleaned out the entire basement behind it. I have no idea where the three or four feet of dirt on top came from. It makes no sense because the house sits squarely on its foundation."

Eve chimed in, "I think they left the space there as a sound barrier."

"Sounds reasonable," Terrill said.

## Chapter 57

When we returned the next morning, Charlie had two more hills of fresh dirt for us to go through. He couldn't go any further because of something behind him.

I was convinced it was the storage cellar I believed buffered the chamber in the back. We hired some men Charlie knew to dig out whatever blocked the backhoe. They also put in beams and side walls to reinforce the tunnel and keep it from collapsing while we were in it.

We knew we could get out through the top hatch but it could trap some of us if we were all down there.

Agent Wade showed up about four. "Wow, look at all the progress you've made." We had the tarp rolled out and had assembled nearly the entire body except for three fingers of her left hand. "What is that?" he'd nodded toward the tarp.

Addy answered, "We believe it to be Judith Izzard's remains. If so, then Professor Thompson didn't tell the truth about the bones at Lexi's very first dig on this property. There is an entire skeleton here except for the three fingers Lexi found."

Blake smiled, "Makes life easier for me. I've been spending my days tracking down each and every girl over sixteen who has been missing six years or less."

"We were wondering where you were," I said.

"I thought about calling several times, but I figured you're not only tired from all of this, but had company. I wonder if I could talk Chief Davis out of the evidence he has. That way we could put the whole body all together."

I didn't say anything. Terrill said, "It still doesn't tell us who killed Judith, if that's who this is. But I guess we'll never know. They already hung someone for her murder back then. The new mystery is who put all these artifacts in the cave and where did they come from?"

I patted Terrill on the back. "It might be for you and your buddies and Addy to find out. I was hired to search the farm. Looks like the entire farm will be searched and the guy who hired me is no longer with us."

"Are you going to leave us?" Addy asked. "I hoped you would stick around and help us catalog all of these items and figure out where they came from."

"Come on, Addy, you've been on the job long enough to know it will take years to unravel all of this. Besides, the site now belongs to the college. They'll either keep it or the state will take over. I certainly hope they don't."

"I'd say you have about five years of job security ahead of you," I smiled at Addy.

I took a couple of steps closer to Blake. "Besides, who stole these artifacts many very well become a federal job. I bet most of it ends up in a museum somewhere. And the FBI will take over looking for the thieves full time."

By tomorrow they will have the obstacles up front dug out and the beams in place. I say we close up shop and take a little break until in the morning when we can spend the day exploring all of the contents."

"What will happen to the bones over there?" Terrill asked nodding toward the tarp.

"They'll be buried once they've been identified. We are assuming we know the bones belong to Judith Izzard, but the coroner will be able to tell us for sure. Someone from their office will be here in a few minutes to pick up the skeleton. They're sending it to the crime lab in Kansas City. I don't know how long they'll have it," I said.

"You need to make a plan about what you are going to tell the newspapers and TV folks. As soon as the coroner's van pulls up here, the gossip will begin. I bet there will be dozens of press here before morning," Blake said.

"Lexi can handle them," Addy said. "She's famous for this kind of find. Well, maybe not skeletons, but treasures."

I laughed, "I think we should all talk to them. I'm sure we each have a unique view of the entire ordeal."

"Anybody up for supper tonight?" Adam asked.

I tried not to show it, but the thought of spending time with two Blake Wades at the same time was beyond my compacity. "You guys go ahead," I said. "I'm so tired of being up and smelling like dust this time of day, I think I'm going to go home, take Indy for a walk and call it a night."

Addy asked the guys, and they wanted to go. Blake bowed out so the five of them left for dinner. Blake waited with me until the skeleton was safely on its way to Kansas City.

I knew I was safe because Indy acted like he and Blake were still bonded over the last adventure they had had together. "I'm going to head home," I finally said, "see you tomorrow."

Agent Wade gave me a hangdog look as if he were losing his best friend and stood by my car until I started it and drove away.

I didn't realize how much I missed the peace and quiet of being alone until we pulled in the garage and turned off the car. I closed the door and sat there.

It was short-lived. The doorbell rang and I went to answer it. Blake stood on the stoop. Geez. I thought about not answering the door, but he had to know I was home. He was less than a minute behind me. "Hi, I thought we were going to meet in the morning."

"Call me silly," he said, "but I had the strangest feeling you're not safe."

"It's strange for sure." What I wanted to say was, I was safe until you showed up.

"I don't feel good about you walking the dog alone."

Again, I couldn't say, I am safe as long as you are with me, you can't shoot at me. "Well, let's go then." I locked the door, put my keys in my pocket and watched Indy run around in circles, tired of laying around all day and ready to explore.

For the first two blocks we didn't say a word to one another. Blake looked at me a couple of times but if I happen to look his way, he would act like he wasn't looking at me.

"Lexi," he said, "I need to talk to you." He looked so serious and sincere. He looked less like a killer than anyone I'd ever met.

"What is it?"

He stopped and looked at me. "I don't really know how to say this so I'll just say it. Adam and Eve are not who they appear to be."

"I know. I know the whole story."

"What do you think you know?" he asked.

"That he is the real Agent Blake Wade from the FBI and Eve is his partner. And you are not with the FBI. So who are you?"

He stared me right in the eye and didn't blink. "I am Agent Blake Wade. I've been with the FBI for ten years. They recruited me from the university. The man you think is me, is actually Barclay Simmons."

"Oh, come on. Get real! You told me yourself Barclay Simmons is dead. Burned in a car in Little Rock, Arkansas."

"I know I did. I thought he was until I saw him standing next to you with Maria Young, one of the most notorious art thieves in the country."

"And you didn't say anything? Why?"

"Because it would have been disastrous," he said. "Five possible hostages, six counting your friend with the backhoe. They're both armed and I have one gun. I'd be dead for sure and one or two of you might have been hurt too. Even if I brought in outside help, it could have caused more problems for you and your team. And we need to find out why they are really here. I don't know how much to tell you."

"At this point, I don't know who to believe. You're Agent Man, he's Agent Man, my head is spinning."

"Answer a question for me. Why is it you believe this man you have never met who tells you he is me, but you don't believe me who has been with you since this all began?"

"Okay, one, I only got shot at when you were out of town or not with me. Two, if you are really an FBI agent, why would you be listed on a website with your picture? Wouldn't that make it impossible for you to go undercover? Three, you said you knew who killed the professor, but you didn't make any attempt to keep him from killing again. Want more reasons?"

He shook his head. "You're unbelievable," he said.

We stood face to face for a long time before I turned on my heel and headed back towards the house. He followed.

Once we got to the porch, he took me by the arm. I shook out of his grasp.

"Five, you just showed up after the professor's murder. No one called you, there was no reason for the FBI to be involved."

"I told you why I was involved. The professor had been stockpiling art and artifacts for years. He took at least one or two pieces from every dig or expedition or tour he ever joined or worked on," Blake took a deep breath before continuing, like he'd made a decision about something.

"Barclay Simmons is Thompson's son. He left when he was about eighteen and reinvented himself. He took the identity from a dead kid in Alaska. He's been conning people ever since. I don't know what he used to make the professor stash items for him, but he did. I think it was because the Izzard's hung his uncle for Judith's murder without any evidence that the girl was dead.

"And there are people who do things for their kids out of guilt or a false sense of loyalty. It appears that Simmons is some of the professor's only living family. That can be a powerful motivator."

My jaw dropped but he continued, "We at the agency think Morgan Thompson got Judith Izzard pregnant and when he wouldn't marry her, they fought. It would seem he then killed her and buried her in a space behind the root cellar. The Izzard family knew she was pregnant but didn't want a scandal.

No one will ever know the truth. I believe Morgan's family made up one story and Judith's father made up another. But like I said, we will never know for sure.

"They hung the boy because he was guilty, but a trial could have revealed the pregnancy. Someone found the ring in his pocket. It's said he was going to pawn the ring and use the money to get far away from here.

"After that it was like the Hatfield's and the McCoy's. The two families hated one another but with the professor's grandfather and father both being senators and Izzard being the richest man in his half of the state, it all got buried: even the girl.

"I don't know how many really rich people you know, but it's all about money and power. They would rather ruin each other in secret, shady, unholy deals, than admit a thing like an out of marriage pregnancy cause a scandal, especially in 1929."

"I need to think," I said, the ring wasn't helping me at all. It went from hot to cold and cold to hot more than once during Blake's story. I took the key out of my pocket and unlocked my front door.

Blake, or whoever he was, took a step back and shook his head. He didn't say another word. He turned on his heel and walked off.

Only then did I notice Indy wasn't with me. I turned to unlock the door to call him when he bounded into the room from the kitchen after having used the dog door to come in.

I heard a car pull up out front. Addy, George and Terrill were about to get to the door. I ran down the hall and into my room before they had a chance to open the door. I didn't want to face anyone.

*Think.* I told myself, *think.*

# Chapter 58

I got up early the next morning and went to the farm. It was not yet six, but Charlie and his crew were there to finish up. I went into the tunnel and walked back to the artifacts.

Again, I was in awe. It had to have taken years to amass so much art and antiquities in one spot. Indy, who hadn't been able to follow me down into the cave from the top, seemed excited to come along and not be left alone.

I looked from shelf to shelf and continued to be amazed. Each item had a date of acquisition, country and all other pertinent information clearly labeled on it. The dates went back at least fifteen years. Some of the notes were in the professor's handwriting and others were in writing I didn't recognize.

I heard voices. "Indy," I whispered, "come, quiet."

After my conversation with Blake the night before, I couldn't wrap my mind about what was true and who was who. The ring had been no help clearing any of it up either. Indy and I went to the back of the artifacts, behind the last two rows. I commanded Indy one more time to be quiet. He laid down next to me and put his head on his paws.

"How long are we going to go on with this charade," Eve's voice.

Adam's voice replied, "You mean you aren't having fun?"

Eve replied, "Let's just take some pieces we know are worth the most and leave."

Adam said, "And leave all of this?"

*He must have been referring to the other items in the room*, I thought.

Eve said, "A couple of million is better than the rest of our lives in jail."

Adam said testily, "Hey, it wasn't my idea to kill the professor. That's on you."

Eve snapped back, "And the cop?"

Sounding placating, Adam said, "This is a terrible time to stop and have an argument. Get five items you believe are worth the most but are small enough to get out of here easily. I'll do the same."

He walked to the row in front of me and when I took a tiny step back, I knocked into the shelf behind me and a ceramic bowl fell. Adam stepped back and saw me.

"Well look who it is. Little miss treasure hunter. You aren't supposed to be here. Now I'll have to do something about you." His voice continued to sound pleasant, but the threat was evident.

Indy did his best to go after the man, but he didn't have any room to get purchase with his back feet. Adam grabbed me by the arm and dragged me toward the empty space in front of us.

Indy finally got loose from his spot and went after Adam. Adam pulled a gun trying to aim at Indy. I stepped in front of him and shoved as hard as I could. Adam careened into a shelf that pushed against the two shelves in front of it. The weight of the antique swords, knives and heavily jeweled crowns caused the next shelf to fall against the others until they all went down like a domino display.

In the back of my mind, I wondered where Eve was. I got my answer when Eve screamed once and finished falling. Then silence.

Adam called out for Eve from under a pile of shelving and artifacts, "Marie, where are you? Are you okay?"

No answer.

He turned his attention back to me. Indy took the opportunity of Adam's momentary distraction gave him time to take a big chunk out of the hand still holding the gun. I heard it clang to the floor. Indy would not let go of Adam's hand.

Adam thrashed around and as he did, he moved closer to the new beams and side walls. Dirt began to fall in clumps. The dust thickened until I could hardly see and breathing got more difficult with each inhale.

Indy released Adam, came to me and put my hand gently in his mouth to lead me toward the doorway. Adam crawled around on the floor I guessed to try and find his gun. Indy let go of my hand and lunged with the full force of his eighty-pound solid, muscular body.

It pushed the man hard against the side wall and the ceiling beam began to give. Indy resumed pulling me toward the door. I no sooner got through it than the entire section behind me gave way and closed off the room I'd been in a second before.

I couldn't see. I yelled for Indy, but I didn't see him. There was no bark to tell me he'd heard me. Tears began to run down my face. When they mingled with the dirt and turned into mud.

Indy," I called. Someone had my arm and began pulling me away from dust and debris that still rained down. "No, no! Let me go! I need to get my dog."

When I finally could take a breath, I saw the hands still holding me. Blake Wade sat next to me, his suit filthy. He choked on dust, muddy streaks on his own face as his eyes watered.

"Please let me go. I need to try and find Indy."

"I'll go," he said and disappeared into the dust.

Nothingness enclosed me. I needed to get farther out of the dust storm created by the collapse, and I needed to get my dog.

I squinted and saw Indy as he crawled on all fours, covered with at least three inches of dirt, he managed to come to me. I hugged him, rubbed the dirt from his coat. The entire time, I looked down the tunnel. Blake didn't come back.

George came out of nowhere and asked if I was okay. "Yes, but Blake went to get Indy and he hasn't come back."

George took off down what was left of the tunnel. It seemed like forever before he came back. "Blake's down there. He's buried to his neck in dirt and dust. I think he's alive but I need help." George ran off toward the outside.

Charlie, Terrill and Addy came back with George. Addy had a wet rag around her face. They tried to head back into the tunnel but more dirt had fallen, making walking upright impossible. They had to crawl.

Sirens invaded my ears. Soon two EMT's scooted past me and headed down the tunnel with the rest. George, Terrill and Addy came toward me. "It isn't good. He has a pulse, but he swallowed a lot of dust and dirt."

George and Terrill hadn't stopped. They ran on and each came back with an air tank and canula.

They took them down to where I imagine Blake lay with the EMTs working on him. "They about have him out," Addy continued. 'There isn't much room down there. We'll wait here though in case they need anything else."

It seemed like hours before the two men brought Blake back up through the tunnel. He looked white and muddy at the same time.

One of the EMTs sprinted off and came back carrying a stretcher in one hand. He laid it on the ground and slid it down to where Blake had been dragged free. He signaled for the boys to come help them. "We can't put him on here alone; the tunnel is too low to leverage him. Can you help?"

"Sure," I heard them say in unison. Twenty minutes later, they brought him out, put him in the ambulance and left, siren screaming as it went.

"I'd like to know what happened down there," Addy said. "But you don't look much better than Blake, so we'll take you to the hospital as the EMTs suggested."

I didn't complain. I wanted to feel better and check on Blake who had gotten hurt saving Indy.

Addy left to get a vehicle and bring it closer so I wouldn't have to walk far. The rest had gone to see how much damage had been done to the cave's two entrances. As I sat there, I heard a bell, then a tinkling like I heard at the end of *Miracle on Thirty-fourth Street*. I looked around but saw nothing until I looked up. Floating about six feet above me was Judith Izzard. Her hair was brushed, her beautiful green dress clean and bright. She smiled down at me as she slowly climbed an invisible staircase until she was out of sight and all that remained was a gentle breeze and a feeling of contentment. I reached for the chain around my neck. The chain was there, but the ring was gone. I smiled as Judith left my field of vision for good.

After they got me to the hospital, cleaned me up, took an x-ray of my chest, and administered a breathing treatment, they told me I could go home. We didn't leave. The four of us went to the waiting room and settled down to wait.

An hour or so later, a nurse came out and said we were more than welcome to coffee from the kitchen and told us where to find it.

We took turns drinking coffee and sleeping.

At dawn, a doctor came out and said Blake was out of danger but they wanted to keep him a day or two as a precaution to make sure none of the particles got into his lungs because it might cause pneumonia.

Later another nurse came out and said Agent Wade would like to speak to me.

I walked close to him and took his hand. He smiled at me and said, "I guess you aren't mad at me anymore since I saved Indy."

I smiled back, then I leaned down and kissed him.

# About the Author

Susan was born in California but moved to Alton, Illinois as a child and considers it her hometown. After high school she received training and was licensed as a Radiological Technician. Although her love has always been literature and writing, she has had many jobs she considers gave her a well-rounded view of the world. She uses that knowledge in her fiction writing.

She has two popular cozy mystery series, The Kate Nash Mysteries and the Arizona Summers Mysteries. She likes to make each novel in her series such that it will stand alone, but says they are more fun to read in order.

This book is the fifteenth book she's written and she is branching out in subject matter. Although this is the first book in her Alexa Ford Cozy Mystery series, the novel adds the twist of paranormal to the stories.

Susan writes full time, but loves to spend time with friends, her daughter and grandchildren and her two mini-dachshunds and a - Min Pin.

She loves to hear from her readers. You can reach her at :susan@susankeeneauthor.com

While you are there, please sign up for her newsletter which will start in September,